THE BEND

Acknowledgments
For my dedicated Beta readers, critique partners, editor and writers
who helped birth this book, thank you for your support, time and
efforts. A book is written not by one writer but by a team of people
who love reading and books. A special thank you to all my Facebook
friends who put up with my angst during this entire process. You are
the best!

1

She was perfect. Exactly what the Trainer needed. Wide hips, supple curves, and a country girl. Not a city girl. He'd tried a city girl before. Never again. It had been disastrous. She hadn't understood his plan for the perfect life. The perfect—it didn't matter. She hadn't been the one and would never be. Only a stand-in.

He moved closer. Loved the way this one selected her vegetables from the local market. She squeezed the plump tomatoes and ripe peaches, unable to make up her mind. Then she gave a graceful shake of her head, bouncing those soft curls into her eyes.

He groaned. A streak of heat coursed through his body. He wiped sweat from his forehead. Studied her again. He didn't need to squeeze the merchandise. He could make up his mind with no effort.

A few basic rules and they could both be happy. Like in those fairy tales he'd heard as a child. The ones his father read him after his mother passed out on the sofa.

Harlot.

Yes, life could have been sweet if only . . .

He hated unhappy endings. Hated the way they made him feel.

She spun around, her skirt hiking up her sculpted thighs. Another sigh surged through his body.

Yes, her story might start a little rocky, but in a few days, maybe a few weeks, she'd come around. It was his plan, after all. His purpose.

He pinned on his suitor's smile, hooked a shopping basket on his arm, stepped forward.

Showtime.

2

Kate Song checked her watch as she positioned herself on the hard bleachers. She'd already clocked in forty hours this week. The little league play-offs. Did she care who won?

Not an ounce, but a job was a job.

The batter glanced behind him as a fresh roar of thunder exploded over Hunlock Creek park. One more pitch and he'd walk to first. Good. The game would end before the storm arrived.

"Did you get a good shot of Trevor? Can't believe Coach let him play third today after he's missed so many practices." Jackie, Trevor's proud mom, tapped Kate's knee. "He's grown so fast."

"Hard to believe he'll be eleven soon." Kate zoomed in on Jackie's only child. If she had children, would she be as proud? Of course, but the likelihood of her bearing children was about the same as winning the Power Ball. Zilch.

Whack! The ball streaked across the field, striking the first baseman in the leg. That was it. Kate packed up her camera, crushed her soda can. "See you Saturday. Tell Trevor good job."

"Don't forget to bring your brownies. I'm off my diet." Jackie pulled out her Detroit Tigers umbrella then shouted to her son who trotted off the field.

Kate waved good-bye and limped toward the parking lot as the first drops of rain threatened to soak her and her gear. Halfway there, a firm hand clamped down on her left shoulder. She spun around, expecting Jackie with another reminder.

Instead a pudgy, middle-aged man with a camera drooped around his neck swayed before her.

"Aren't you the Miracle Girl of the Canton bomber? I've been looking for you."

His question tore into her like a round-nosed bullet. "Sorry. You've got the wrong person." She twisted from his grip, veered toward the stream of parents. When she reached her car, she dove into the driver's seat, pressed the locks, and fumbled with her keys. The ten-year old engine sputtered, refusing to start. "C'mon!" she begged as her pulse surged. She cranked it again. Another time. When it finally turned over, she shifted into gear and craned her neck to scan the packed parking lot. Then she tore out onto the road.

Kate gripped the steering wheel hard, steadying her racing thoughts.

She glanced into her rear-view mirror as she skillfully maneuvered the back streets of Loreen, certain no one followed her. As the Sun's photographer, she had memorized all the streets. Now she'd have to quit her job again. Move away.

At thirty-two, she was tired of running.

The driveway of the apartment building loomed before her. She searched the lot for strangers. Anything out of the ordinary. One mistake and . . .

She wiped her clammy palms on her jeans.

It would take only a few hours to pack. She'd become somewhat of a pro over the years. Her own private disappearing act.

Kate stashed her camera gear in the foyer corner, and rested her back against the locked door, her bad leg throbbing. The smell of last night's lasagna still lingered in small pools of spicy scent around her. She scanned her home. Too bad she'd fallen for this apartment. High ceilings with ornate moldings. Something out of her dreams. She should have known better.

She pushed off. Enough memories.

First she dug for an envelope from the box she kept stashed in a kitchen drawer. A final rent check. Then a letter of resignation.

After packing her meager closet of clothing, she pulled out a box she'd kept stored for this particular day. In it she placed her knick-knacks, art work, and other memorabilia she'd collected over the years—items that reminded her she had a past before the running began. She picked up the pocketknife her father had always carried on him. The pearl handle soothed her soul.

She slipped it into her jean's pocket.

Once she packed her apartment, she opened her computer and uploaded the ballgame photos. Because she planned to run from her job, didn't mean she couldn't finish her work. She'd send her editor the photos and the write up first. She wasn't a total loser.

Her mouth curved upward as she flipped through the shots. She had been careful to include as many players as she could. She'd also taken a team picture to present to the coach at the picnic on Sunday. Hopefully, Mark would see he got it.

Kate propped her elbows on the kitchen table while memories whirred. Jackie had become as close to a friend as she had ever known. They'd clicked the first time Kate showed up at a school event where she'd taken photos for the paper. Next thing she knew, she was attending all the games with Jackie and her husband and cheering on Trevor like she was his aunt. He was a good kid, always trying to please his parents.

Another photo. Her last one. Trevor, glove in position at third base.

No! Her throat clogged, as though someone was choking her from behind. She lunged for a gulp of water at the sink, tipping over her chair in her haste.

Her hands shook as she stared at her computer. Not again. She should shut it down now. Slam the lid. Walk out the door and forget this town. The people. Her life.

She squeezed her eyes shut. Is that who she'd become?

Swallowing hard, she forced herself to return to the picture of Trevor, forced her eyes to focus. Trevor blurred, then cleared. His prepubescent body squatted, ready for action. His mother's blue eyes peered from beneath his cap. The dimple that Jackie swore came from his dad, filled his right cheek.

A handsome child. A child full of life.

Kate blinked. Touched the screen. She couldn't deny the truth that screamed to her.

The faint white glow. It had returned. Again.

This time the aura surrounded a little boy whose only dream was to become a major league ballplayer.

She gagged, turned her head away as hot bile rose to the back of her throat.

She hated that glow. What it meant. What it promised.

Certain death.

Not Trevor. A primal ache erupted from a place deep inside of her heart. She remembered the cough. The one Jackie said had kept her up for a month of Sundays. The visit to the town doctor who declared it a cold, nothing else.

She glanced to her phone. How could she not say something? She punched in her friend's number, hoping Jackie wouldn't pick up. A message. A short message and that would suffice. Then she'd run to another town where she would know no one. Where she might never see the aura again.

The phone rang three times. Each ring pounded into Kate's ears like a sledge hammer. *Don't let her pick up.*

"Hey, did you make it home without drowning? Trevor and I are soaked." Jackie's velvety voice answered.

Kate clutched the phone to her ear. Ordered herself to breathe normally.

"Listen, I've been thinking about Trevor and his cough. Why don't you take him to a specialist in Lansing for me? I had a friend once who had a cough like his. I don't want to scare you, but I would take him again. Make them run more tests."

"Now look who's worrying."

"Please?" Kate turned back to her screen. Slammed down the lid.

"Okay. I wanted to anyway, but I didn't want to come across as overprotective. I'll call tomorrow."

Kate's stomach dropped into place. "Thanks. Oh, and I found out I need to leave town awhile. An emergency. My aunt. She fell and needs my help."

"I'm sorry. Can I do anything while you're gone? Get your mail?"

"No, no. I'll put a stop on it. Just take care of Trevor for me, okay? Kiss him bye."

"Sure, I'll do that. Kate, take care of yourself. I'll miss you."

"Me too. I'll miss all of you." She clicked off. Dropped her head into her hands.

She could deal with the running. The leaving. The hiding.

What she couldn't deal with was much worse—being the person who predicted death.

3

A sense of hopeless gloom permeated the air.

Bend, Pennsylvania. A pimple on the map. The place reminded Kate of the dismal battle pictures she'd seen while visiting Gettysburg with her parents. Drooping store fronts decayed from too many years of poor upkeep. Skinny hounds rooting for a sliver of shade or a handout. A spattering of tired-old men in bib overalls and women dressed in drab forgotten colors following one step behind.

She toyed with the idea of turning around as she consulted the GPS on her phone.

When Kate had called about the job, the editor warned he couldn't pay much, but he had an opening. She would cover social events and funerals. Shoot photos and write short copy. If she wanted the job, those were the terms. Apparently the other reporter covered everything else.

She wanted work, and her choices had run out.

Running was no longer an option. She needed to eat.

She continued south through town, crossed a rickety bridge and slowed as she neared the address for her new home. The real estate agent called it a fixer upper. A gross understatement.

Egg-shell blue paint had been used to hide a rotting front porch. A tin roof patched with rust spots topped the deteriorating building. Windows like gloomy eyes stared at her, dared her to enter. But it *was* in her price range. Plus, towering oak trees bordered the property so she would not easily be detected.

She parked by the back door. Hoisted her suitcase and box through the back door.

Time to check out the rest of the place.

A prickly horsehair couch dominated the living room. Not exactly her style. Or anyone's, she guessed. The one saving grace—a comfy looking chair with a three-legged stool in front of it. She quickly toured the bedroom and antiquated bathroom and found it livable. After she stashed her groceries into one of the two kitchen cupboards, she collapsed on the front porch in a high-backed rocker that wheezed from age.

Her new job started tomorrow. She'd meet Tim, the editor, for the first time. He'd agreed to hire her using only Skype. An added bonus when she'd been holed up in a motel in Ohio, searching the online want ads.

Her first assignment: an event being held at the Brickhouse Church on Spencer Street. Tonight. Everyone in town would be there, he'd said. Make a few friends. Snoop out a few stories.

She didn't want to make friends again. Or be seen in public any more than necessary, but it was part of her job. She couldn't be alone forever. Or could she?

She thought of Jackie and how devastated she would be when she learned of Trevor's illness. How she could never explain how she knew.

Even she didn't fully understand.

Her gift, her grandmother called it. More like a thorny curse. A curse to remind her of the day her life changed forever.

She gave the rocker a hard push. She would start over. *She'd* chosen this town. Not her curse.

###

Two hours later, Kate drove through the dismal town again. The BC, as Tim had called the church, sat on a sizable hill on the other side of town. She found it easily as it appeared everyone was headed in the same direction. She followed a dented, blue Ford truck and parked next to it in one of the few remaining open spaces.

Her stomach twisted as she unhooked her seat belt. Second thoughts gripped her. She should have skipped this meeting, waited to meet her coworkers first. She hated crowds, preferring to remain in the background. She exhaled. This was her job.

She watched as women and children clustered near the front entrance. Long skirts for the girls, ties for the boys. Kate groaned and brushed the lint from her best pair of jeans. Why hadn't she worn her black skirt she used for interviews? She'd stick out like a pickle in a plate of olives.

At least she'd dabbed on makeup. She checked her face in the mirror one last time and slid from her car.

"Evening, ma'am." A cherub-faced boy who looked close to ten spoke as he passed.

"Evening to you too." Kate smiled at being called ma'am. Cute kid. Like Trevor. She hooked her purse over her shoulder and followed him up the walkway toward the country church, being careful to mask her limp.

Stale air like moth balls blasted her senses as she entered. Up front, the organist played a tune she vaguely remembered from her youth. "Bringing in the sheaves, bringing in the sheaves. . ." The forgotten words tested her tongue and then fell off. Another time.

She veered around a hunched over gentleman, steadied only by a cane, and selected the last pew, sitting next to a matronly-looking woman with sparkling blue eyes. "I'm Ethel," the woman offered, as Kate settled beside her. "Can't wait to hear Brother Earl speak. We need change in the Bend. Can't come too soon."

"Kate. It's nice to meet you, Ethel." Kate grasped her hand, shook it, then turned her attention toward the front. Already the townspeople had filled the church to the bones, the music working overtime to energize them. A large wooden platform occupied the center of the church. The sturdy podium on it resembled the one Kate once stood behind as a child in school. A speaker. That's what Mrs. Bing said she would become.

Her sixth-grade teacher had gotten that wrong.

"Find your seats, please. We're ready to begin tonight's program. Gentlemen, corral your wives and children." The balding spokesperson, whom she assumed was Brother Earl Foreman, anchored himself behind the podium, his fingers gripping both sides as he swayed as though on his own ocean. His bushy mustache curled to his chin.

"Do you mind?" A man closer to her age, slid in on her other side, blocking her only means of exit—something she always planned for when she went out. A habit that gripped her still.

Kate eyed her seatmate. Pressed khakis. A Polo shirt with a pen tipping out of the breast pocket. His sandy hair had been cut tight and when he smiled at her, he showed bleached white teeth. He also cradled a floppy notebook in his arms.

Kate eased closer to Ethel.

"I don't have cooties."

Kate's cheeks burned. "I was making more room," she said. "That's all." She steered her attention once more to the front where Brother Earl spoke in tones that grew increasingly louder.

"We own this community, don't we? We *own* the Bend because we are its people. Our goal is to make this a town we are *proud* to raise our children in. Even if that means *giving up* some of those creature comforts you thought you couldn't live without. A town where we respect family values. Respect the men and women who created this town. A town where men and women live how God intended them to live. Not how the world intends. Not how the world is corrupting us."

The crowd cheered at his words. An electric charge shot around the room, forcing Kate to take notice of the rapt expressions on the faces nearest to her. Ethel practically glowed. The man in front of her whistled through his teeth.

A wave of uncertainty swept through Kate. Brother Earl's message struck a flat chord.

"Tonight, we're taking a stand. Fighting the devil right at his doorstep. Clutching our crosses and saying, "No more!" He shouted the final two words in a thunderous voice.

Kate took a deep breath. Clamped her jaw together. Told herself to relax. This was the Bend, after all. Not Canton.

Beside her, Ethel raised her arms and added her loud amen to the choruses. Kate had been to revivals in the past, but something about this one told her it wasn't a revival of faith but a revival to save the town.

From what? Who were they standing up against? The world? She dug into her purse and pulled out her notepad. Tim might want the scoop tomorrow. She should get her camera and take Brother Earl's picture too. Her editor would see her potential and move her to meatier stories. She'd finally earn enough money to make a decent living. Perhaps she could settle down in a place like this, far from the rest of the world.

Brother Earl's voice escalated, yanking her from her hopeful thoughts.

"Movies are for the dead! You won't get to heaven watching movies, dear people. Nor will your children find that perfect mate by going to theaters. No, they won't. We need to demolish movies and DVDs and anything else that will destroy our precious community and distract from the good this community offers. We need to put our feet *down* and *refuse* to be mollified by the present trend. We need to *stand* up for good! It's the only way!" At Earl's final thrust of words, the people vaulted to their feet and cheered.

But she didn't. Nor did the man with the green toothpick sticking out the side of his mouth next to her. He scribbled in his notebook faster than she could think.

When the rally finally ended, Kate followed the crowd outside where the cooler air fanned her fiery cheeks. She peered upward. The moon showed behind the steeple. She preferred to be safely locked in her new home before darkness descended, but she wasn't quite ready to leave. She glanced at her notebook. Pictured a heading: *Determined Folk Take Back the Bend.* Maybe her editor would run her story on the first page.

She studied the women who gathered in a tight group in the parking lot. Then the men who had done the same but on the opposite side. Why the seriousness? Again, she thought of Canton and how her home town had fought against the growing cultists among them. But those followers had been crazy—filled with anger toward the Christian faith.

The Bend and its people loved God. Didn't they?

She scanned the parking lot for the stranger who had sat beside her. There, standing by a two-toned van. Deep in conversation with a man. As the crowd thinned, she made a quick decision. Get her story.

Brother Earl stood in the dimly lit sanctuary gathering a sheaf of papers by the platform, his huge ring catching on a folder. He huffed, then pulled up straight when she tapped him on the arm.

Dark hooded eyes glared down at her.

"I don't think I've met you before. Are you new to the Bend?" His words came out softly, sounding not at all like the man who had riled the crowd with such fierceness earlier.

"I work for the newspaper. This is my first rally, actually. I was hoping I might conduct a short interview with you, take your picture and write up a story about your plans for the B-b-e-bend." She stuttered on the name of the town. What was wrong with her? She licked her dry lips. Normally, she wasn't nervous doing her job, but something about him put her off her game.

He grew larger by the minute, soon towering over her. His chest expanded. She couldn't help but think of a grizzly bear and found herself shrinking backward. "The Bend is falling into evil hands, Miss. It's the town's job to see it doesn't happen. We've failed. We've failed miserably. My hope is to turn the corner on the corrupt, sinful, and wrongdoings that have put our community at risk. We must be the salt of the earth. Be different than the world. Put that in your paper. Maybe the pack of wolves devouring our community will realize we mean business." With a curt nod, he brushed past her and tromped down the aisle to where a group of older men gathered. A few slaps on the back peppered with a few more amens and they moved outside.

Kate followed trying to overhear their conversation. When it appeared she'd get nothing more, she trekked to her car, favoring her bad leg. At least she had something. Maybe with further digging tomorrow, she could whip up a printable story.

"Ma'am." The same sweet boy who had greeted her on her arrival ran up to her car door. He held out a delicate daisy, probably plucked from one of the many fields surrounding the church. Kate took the wilted flower.

"Thank you. What's your name?"

"I'm Brother Earl's son. He asked me to invite you to our home next week for dinner." From his other palm, he produced a blue business card. "Call him tomorrow." After he planted the card firmly in her hand, he scuttled toward a large van where several women and children waited.

She raised the embossed card to her face and read it in the waning light.

FOREMAN'S FUNERAL HOME. Visitors always welcome.

4

Seth Abrams peeled his Jeep onto the highway, roaring away from the church. If only he'd had a chance to speak with Earl again. But that redhead beat him to it. It wasn't his style to butt in but maybe he needed to change his style. It was his story, after all. One he'd been working on ever since arriving in the Bend last year.

He tore down the steep hill, navigating his vehicle through the darkened streets. As he passed through the center of town, he stared at the local movie theater. Poor Mr. Jeffers. After tonight's rally, he might be the only one watching his movies.

His foot hit the brake. A basset hound glared at him from inside his headlights then continued his path across the road. Stupid dog.

Stupid owner.

Seth groped the seat next to him for his opened bag of Tootsie Pops. He unwrapped one and shoved it into his mouth. Not as soothing as a cigarette but it helped. He reminded himself to stop at the grocery store tomorrow for another bag. Between pops and flavored toothpicks, he'd managed to kick his pack-a-day habit.

He tapped the steering wheel as he rounded the final curve to his rental house.

The one-story log cabin wasn't much but he could afford it. The silhouette of pine trees greeted him as he pulled into the short driveway. He glared at the unlit porch

Thankfully, he left a light on over the sink in his laundry room. His crazy tabby cat, Daisy, greeted him with a scolding meow when he came through the back door.

"Hold your mouth. I'm getting your dinner." He reached into the cupboard over the washer and dumped a handful of cat food into Daisy's blue dish. Patted her head. Then he moved into the kitchen and opened the refrigerator for a soda.

Seth next flipped on the desk lamp and fired up his computer in the spare bedroom. Not really an office, but it would do for now.

He should have taken pictures tonight. Earlier in the day, his editor told him he'd finally hired a photographer. Maybe once the guy started, Seth could bring him to events like the one tonight. A few candid pictures of the crowd getting all riled up. Maybe a few of the women with the up-do hairstyles piling out of the vans while their kids clung to their prairie dresses.

He gulped his soda, burped, and shoved it aside.

When he finished this story, he'd win the Pulitzer. At the very least, a page in the *New York Times* or a guest appearance on the *Good Morning Show*.

He'd waited his entire life for this opportunity. Made working hard all through school worth it.

Seth flexed his fingers. Hit the keys.

A little more digging. A little more nose-poking. He would expose the evil that was growing in this town.

He had to.

The story of the year—*his* story of the year—was unfolding right here in little old Bend.

5

The alarm clock jarred Kate awake. Another bad dream. This one found her racing down the street with her clothing on fire. Would they never end? The same one all the time. The man with the black hood over his head. Chasing her. Each time she escaped by jumping off the bridge into a swirling icy river. She'd kick, fighting to rise to the surface, her chest constricting from no oxygen. Gasping, she'd finally awaken drenched in sweat.

And the press wanted her to remember that time? Right.

After a quick shower, a breakfast of cold cereal and buttered toast, Kate drove over the bridge and down a few narrow streets until she found her new place of employment. Starting another job stunk. She'd lost count of how many times she'd done this before. Too many. Hopefully, her new boss and coworkers would go easy on her like they did in Michigan.

She slowed, eyeing the dilapidated building. A dump from the 1800s. A faded sign. A scuffed white entry door. A folding chair and dead flowers in a plastic pot.

Who was she to judge? After parking out back, she hiked around to the front door, her briefcase stuffed under one arm. She'd stayed up too late last night jotting down her thoughts from the meeting. She'd added the photo of the church she snapped before leaving but knew the story needed more detail. She would set that dinner date with Brother Earl. An interview with the man who fueled the town's pulse. Perfect.

A bell tinkled from overhead when she entered. "May I help you?" A woman with streaked blonde hair sat behind a desk painting her nails a bright red.

"I'm Kate Song. I start work here today." She held out her hand then withdrew it. No need to ruin the girl's manicure or her own hands.

The receptionist greeted her with a wave and gestured to a nearby chair. "Have a seat, Kate. I'll get Tim for you. He's eager to meet you in person."

Kate did as instructed, drawing a deep breath to steady herself. Hopefully, Tim would like what he saw and skip past the particulars of her previous employment.

The bell tinkled a second time.

Kate looked up. The man with the cooties from the rally. She gulped and tried to look away, but his strong gaze held hers.

"We meet again. Too bad there isn't another chair. I'd sit by you, cooties and all." His tone was warm, but his smile didn't quite reach his sparkling eyes. He tipped his head and strode through a doorway.

The receptionist soon returned with a familiar-looking older gentleman in tow. Standing, Kate waited for introductions to her new boss.

"I see you made it to the Bend. Come on in. I'll show you your desk. Oh, I'm Tim." Tim stood at least six feet, a good half foot taller than Kate. Broad shoulders. Wavy hair. Glasses. All in all, a friendly face. The kind one instantly trusts. Just like on Skype.

Kate held out her hand. "It's great to be here. Thank you."

"You've met Rhonda?" After a firm grip he gestured toward the woman who first greeted her. Kate smiled at Rhonda again before following him into a large room cluttered with metal desks and outdated computers. A smaller space looped off to the right. Tim's office, she assumed, as he tapped a desk for her near an opened window.

When she'd settled into her seat, he pulled up a nearby chair. He gave a few instructions and told her she would be given assignments as they came. When she wasn't busy with those, she was to drive around town to scout out news, take calls as they came, and assist Seth.

"Seth?" She scanned the room in search of her fellow reporter.

Tim looked over his shoulder, let out a high-pitched whistle. She heard the flush of a toilet, running water, and then a door opened in the far corner. Mr. Cooties stepped out. He wiped his hands on a paper towel, tossed it in a nearby paper can.

He wound his way toward them.

Kate squelched a groan as understanding filled Seth's eyes. She stood and put her hand out. "It's nice to officially meet you. I'm Kate Song."

Seth shot Tim a wary look before he shook. "All clean."

A smile found her mouth. Thank goodness. A sense of humor.

"Have you two met already?" Tim looked from her face to Seth's.

"Briefly," she said. "We were at the same meeting last night." She remembered her notes. "Oh, and I have the beginnings of a story for you if you're interested. I need to gather a little more information, but I think you might like it. Saving the Bend."

Seth's face reddened. Was he embarrassed that he hadn't offered a story too?

Tim clapped his hand on her shoulder. "Good work. I like a reporter who jumps right in. Give me the details on paper and we'll see where you go with it. Seth can help with the writing. I know you're better at taking pictures." He slapped his palm to his forehead and shut his eyes briefly. "Let me think. I've got a list of upcoming functions for you to cover. Where did I leave that list?" He wandered away from them, mumbling about too much to do and why couldn't Rhonda file better.

Seth tossed her a half-smile. "Welcome to the club. Coffee?" He pointed to a setup on a counter.

"Thanks. I'd like that."

She followed and poured herself a cup. Black. Like she remembered her parents drinking. Seth poured himself one as well, then led them back to their desks. His butted up next to hers. Handy, but she'd have preferred her own cubicle like at her last job.

"So, it's your first day on the job. Where are you from?" He took a long sip and rocked back in his chair, the ancient coils groaning from his weight.

Kate shuffled the pens and pads on her desk and placed her coffee next to the computer. Stalling for time. Her best defense. Whenever anyone asked her where she came from, her throat froze. She'd yet to come up with a great answer.

She gave the usual. "All over. I saw this job online. The area sounded pretty."

"Pretty." He smiled showing his nice even teeth. Kate's tongue ran over a chipped tooth she still hadn't found the funds to fix.

"Very pretty. Mountains, lakes, rivers. What more could a girl want?"

"Pretty," he said again as he uncrossed his legs and leaned forward—uncomfortably close. "Do you know where you are? This is the Bend. I'm sure you didn't read about the Bend in your studies of Pennsylvania." He inched closer, lowering his voice.

A strong sugary odor danced between them. Chocolate.

"This is the place time has forgotten. The place maybe even God forgot. You saw those people last night. Long skirts, hair pulled up in buns." He nodded toward her attire. "You might want to trade those slacks for an ankle-length dress. You'll fit in better. Forget about going to the movies or walking around town with a cell phone. Didn't you hear the old man last night? Change is in the wind and anyone who gets in the way is begging for trouble."

She drew back. A menacing tone or giving her the facts? Probably more like a sore ego because she'd scooped a story. She'd run into a lot of reporters like him in her years working at newspapers. Ego-filled. Looking for the story that propelled their career. Didn't matter who got in their way.

She'd met another.

Kate steeled her voice.

"What I saw was a group of people eager to keep the town simple and clean. They care about where they live. The morals. Family. God. Country. All-American. Trust me, that doesn't happen too often. People don't care who their neighbors are anymore or what's happening to their community. Not from what I've seen." She was not about to admit that strange feeling Earl's speech gave her.

He frowned—long and hard. "Give yourself time, Red. You might sing a different tune."

His use of her childhood nickname irritated her. She gripped her mug— imagined his throat. "How long have you been here?" Seth definitely didn't fit her picture of a Bend resident. He was probably from New York City where people smacked into you on the street without apology. He wouldn't be able to appreciate a small-town atmosphere.

"Long enough to know something about this town." He turned toward his computer, cutting off their conversation—thrusting up a brick wall more like. Kate wanted to ask him another question but decided against it. Maybe after she went to dinner with Brother Earl.

The day spun by with Rhonda giving her forms to fill out and Tim instructing her to follow his schedule. She devoured a quick tuna sandwich at her desk at noon, then grabbed her gear at one to catch the meeting at the library.

She found the place easily enough. A plain brick building tucked behind the laundromat. The musty odor of mildew greeted her as she stepped over the threshold. Already, a group of young mothers and children had gathered toward the front of the main room. The kids who read the most books during the past school year were receiving an award.

Kate introduced herself to the woman in charge.

"They call me Miss Lillian." The woman with the twist of hair on the back of her head informed her. A pair of pink readers hung from a chain around her slender neck. Her dark skirt folded like a blanket when she leaned against the counter. Kate couldn't help but notice the quick glance Miss Lillian gave her pants.

"After the presentations, may I speak with you to get the proper spelling of names and other information?"

Miss Lillian nodded. "Of course. We are grateful to have children's accomplishments published in our local newspaper. The Bend needs to applaud these fine young residents. They are our future, you know. We are nothing without our children. Nothing. It's every woman's job here to see to that. Every precaution must be taken with them."

Kate nodded, anxious to get away from over-the-top Miss Lillian. "I'll sit over there and take pictures as they come forward." She limped toward a bright display of first readers and dropped onto a wooden bench.

The children appeared to be in the age range of six to ten. Five girls and three boys. The best of the best readers. Kate set up her camera.

"My mother said she'll cook your favorite meal when you visit us." Kate looked up. The boy from the night before. Today he dressed in dark black pants with a button-down shirt. No tie. His brown eyes sparked like he knew something she didn't.

"That's kind. I haven't set up the dinner yet, but I promise you I'll call later today."

He matched her smile. "My mother says she can't wait to meet you." He nodded toward a petite woman on the left bank of folding chairs. The woman appeared to be in her early twenties. Brother Earl's wife? So young?

"Your mother is the woman in the navy-blue skirt?" She couldn't be. She must have been a child when she married.

The boy nodded. A solemn look overtook his previous smile. "My other mother couldn't come today. She's feeling poorly."

Kate caught the camera that almost slipped from her fingers. "Your other mother? Do you mean you have two mothers?" Surely he was confused. Although Kate once thought of her grandmother like a second mother. Maybe that was the case here, too.

"Don't you?" He gave her another sweet smile and skipped over to the assembly. Miss Lillian had already started directing everyone with a firm voice.

Concentration came hard as the awards were presented. Kate's thoughts kept colliding on the woman in the third row from the front. The woman who kept her head lowered the entire time, never once raising it until her son received his certificate. Then a ghost of a smile appeared, and she applauded softly.

When the gathering ended, the boy's mother hustled her son through the doors without stopping to speak to Kate or acknowledge her presence. Kate watched them climb into an older model vehicle parked along the curb. A man with longish hair sat in the driver's seat. He frowned in Kate's direction.

She ducked her head, embarrassed to be caught snooping. Yet why wouldn't the woman speak to her knowing Brother Earl had invited her as a guest to their home?

The only explanation that made sense was the woman was shy. That's why she'd sent her son over today and last night as well. That had to be the reason for her reserved manner.

Kate packed her camera and notes and dug into her purse for the business card. She'd call Brother Earl when she returned to the office and schedule the dinner. Although she hesitated to make friends in the Bend, it was obvious Brother Earl's wife needed one. And what better friend to have than one who kept quiet.

6

If only she'd shut up. He tightened the rope that constrained her wrists. His new candidate twisted, screaming beneath her tape. He hated to damage her, but, in some cases, it was the only way they learned.

Pity.

Who knew that outing to see the circus trainer when he was twelve would change both his father's life and his forever? And now this woman, Cindy, would reap the benefit of his lessons.

He plied his fingers across her pale throat. She'd offered her name when he carried her groceries out the door. Naive, stupid Cindy. Look where flirting got her.

Another caress. She squirmed away from his touch, her arms banging against the sides of the box.

Fire shot from her eyes. He would douse that soon. He would douse everything very soon.

"You'll play nicer tomorrow," he whispered. He flicked one finger under her chin.

If she made it until tomorrow.

He pulled a chair from the dark corner. Straddled it. Looked down at her lying in the pine coffin.

Good hips. Nice for bearing offspring.

Cindy moaned, banged her feet against the base.

"No one can hear you. No one. The faster you play by my rules, the faster this will go."

He reached for the lid, let it slam shut. "Nap time, darling."

7

Seth checked the time again. He couldn't keep his thoughts off last night's meeting and the redhead who stole his thunder. Sure, Kate seemed nice enough. She'd offered to run out and buy more coffee when the supply ran low. She also suggested they meet the next day at the theater and interview Mr. Jeffers. "Get his thoughts on what he's showing and how he's accepting what the town is saying."

The last thing Seth needed was someone telling him how to do his job. Been there before. Not going there again.

He reached for a flavored tooth pick. Peeled the paper back and jammed it in his lower jaw. It was a wonder he never drank.

Anyone would after losing a woman like Lisa.

Images of his lost love fired through his thoughts.

Someday she'd see his picture on the front page of the news or on TV when he accepted his award. She'd regret dropping him. Maybe she'd even cry a little. He pictured her calling her girlfriends to tell them how Seth and she were once an item. Maybe she'd call him.

He crushed his paper cup.

Who needed this little redhead to come in here acting like a star reporter? He spun around, eyed the office doorway and the clock over it once more. Where was she now? Barking up another tree in hopes of putting him out of a job?

"Where's that story you said you'd have for me by now?" Tim trotted out of his office, his glasses pushed high on his head, his lips turned downward. "Daydreaming out here again, huh?" His voice sounded gruff, but Seth knew his boss well enough to know he was all air.

"Almost done. You'll love it." He returned to his computer, tapped a few keys.

"Yeah, yeah. That's what you always say. Just so it pays the bills."

"Speaking of bills, have you thought about raises? My yearly anniversary was last month."

Tim stopped sorting papers on a nearby desk. "Told you and I'll tell you again. Get me a story worth selling and I'll get you that raise. Then you can buy yourself a decent car instead of that piece of junk you call a Jeep."

Seth laughed. "You don't like it?" He loved his Jeep. It had been his father's. Parting with it wouldn't be easy.

"Just get me my story." Tim returned to his office, leaving Seth staring at a blank computer screen.

He had nothing new to report on his story. Last night's meeting hadn't revealed much more about Brother Earl than he already knew. The guy lived like a king in his funeral home surrounded by more women than Seth cared to count. Young women. When Seth tried to check the marriage records, the staff at the county office politely told him they were none of his business. The next day he saw the Recorder of Deeds eating lunch with Earl at The Cow's Cafe. Neither spoke to him when he walked past.

He'd need to be more careful if he wanted to uncover the truth.

He shut off his computer. The only event for him to cover today was the bowling derby at Starburst Lanes outside of town. He picked up his phone. It wouldn't hurt to take a photographer with him.

Kate answered on the second ring. "This is Kate."

"Meet me at the bowling alley in ten. I need pictures." He didn't give her a chance to refuse, hung up and gathered his belongings. He was the real reporter at this paper.

###

The temperature inside the lanes registered eighty degrees according to the cowgirl thermometer that hung over the front counter. Seth pushed his way through the crowd of wannabe superstar bowlers until his gaze landed on Kate. Bent over a bowler, her hand clutched a pen and pad. Seth dug for his recorder. He gritted his teeth as he approached.

"What are you doing, Red? Where's your camera?"

She straightened, jutting her chin out as she did. "I brought it. Jack and I were just discussing the way the tournament is going to run. I thought that information might be useful."

He could tell by the way her lips moved, he'd offended her. But who cared? She was hired as a photographer and needed to go on his leads. "Great. Get some pictures of the teams as they warm up while I meet with Jack."

Kate nodded her apologies to Jack and shuffled over to the other side of the lanes where she pulled out her camera. Seth shrugged. Maybe she'd get tired of the Bend and pack up and leave. Others had. What made her any different? Once most newcomers got wind of this town, they took off running like a bad case of diarrhea. He'd seen that happen a dozen times in the past year.

Faith, the last photographer, had not even said good-bye. She never showed up at work the next morning after a big rally on the hill. Rumor had it she'd run off with a local, but Seth thought otherwise. She hadn't liked his warnings. He didn't want to think about the other possibility—the possibility that ran through his brain when he lay in bed at night. He shook his head. Idiot thoughts.

He glanced again at Kate. How long before she ran off too? Maybe Tim would let him pick the next photographer. Someone who wouldn't compete with him.

He shelved his dismal thoughts for later when the announcer came over the PA system. Time to do his job.

The event rolled to a stop after three hours of bowling and a lot of hoopla in between. Kate took the pictures he suggested while he took notes. He almost pulled the plug an hour into it but didn't. He needed a complete story and might as well keep his eyes open for one here. Besides, she seemed content to hang out. She'd struck up conversations with several of the locals.

"Soda?" The bar maid wiped down a wet spot in front of him when he stopped at the counter.

"Root beer, please." Seth took a long sip through the foam and eyed the remaining patrons. To his far left, a group of older bowlers gathered. Their heads were bent close, foreheads almost touching. Seth watched with interest as Kate approached them, notebook in hand. He took another long sip as she sidled up to one gritty farmer. His scraggly bearded face scowled when she said something to him. Kate stepped back, nodding, her cheeks turning crimson. Even at this distance, Seth could tell that whatever bearded face said to her it wasn't nice. He set down his glass with a sigh.

Seth ambled toward the group of men and Kate with a smile pasted on his face. Hopefully he could diffuse whatever mess she'd gotten herself into without a fight. Gritty Farmer, aka Mole, looked up at him. "Hey Seth, tell your sidekick here that women ought to dress like women. Not hang out in bowling alleys asking questions they have no business asking." He spit a wad of juicy brown slop into a nearby cup.

"She's new to the Bend. Give her a break, Mole."

Mole frowned. "Slow learner and an outsider. Better have a talk with her." He spit again, this time giving Kate the stink eye. She'd had the decency to step further back from the group, but Seth saw her jaw tighten.

She would not be easy to convince. But he owed it to her to try.

8

The last time a man spoke to Kate like that she'd told him off. Today she took a deep breath, wishing her face didn't burn so much. She must look like a school girl who heard her first bad word on the playground. Too bad she needed this job. She would like to walk right out the door, get her belongings and head south.

"I'm sorry to have bothered you," she said to Mole after Seth finished his rescue.

"Maybe you better think twice about going around and asking questions about the Bend. You might not like the answers." He snorted and turned back to his group of cronies, laughing as he did.

Kate limped to a corner where she'd set her belongings. She shoved her camera into its bag harder than she should. So what if she asked a few questions about Brother Earl. He seemed to be the man of the hour and she wanted more information for her story.

"Can't say I didn't warn you." Seth stood next to her. She fisted her hands. Forced herself to not slap him. Let alone thank him.

"Are we done here? I've got a few calls to make and I'd like to check my photos."

He shrugged as though he had nothing better to do than remind her about her humiliating moment. "Fine with me. I'll meet you back at the office. Everyone should be gone by now. If you beat me, there's a key under the front mat." He turned and returned to the lanes where he stopped and chatted with a few younger bowlers who were packing up.

Kate gritted her teeth. Seth would take getting used to as much as this town, but his arrogance would not get the best of her. What Seth didn't know was she was a survivor.

The key sat right where he said it would be. Kate felt for the light switch. The front room illuminated with a soft glow casting enough light into the next room to find the next switch. She went directly to her desk and fell into her chair with a sigh. Was it too late to call Brother Earl and set up dinner?

She dug for her cell phone. She still couldn't rid the boy's comment about his mothers from her mind. That's what she'd asked old scraggly beard and his friends at the bowling alley. "Do you know Earl's wife?" They clammed up like someone had threatened to take their paychecks from them. All except the guy whose shoulders outsized a grizzly and smelled like he needed a long overdue shower.

She flicked the embossed card with her finger. A funeral home director. The kind of man she'd want to go to if she needed those services. Brother Earl didn't exactly ooze compassion. She couldn't imagine him assisting a broken-hearted widow with the coffin selection or choice in music. Perhaps he owned the home but didn't run it. That had to be the answer. Maybe his wife performed all the empathy scenes. Or one of his wives.

She set the card in front of her. What kind of meeting would it be? Would he allow her to question him about his plans for the Bend? Or would she be expected to sit meekly and sip her soup?

She wouldn't go if that was the case.

Her phone in hand, Kate punched in the numbers. She waited. On the fifth ring, a woman answered. "May I help you?"

"This is Kate Song from the paper. Brother Earl invited me to dinner at your home this weekend. Could you give me a time and directions, please?" Getting right to the point seemed the best tactic. She waited while the woman put her on hold.

A second later, Brother Earl's fiery voice boomed into her ear. "We eat precisely at six p.m. This Saturday will be fine. Sunday is the Lord's Day and I reserve that for my family. I will see you then, Miss Song."

The phone died.

Precisely at six he'd said. She'd arrive at 5:45.

9

Seth frowned. It wasn't like him to eavesdrop on someone, but he couldn't help it when he heard Kate mention Earl. Mole was right. She was a slow learner. Stupid wouldn't win her any Pulitzer Prizes. For that he should be grateful.

He pretended to cough twice before he entered the office, giving her time to pull herself together. He hated a weepy female. "So how did the pictures turn out? Get any we can use?" He didn't care, but one glance told him now wasn't the time to ask. She looked like she could eat a bear for dinner. Raw.

"How much do you know about Brother Earl? Really. Is he always so polite?"

Seth plunked down in his chair across from her. He turned on his computer. "You heard him at the rally. The man is intense." In some ways, like himself. But Seth didn't go around in public acting like he was God.

She turned back to her desk and punched some keys. "I'm surprised he's so well received. He has the personality of a shark." She pulled out a cable and attached her camera to the computer. Another few clicks. "So do his cronies."

"Still brooding about your encounter with the boys? Get used to it. In this town, you're either on the inside or the outside."

"Where are you?"

She was looking at him again and he couldn't help but admire the fine shape of her lips. He tore his gaze away. The last time he became involved with a coworker, he lost a major story because he was too wrapped up in the chase. Nothing would stop him this time. Not even emerald green eyes that glowed like gemstones.

"I prefer to stay neutral. If you have any sense at all, you will too. Consider that my free advice for the day. Now if you don't mind, I have a story to write." He placed his hands on the keyboard and typed two lines.

"Of course. Don't let me stop you."

Icy. He had almost felt sorry for her. Forget that. Let her find out on her own what the Bend was like. He'd tried to warn her, but some fools needed to wade knee deep in it before they learned.

Kate glanced at Seth again. Stuck working with Mr. Macho. A sigh wormed itself out of her lungs. Hopefully, he hadn't heard, but just in case, she stretched her arms over her head and let out a huge yawn.

Next, she scrolled through the photos she'd taken earlier that day. She held her breath. Please no auras. But she never knew when they would appear. That was the hard part about this curse—never knowing when she'd see the white glow and who it would surround. She leaned in to peer at one particular shot. Mole. She'd taken a picture of him wiping his ball after throwing it. Was that a ring on his right hand? He didn't look like the kind of man to wear one. She zoomed in. It *was* a ring. A ring with a hawk emblem. She tapped her fingers on her desk. Glanced again at Seth who was typing. Better not to ask him. He'd give her a flippant answer—something that meant nothing.

She studied the ring again. Why did it look familiar?

It didn't take her long to remember where she'd seen that ring before. The answer sent shivers racing across her neck.

Brother Earl and Mole wore identical jewelry.

10

There were distinct advantages and disadvantages to being the only reporter in town. Either people liked you or they didn't. Most people Seth got along with. Most people.

On Friday night Seth scanned the mixed crowd at Selma's Pizzeria before choosing a secluded seat in the back. The smell of baked dough made his stomach growl. He usually ate at home, but his refrigerator lacked food, and the last thing he wanted to do tonight was shop. He also wanted to interview Selma, the pizzeria owner. He'd heard Earl had paid her a few visits.

The cute waitress with a butterfly tattoo on her wrist dropped a menu in front of him.

"Two slices with pepperoni and extra cheese." He gave his order doubting whether she heard it. She seemed more interested in the gamers along the wall than her customers.

He should have gotten it to go.

"Late night for you? Or do you have another town meeting?"

Seth recognized that voice. He looked up. Heads turned. Feet shuffled. The room quieted. A couple next to him grabbed their drinks and moved to the front.

"Are you deaf?"

His gaze crashed into Harley White's iron stare.

He could have spit and heard it splat on the floor.

Harley slammed down his drink and shoulder-bumped the guy next to him. Looking for another fight.

Seth usually managed to avoid the low-life, but tonight he had no choice. Seth remembered what Tim told him after his first run-in with Harley. Play along. Don't let him get to you.

He didn't want to pretend tonight.

"Go home, Harley. Play with your dolls."

A buzz circulated around the other patrons. Small-town entertainment. Seth sipped his soda. Slowly and deliberately.

"You don't know who you're messing with, boy." Harley's threat reverberated off the walls.

Seth's heart picked up speed. He unclenched his drink. "I know exactly who."

Harley hoisted himself from the chair, bolstered by the catcalls of his two buddies. More low-life. Seth steeled himself. He'd lose the fight, but at least he hadn't put up with him.

"You think you're something, do you? Writing fancy articles about a town that isn't even yours. Why'd you come here? No place else want you?" He laughed at his twisted humor.

"Maybe a hole-in-the-wall town like this needs someone like me to boost its image. You certainly don't help."

Harley's friends whistled. Maybe he was getting the hang of this trash talk.

"Now, now. Cut the crap. Take it outside if you can't settle down." Selma, a rumpled-looking woman wearing a spattered apron, came around the counter, hands on her hips. Eyes burning fire.

Seth glanced away. No use antagonizing Selma—he'd never get his story.

Harley must have not wanted to upset her either because he plunked down in his chair with a groan. Relief surged through Seth. The threat of a black eye dissolving.

He gulped down the last of his pizza and drained his can of soda. Selma was nowhere in sight by the time he crushed his paper plate. When he went to the counter to pay, he gave Harley and his men a wide berth. "Does Selma have a minute? I need to talk to her." He leaned close to the cashier. Smiled. "I want to apologize for my behavior."

She rolled her eyes and gestured toward the office behind her. "In there."

Seth tipped his head and walked to the open doorway. He found Selma working at her computer. She glanced up and grimaced. "What are you doing back here? Don't have a home to go to? I saved your butt once. Don't make me sorry I did."

Taking her good-natured comment as an invitation, he perched on the edge of her desk. "Selma, sweetheart. Mind answering a few questions?"

Her fingers left the keyboard. "Depends. Going to push me about Earl? That man is going to ruin me yet."

"He's out to ruin the whole town. How will it feel when he closes you down because of your games?" Might as well put it all out there. He'd either get her to talk or she'd call the cops to get him to leave.

"Think you're pretty smart, do you?" Selma shoved back her chair, anchored her arms on her ample chest. "You don't know what smart is. The person you need to be talking to is Earl's brother. That character is the one who runs the whole show. Earl's nothing but a puppet. A mean puppet—but he don't have the guts to do what he says. That's why he keeps that weasel brother of his around."

"What are you saying? David threatened you?" He should have brought his recorder. Or maybe Kate to take a picture. Yet he doubted Selma would have approved of either.

She frowned as she spoke. "You really are dumb. He didn't threaten me like you think. No, they've got other ways to get what they want. And without a good police department, business owners like me have to fight our own battles. I'm sick of it."

"What's your plan, Selma? You can't let him shut you down. He'll put another church in here where he can spout off his own form of religion." Was she crazy?

She laughed. Short and hard. "Maybe that's what I should do. Sell out and join his cult. What do you think I'd look like with a bun?" She patted the back of her head, but Seth recognized the sarcasm in her words. "Go home, Seth. You aren't getting your story tonight." She rolled from her desk and patted his knee. "If I get chased out of here, you'll be the first I call."

Disappointed, but he didn't dare push harder, Seth shuffled to his feet, reluctant to end their conversation.

At the same time he stood, the cashier stuck her head inside the doorway, eyes wide. "Better get out here, Selma. Brother Earl's got a sledgehammer and is threatening to smash your machines if you don't unplug them."

Seth met Selma's thunderstruck look before he rushed out of the office. Selma followed, cursing as she did.

The scene at the back of the restaurant resembled a standoff from an old western. Earl and two of his men welded sledgehammers as they stood in front of the four machines against the back wall. The gamers had dispersed; probably wet their pants as they did. Seth scanned the front where the patrons that hadn't run were huddled in a group near the door. Even bad-boy Harley.

So much for help.

He glanced at Selma. The fire in her eyes burned. "What do you think you're doing, Earl? You don't own this place. I do, in case you've forgotten." She gripped her hips and marched up to him. Not a smart move but then no one told that woman what to do.

Selma growled at Earl's sidekicks who had the decency to shuffle away. Earl didn't. He glared down at her, puffing like a snake poised to strike. "You know the rules. Break them, you pay. God didn't intend for our people to spend their money and time on mindless machines."

"God didn't tell you nothing. You better get your butt out of here or—"

"—What? You'll call the mayor? Your broken-down son-in-law? Guess you aren't up on things. His wife joined our cause. Lock, stock and barrel."

Selma's expression faltered then her jaw hardened again. "Get out. I'll take care of it." Her voice raked Seth's nape like fingernails. But Earl had her. Like he did everyone else in the Bend.

And he had stood by and watched it happen.

His cell rang. Earl's gaze sliced into him.

"Sorry." Seth pointed to his hip. "Work." He ripped his phone from his hip and bolted out to the street where everyone now congregated.

"I'm on a big story here, Boss." He glanced over his shoulder, hoping to see Earl exit.

"Forget your big story. I'm tired of hearing about Earl."

"I didn't say it was about him." The crowd thinned but no Earl.

"It's always about him. When you can give me something concrete, I'll run it. For now, it's a waste of paper."

"Tim, I'm at Selma's pizzeria. Earl is threatening to shut down her games. That's news."

He could hear Tim shuffling papers. Couldn't an editor recognize a hot story?

"She didn't pay her taxes last year. He's got every right as the deputy collector. Go home and work on something else. In the meantime, I won't be around for a few days. Run the place for me. You know how to put the paper to press. Go with what I've laid out. If you hit a brick wall, call me. Otherwise, I'll be back on Wednesday."

Seth gripped the phone tighter. Taxes? Deputy collector? He yanked open his car door. "What about the photographer? Want me to send her out on stories?"

"That's what she's paid for!" Tim's irritation with his question ripped through the phone lines.

"Got you." He should have stayed home and eaten cat food. So Kate was a keeper and he was being shut out. Seth would have to live with it, but he'd be more careful in the future with any attempts to shed light on what he found in the Bend. An inexperienced girl was not going to scoop him.

11

After lunch on Saturday, Kate sorted through her meager wardrobe for something appropriate to wear to Brother Earl's that night. Tossing clothing after clothing onto her bed, she finally settled on a denim jumper bought at a thrift store in Michigan. She'd never worn the bland thing once she got it home but hadn't the heart to throw it away. She slipped it over her head, tugged it down over her hips.

She checked her image in the wall mirror. Turned and twisted. Would she fit in? Would Brother Earl point out her differences and ruin her chances for an interview? The soft folds fell well below her knees, hiding the hideous scar. Another reason she preferred pants. But not tonight.

When the time arrived to leave, her confidence soared. She'd convince Brother Earl to share his plans for the Bend. Why he didn't like progress. Why he thought the Bend was filled with depravity. And most of all, what he believed about women and their roles. She'd get that front-page story.

She pulled out onto the road. Already she noticed her house received little drive-by traffic. She preferred it that way. Fewer people. Less to find her. With a hard press of her foot to the gas, she gunned her car, following the directions she'd memorized. Six miles, Google said. Part of her wondered why someone would build a funeral home so far outside of town, but the other part figured maybe Brother Earl preferred the quiet too.

As Kate rounded a curve, a loud pop sounded from the right rear area on her car. She gripped the wheel and steered to the side of the road. *Not a flat.* She didn't want to change a tire in her jumper. Or in anything else. Besides, she was already later than she preferred.

Her mood plummeted as she left the car and strode around to the other side. "Great," she said as she glared down at a flat. Where was AAA when she needed them? She pushed up her sleeves and popped her trunk. She could change the tire, but it wouldn't be pretty.

As she bent over, a honk startled her. She looked to her left. A pickup truck had stopped across the road. A white-haired man climbed out of the cab and crossed the road grinning from ear-to-ear. "Got yourself some trouble, do you?"

"A flat tire. You didn't need to stop. I've changed them before."

"Doesn't mean you have to this time." He struck out his hand. "Doc Brown, they call me."

"Kate. I live a few miles down the road. And you?" A strong grip.

He nodded toward the white farmhouse she passed minutes ago. "Been practicing medicine in the Bend going on forty years. I know about everyone." He squinted, making his bushy eyebrows more prominent than they already were. "What brings you here?"

"I'm the new photographer at the paper." She glanced at her watch. Doc wanted to chat. She didn't. He leaned against her trunk.

"In a hurry?"

"I'm having dinner at Brother Earl's tonight. I'm sure you know him."

Doc's eyes darkened. He pushed off from the bumper and reached for the jack in her hand. "Then you don't want to be late." He bent on one knee and in a few minutes had the damaged tire off and the spare one on.

"Thank you. You saved me from showing up filthy." She gave him a grateful smile as he wiped his hands on a white handkerchief pulled from his shirt pocket.

"Wouldn't want that. Not with Brother Earl." He glanced downward. "Where did you get that limp?"

She hadn't realized her limp showed. She usually tried to cover it up, but sometimes it wasn't possible. "An old injury," she said.

"Too bad for someone as young as you." He stretched, arching his back. "I best be on my way but now that I know we're neighbors, I want you to feel free and call on me whenever you need something again. It isn't good for a young girl to travel around this area by herself. Even if it is the Bend." He spoke with a gentle tone.

"Thank you. Maybe I can stop by some day and interview you for the paper. You must have seen and heard a lot over the years."

Again, his eyes darkened. "Sometimes more than I wanted. But yes, you do that. I'm fairly retired now. Only go out to see patients who refuse to move on." He chuckled.

After Kate returned to her car, she watched Doc pull out first, his truck rumbling with effort. Maybe she'd ask Tim about that interview. It might be newsworthy to take pictures of the doctor and share some of his stories from the past. A real human-interest story.

With her mind filled with possible leads, she missed the turn to Brother Earl's but backtracked after she turned around. A packed dirt road appeared.

It narrowed sharply as she drove deeper into the flickering sunlight. She double-checked the address. A sign announcing the funeral home appeared. She rounded a blind corner and swerved to a stop in front of a dark metal gate. A buzzer with a sound system waited to her left.

Kate unrolled her window, pressed the buzzer. "This is Kate from the paper," she spoke into the speaker. The gate swung open before she could roll up her window. Kate shifted into gear and drove forward toward a yellow and green Victorian. She eyed the dense woods that surrounded the two-story house, complete with stained glass windows. The front yard looked cleared and meticulously mowed.

A matching sign swung from a pole near the parking area. Visitors. Upon closer inspection, Kate discovered two sets of steps climbing to the porch. One set led to the office and the other set led to a door marked private.

She grabbed her purse. A smoky haze clung to the tree tops behind the house, but otherwise, nothing around her moved. Her nose crinkled. What was that smell? Hopefully, Brother Earl wasn't serving venison as the main course. She'd politely decline.

"Come this way, please."

Startled, Kate turned in the direction of the voice. The woman she'd seen at the library stood near the door marked *Private*. She hooked the air with her delicate hand. Twice.

Kate checked her watch as she made her way up the walkway and across the worn porch floor boards. Ten minutes late. She swallowed hard. Composed herself.

"Come this way." The young woman frowned. She didn't stop to greet Kate. Like the day in the library, head-to-toe, dark-blue garbs covered her petite figure. Kate glanced see what kind of shoes she wore. Work boots.

She motioned Kate to follow her through a maze of dimly lit hallways. One room looked like a parlor, complete with wall-to-wall bookshelves.

Finally, they arrived in a brightly lit dining room.

Brother Earl waited at the head of the table for her.

A butcher knife in his hand.

12

The selection process could be time consuming. He couldn't choose just anyone. She must fit in. And she must be like her. The wrong person messed with his head. He'd learned that early on. It got too messy.

And he never liked messy. His father hadn't either. Especially on that day with his mother.

His mother loved her soaps. *As the World Turns. The Young and Restless.* Every single day. Gagging on her foul cigarettes. Ordering him to bring her another cold beer. He remembered how she looked dressed in her red silk nightie. The one his father gave her for Christmas. The same one she threw against the tree when she opened it. "I told you blue. I wanted the blue one, you idiot. Not red. Can't you do anything right?"

Dad finally did something right.

But he made him help. A twelve-year-old trusts his father. Trusts he'll do right by him. Trusts what his father teaches him will advance him.

That's when he learned to use his first tool. The whip.

But now he must store away his memories. He had work to finish.

He moved to the shadows, studying Cindy. Her screaming had stopped. Good. His newest place wasn't sound proof. Not solid and made from block like the one in Michigan. The street where neighbors ignored his comings and goings.

Yes, he was good at what he did. A good trainer. He could flick a whip like the circus man. Like his father.

He stepped closer, grinning with anticipation. He always looked forward to this part in the process. Hopefully Cindy would too.

He reached for the worn leather handle that hung on a hook next to the door.

Crack!

Cindy's eyes widened. Her chest heaved where her cleavage met her neckline. Sweat gathered on her brow.

He'd show her what it meant to obey. He'd show her because he was the Trainer.

13

"You're late. It's bad manners to keep someone waiting. Where I grew up, parents frowned on bad manners. Adriana, show this woman where to sit." Brother Earl pointed to the chair directly across the table from him with his knife. Then he positioned it on his empty plate, sighing deeply.

Was she to be treated like a child? She came here for a story at this man's invitation. But yes, she was late.

"I'm sorry. I had a flat tire."

Brother Earl remained quiet until Adriana took her place beside him. He cleared his throat. "I see you were able to fix it. Resourcefulness is next to godliness. I like that." Was that a hint of a smile? Kate nodded her agreement but fixed her eyes back on Adriana who studied her empty plate as though it held the universe's answers. Only three of them were seated at the massive oak table. Where were the children? Where did they eat?

The door behind Brother Earl opened. A man, who looked near Kate's age, dressed in a T-shirt and well-fitting jeans, entered the room. He brushed past Brother Earl and flopped into the chair next to her. "Earl said you were coming." He stuck out his hand. "Nice to meet you. David Foreman."

Brother Earl gave a short laugh. "And now you've met my illustrious brother, David. He, like you, lacks the fundamentals in life—like showing up to dinner on time. In case you're wondering, David does our accounting. Among other things." Brother Earl shot David a frown, but Kate noticed the twinkle in his eye as he spoke.

David shrugged off the comment.

"At least I earn my keep. But enough about us. Tell us about you. The newest reporter in town."

"Actually, I'm the photographer. But I'm allowed to write stories as they come. That's one of the reasons I accepted this invitation. I attended the rally the other night and found myself intrigued by your concern for the Bend." She refocused her gaze on Brother Earl who passed steaming dishes of vegetables to his left, after shoveling a hefty amount onto his plate. Kate accepted the potato dish from Adriana's hands when she passed it her way.

She placed an appropriate amount of the remaining food on her plate before passing the dishes to David. He emptied the bowls, scraping the sticky potatoes with the spoon.

"So you're a photographer?" David filled her water glass from a nearby pitcher. "You like working?"

"I enjoy taking photos. And yes, I enjoy working." She took a bite of the mystery casserole, pleased it tasted delicious.

"You mentioned the rally." Now Brother Earl spoke.

He shoved aside his half-eaten food, nodded toward Adriana to fill his glass. She did as ordered with her eyes cast downward. She remained quiet, taking her cues from Brother Earl, making no movement unless sanctioned by him. Maybe Kate would get a chance to speak with her later.

Brother Earl cleared his throat a second time. "I deal with death every day. It isn't pretty. I went into the business after my parents gave it up. David didn't have the heart or stomach for it. Preferred numbers." Brother Earl belched. "Seeing death each day does something to you. It makes you take a fresh look at life. A hard look, if I can say so. You look at the way people are going about their day-to-day existence and finally decide enough is enough. Someone must take a stand. Someone must do something before evil takes over. Someone must care for the babies coming into the world and provide them with a place they are free to live in. A healthy environment."

Kate glanced at David who seemed more interested in his last piece of bread than what his brother said. Maybe he'd heard it all before, but she hadn't. Dare she ask if she could take notes? No, she didn't want to stop his monologue. Her memory would have to suffice.

Brother Earl continued about how the culture was ruining our children. Shaping the world in a way that perpetrated evil. His job was to stop it. No matter what it took.

"What do you mean by that? No matter what it takes?"

Deep lines traced Brother Earl's jaw. "Just what I said. Whatever it takes." He downed his glass of water.

David finally spoke. "You can see how passionate my brother gets. I, on the other hand, find other things to get passionate about." He gave Kate a sidelong glance, and winked.

When he stood to help Adriana pass dishes of vanilla ice cream around the table, Kate noted the way his dark hair curled at the back of his neck. He was no black sheep. Rather the swan in this family. She studied Brother Earl's boxy build. She would never have guessed the two men came from the same family. David spoke in a gentler tone and acted as though what she said mattered. Brother Earl never asked her any further questions once qualifying her as a photographer. It appeared she was present only to listen to him ramble. Like poor Adriana.

Once Brother Earl finished slurping up his dessert, Adriana gathered the dirty dishes and vanished through the nearest door as though she had never been in attendance.

Kate watched her leave and sighed.

"Do you mind if I use your restroom, please?" She wanted a better look at the house. What better excuse?

"Of course. Take a left. Two doors down. I'm afraid you'll find it quite outdated to what you are used to. I tried to keep the original character of the home. I do that in many aspects of my life."

Rising, she took her purse with her. After shutting the door, she scanned the small bathroom. Earl hadn't lied. The decor looked like something out of the forties. At least running water dripped from the faucets. She washed her hands and peered out the back window. It was close to dark, but she could make out a small clearing and what looked like a dirt path leading into the woods. Was that a swing set behind that clump of trees? The green and yellow pattern sure looked like it. Where were the children? An early bedtime? As she was about to turn away, she noticed a slouched woman walking on the path toward the woods. Adriana? She held what looked to be buckets with ladles.

Kate grabbed a towel and dried her hands. Maybe Seth would know what's going on.

When she returned, she gave a quick good-bye to Brother Earl and thanked him for her meal. For the second time that entire evening, Brother Earl looked directly at her. "You come visit again."

She nodded, wondering if that was a request she wanted to fill.

David offered to walk her to her car. "We've got some wild creatures in these parts. In case you hadn't noticed, the woods behind the house are pretty dense. When I was a small boy, I got lost out there. Took my father two days to find me. Never did it again."

David guided her through the same hallways to the front porch. Someone had turned a light on over the doorway. She glanced to her car in the settling darkness. His offer to accompany her made her breathe easier. "I can't imagine going through that nightmare. I bet your parents were out of their minds with worry."

David nodded. "My dad was. I got the whooping of my life when he found me. After that, I made it a point to study my surroundings." His voice

tightened. "You should too, Kate. The Bend isn't the easiest place to live in."
He stood motionless next to her.

"I can take care of myself. I've been doing it a long time now." She
thought of her parents' untimely death and how she hid from the press. Yes,
she could take care of herself. David didn't need to give his warnings.

"That's good to know. I should have realized you had spunk. Anyone
strong enough to sit through an entire meal listening to my brother's rants
knows how to take care of themselves." He chuckled.

When they reached her car, a certain sense of relief filled her. She didn't
know if it was because of David's kindness or because she was no longer
inside that house. "Was it hard growing up here? In a funeral home?"

He shrugged. "When that's all you know, it's okay. My brother might
come across as brash, but he does a good job."

"Do you think he'd meet with me again? I would love to write a feature
story about him."

David reached for her car door and opened it. "A word of advice, Kate.
Earl does what Earl wants. He'll contact you if he deems it in his best
interests. But word of caution again—if you write a story, print the truth." He
stepped aside. "Now drive safely. You never know what you're going to run
into this time of night."

He gave a half-bow and left her standing by her opened door. Kate
watched him climb the porch steps and disappear into the darkened house.
She scrambled into the driver's seat as the porch light went out. Blackness
surrounded her like a wool blanket.

She started her car and flipped on her headlights. Her gaze traveled back to
the house one final time. A faint light flickered on in the second story. Kate
rolled down her window for a better view. As she did, the light snapped off,
thrusting the house into a final darkness.

14

An unexpected shadow swooped over her desk.

Seth. He pulled the ever-present lollipop from his lips. "How was your dinner with Earl?"

Although she'd worked at the paper only a short time, Kate had come to the conclusion that she and Seth would never be best buds. More the contrary. It didn't matter what time she came in or from where, he questioned her whereabouts.

He wasn't her keeper and he should stop acting like he was.

She grabbed her coffee mug and headed toward the fresh pot. "Why? Writing a story?" As soon as the unkind words left her mouth, she regretted them. Just because Seth annoyed her didn't justify her meanness. "Sorry. That was rude." She returned to her desk. Seth was already typing at his computer. "I had an interesting evening. Want details?"

He typed another moment then spun around to face her. "Tim is out of town on business for a few days. That puts me in charge. If you've got a story, give it to me. If not, find one. In the meantime, I'm going to need your services at one. I've got an interview scheduled with the owner of the First Time Daycare on the edge of town. Seems like Brother Earl put his finger on her too."

The hours ticked by until she joined Seth in his Jeep. He spoke barely two sentences to her until they pulled in front of a yellow with white trim cottage. A pink sign in the lawn announced the day care's name and phone number. Except for an assortment of swings and a turtle sandbox in the side yard, the grounds looked empty.

"Where is everyone?" Kate searched for signs of children as she shut the Jeep's door. Seth came to stand next to her. "It looks deserted."

He waved his hand in front of him. "Compliments of Brother Earl."

###

Their interview with Debbie took place inside a living room filled with empty playpens and discarded toys. Debbie picked at a cross necklace around her neck and a ring on her finger while a frazzled look rode in her deep-blue eyes. Her slacks were stained, and her top was beyond wrinkled. Kate smelled stale milk and noticed a few loose animal crackers tucked into the couch cushions. Maybe Brother Earl had done the Bend a service. She wouldn't bring a dog here for the day.

"Thanks for meeting with us. Do you mind sharing your story, so others can be made aware of Earl's methods?" Seth pulled out a small tape recorder and clicked it on. Kate readied her camera and, as quietly as she could, snapped a few photos of Debbie speaking with him.

By the third question, tears fell from Debbie's eyes. "He's a mean one, he is. He told me no mother in her right mind should ever take her child out of her home to stay in a place like this. What's he think I am? A child molester? I've watched kids since I was a kid myself. My mother watched kids in our home when I was growing up. What gives him the right to threaten me if I don't close up shop?"

"How did he threaten you? Did he give specifics?"

Debbie reached for a nearby tissue, dirty, by the way it was already scrunched. Kate glanced away.

"No specifics. He wouldn't do that. Just general threats. Next day I found my Buster dead as a doorknob down by the pond."

"Buster?" Seth leaned forward. Kate gave him credit. He had perfected his interviewing skills.

"Who is Buster?" he asked, concern oozing from his voice.

"What is Buster, more like," Kate said, as she passed Seth the photo of Buster she found on the mantle. Someone had taken a pen and written his name, and rest-in-peace below his body.

"That's him." Debbie reached for the picture and cradled it in her arms. "Best dog in the county. Wasn't more than fifteen years old if that." She sniffed and wiped her sleeve across the dusty frame.

Kate snapped another picture.

"Can you be sure Earl hurt him? I mean, the dog was kind of old, wasn't he?"

Debbie stiffened. "I took good care of my pets like I did my kiddos. It was Earl that did it, and I'd swear it in court. That is if I could ever get the judge to listen. All they do is tell me to go home and forget about it. How can I forget about it when I have no business left? I swear Earl has got that judge in his pocket too. What am I going to do? All the mothers who used to bring their kids here have stopped. They're afraid of that man, that's what I'm telling you. Afraid."

"Did he give you a reason why he felt the children shouldn't be leaving their homes?" Seth laid his hand on Debbie's arm. Nice touch. What he wanted was the lead—the headline that would sell the story. She aimed her camera and crouched closer.

Click.

Debbie glanced out the front window. She clasped her hands in her lap on top of the photo of Buster. "He said women belonged at home taking care of their children. That's the role God made for women. To nurture. To take care of their offspring. That's the word he used. Offspring. Like kids came from a litter. But what got me worse was he said women are meant to serve man. Period. Not only was their place in the home but at the man's feet. He said the faster I learned that, the better a life I would lead." Her voice dropped to a whisper. "So that's why I called you. I can't survive without no man taking care of me if I don't have my business. I'll lose this here house too." Her eyes grew wider. Kate looked down at Debbie's hands. They were shaking.

When they said their goodbyes, Debbie clung to Seth's arm. "Don't wait too long. Write your story so someone will stop that man. And for me as I'm running out of time."

Seth gently pried her loose while promising to do his best. Kate gave the poor woman a quick hug and whispered she would check on her in a few days. She didn't know why she promised, but something about the look in Debbie's eyes worried her.

Seth took a short detour on the way back to the office. "One more stop. That's all. I'll get you back to the office soon."

She had no place to be except work. That's the kind of life she led. Alone until she made new friends. Friends who didn't ask questions. As far as she was concerned, she had all day to ride around the county chasing another story.

He slowed on approach to a wooden bridge that crossed a narrow creek. The Jeep crept along in second gear. Was something wrong with the engine? Finally, Seth turned right onto a dirt road. About fifty yards in, deep inside heavy brush, they came upon a rusty wrought iron fence. It surrounded tombstones.

15

The Trainer enjoyed taking his meals at local cafes. His favorite booth in the back corner of this one allowed him to observe the patrons. And the waitresses.

He liked to watch people. Study their reactions to situations. His father once told him he needed to read people as much as his books. That's how one gained control. Made it that much easier to train them.

"Don't waste your life like I did mine," his father told him after they carried his mother's dead body to the freezer in the garage. "Make it count."

He'd taken his father's advice. All his advice.

Today he spent most of his time, between bites of a tuna sandwich, reading the expressions of one particular woman. He called her over twice to refill his coffee. Both times she tittered like he was asking her out to her senior prom. Wouldn't that have been nice if that's all he wanted?

She had good bones, too. Carried a tray full of platters without any effort. Her hips swayed as she sashayed between the tables. He smiled. Another one. But he was running out of time. He needed to move on to the one he most wanted. To complete his final purpose.

"Miss, do you mind bringing me a slice of that blueberry pie?"

"Sure thing. Is there anything else I can get you? Coffee? Soda?" She hung over his table, her ample chest heaving in his face.

He'd take care of her.

"No thanks. Maybe later." He tossed her a flicker of a grin. She grabbed onto it like a child to a rattle.

He drank from his cup, deep and long. This part of the plan was his favorite part. Well, maybe not. He did derive a certain pleasure from seeing their expressions when he told them what he expected from them.

16

Seth parked as close to the gate as he could get. "This will take only a minute." He got out of his Jeep and stepped into knee-deep weeds. It appeared no one maintained this cemetery from the looks of the fence and the ground. It would be harder to find what he was looking for.

Kate got out and stood by his side.

"What are we doing here?" she whispered.

"You don't have to whisper. Everyone is dead, in case you hadn't noticed." She clamped her jaw shut while he pushed through a couple of low-hanging branches. He wasn't one for traipsing around in the woods. Never liked Boy Scouts, although his mother made him join. Never liked camping or hiking.

He slapped a bug off his arm. Or insects.

Last night, he'd done his research. Now he dug into his jean's pocket and pulled out a sketchy map. Kate stayed close on his heels, despite her noticeable limp, as he pushed forward past crumbling tombstones. Tall weeds whisked his legs. He tripped over a dead branch before he could catch himself.

Kate giggled behind him.

"I didn't see it. Be careful or you might fall as well." He raked his hands through his hair. Hmm, she was a smarty as well.

"I'd have worn my hiking boots if I'd known we were doing this."

"Just be quiet, okay? I'm concentrating."

One by one, he scanned the almost-unreadable names.

It was here, somewhere.

"What are we looking for? I don't think anyone has been buried here in years." Kate pointed to the date on a nearby cross.

"Has anyone ever told you patience is not your best virtue?" He gave her a hard look and turned forward again. He should have come alone.

Overhead, a lone crow hawked, fluttered near them. Kate ducked and stifled a scream. He grabbed her hand to catch her and then steered them toward an area along a back fence.

He stopped. Let her hand fall. What was he thinking?

"Someone mowed it." Kate's voice cut into his senses as he took in the scene.

A patch of lawn about 600 square feet had been perfectly sheared. In the center of the cleared area sat an enormous tombstone sculpted in white marble.

The name engraved on the smooth finish spelled Foreman.

He'd found Brother Earl's family plot.

17

The Trainer called good-bye to the pretty waitress and crossed the street, neatly avoiding a passing school bus. He'd wait outside for her shift to end. An hour. She said she finished at five.

Nice of her to be so talkative.

But then most of the women he chose were that way. Like her. Friendly. Made his part in the plan that much easier. He relaxed by his truck. Watched the sky darken. Few people spoke to him since he easily blended in to the Bend. Most skirted past him on a mission to get home.

Where they should be.

He checked the restaurant doors. From where he stood, he could see the clean-up start. The blinds lowered. The lights shutting down. His newest candidate descended the front steps, calling back to someone as she did. She glanced down the street. Looking for him? He stepped into the shadows, not ready to spoil his surprise. Not yet.

The waitress tapped her foot, slung her purse over her shoulder. Did she know he'd be here? A shiver of anticipation raced through his limbs. His legs grew weak. He moved forward then stopped. Patience. That's what he needed.

She waved. Stepped onto the sidewalk.

So easy. So very easy.

Now was the time. He left the shadows. Put on his suitor's smile.

A dark sedan pulled in between them, blocking his view of her. The Trainer clenched his fists and stepped back under cover.

She called out to the driver and sprinted to the car. Smiling. Like she was supposed to with him.

She joined the young man behind the wheel. Kissed his waiting cheek.

No! The Trainer jammed his fist against his leg. She was his. She would be his.

He backed up, his plans fading fast along with his adrenaline.

He breathed deeply. Yes, he'd be patient. That's what he would do. He would be patient like his father had been with his mother. Catch her

unawares. Catch her when she trusted him the most.
That's how he played his game best.

18

They were standing in the middle of a family plot. Brother Earl's to be exact, and Seth was acting like Indiana Jones. Kate edged closer to read the dates engraved in the marble slab. "Looks like they died a long time ago."

Seth pointed to the dates next to the names. "On the same day."

"Couldn't you have found that out in the records in town? Did we need to come all the way out here to see it for ourselves?" Her bad leg was throbbing from their trek through the overgrowth. Her hand stung where he'd grabbed it.

Seth brushed past her. He peered at the words written out below the dates. "Let those who seek the truth find it. Let those who don't, forever suffer." He straightened his back. "Who puts words like that on their tombstone?"

They *were* strange. Kate had requested a Bible verse for her parents' stones.

"Don't you see what I see? They died on the same day. How often does that happen unless they were in a car accident or something?"

Kate swallowed hard, remembering her parents' death from the bombing. "It happens. Things like that happen."

He shot her a look. "Not in the Bend they don't. One day they were here, the next day gone. I've heard different stories. They retired in Arizona. They died together, and Earl didn't want a fuss. They left and didn't tell anyone." He looked upward. Kate followed his gaze. A dark cloud covered the sun. It would be raining by the time they returned to town.

"Don't you find that strange?" Seth asked.

She didn't want to tell him that she found living strange. What could be more strange than having your family torn from you by a crazy bomber or seeing auras in photos around people meant to die? "I don't know what you mean. What is it you're looking for?"

Seth let out a sigh. "Let's go. There's nothing more to see here."

His moods irked her. She gave one final glance to the well-maintained headstone and then clambered to follow him back to the Jeep.

Like before, Seth spoke little on the return drive to the office. A fitful storm let loose by the time they reached the building, so he let her off near her car. "See you tomorrow," he said and peeled out onto the street.

Early Saturday, the phone woke her. She recognized the number and held her breath. "Jackie? Is everything okay?" They hadn't spoken since she begged her friend to take Trevor to the doctor's.

"Kate? I'm thankful you told me to get a second opinion. It's cancer, Kate. Trevor has cancer." Her voice broke.

Kate sank back against her pillows. "I'm so sorry."

"Don't be. If it wasn't for you, we wouldn't have found it. But it's treatable. Trevor will be fine. They said we caught it early enough to cure him. You don't know how scared I was. I wish I could give you a big hug."

"Treatable? Oh, I don't know what to say. I'm so relieved." Kate threw back the covers, slapping her bare feet onto the cold floorboards. No one lived once she saw their aura. How could it be treatable? Had the doctors given Jackie false hope? Did that mean seeing the aura early meant hope?

"Listen, I miss you like crazy and wish you were here. Any chance you'll be coming home soon?"

Home? Kate couldn't remember calling any of her stopovers home. "Not yet. My aunt still needs me."

They talked for a few more minutes more. Finally, Jackie said she had a zillion errands to run now that Trevor would be spending so much time at the hospital.

As soon as they hung up, Kate raced to her computer. She turned it on, opened her photo program. Where was it? Click. Click. There. Trevor's smiling face stared up at her from the screen.

With no glow. The photo showed only a happy player.

She covered her mouth.

Could it be? Was she losing her curse?

She flipped through several past photos, the one taken of her neighbor who'd been diagnosed with a brain tumor right before she fled. The one of the man with cancer who won the award at the fair for his sheep last fall.

Yes, the auras were all still there.

Her fingers slid off the keyboard.

She should have known not to get her hopes up. Yet, why Trevor? Had she looked at the photo and only imagined the faint glow? She'd been stressed about the reporter. Worried that the press had found her again. She tapped her fingers against her knee. A glitch. That's all. A good glitch though. She needed to put her fears aside and concern herself with the present. That's how she would survive. That's how she always survived.

Kate reached for her camera and plugged in the cable. She uploaded the pictures she'd taken the other day at Debbie's house. Seth said he'd be writing the story when he had more information. What he'd write about, she didn't know. That Brother Earl believed women should watch their own children? Stay at home and raise your own kids? Maybe a little old-fashioned but nothing criminal. Sometimes it seemed to Kate that Seth was intent on proving that Brother Earl was a bad guy when all he wanted to do was improve the community even though some of his ideas were archaic.

She brought up her pictures, pleased with the one she'd taken of Seth crouched near Debbie. He photographed well. Then her gaze caught on a close-up of Debbie. The one where she was holding the photo of Buster.

Kate sucked in her breath. No. She slammed the lid down and pushed off from her chair, pivoting in the tiny room. The aura. Would she ever be free from seeing it? And why poor Debbie?

She'd visit Debbie later today. That's what she would do. Maybe suggest that Debbie pose for a better picture. Get her to relax. Maybe then that stupid thing wouldn't show up. Maybe Debbie's anger caused it.

A hot shower didn't ease her fearful thoughts. She knew what the aura meant in the past. Any amount of reasoning on her part wouldn't change that. But she still would go see Debbie. Maybe she could suggest she see a doctor based on her stress over her situation.

Kate dressed in old jeans and a T-shirt, grabbed her gear and purse and headed to her car. When she caught sight of the spare still on it, she groaned. She'd need to stop at a tire place in town first before she ventured anywhere. Debbie would have to wait.

19

A little action. That's what he needed. Weekends in the Bend reminded Seth of reruns on TV. Nothing new. Same old faces and places. Not even a good twist to rev up the plot. With few friends and no family in the area, his usual recourse was to fish or hole up in his place with a movie and pizza. This Saturday morning, he pulled on his clothing with different plans in mind.

He was going hiking. Not just any hiking but hiking with a purpose.

He'd stayed up last night researching the local topography. It appeared the land around Earl's funeral home was privately held but not by the infamous funeral director. Shortly after Earl's parents died—*together*—Seth still wanted to know how—Brother Earl sold a parcel of land for quite a sum to man from New Jersey.

After a quick phone call, the owner gave Seth the go-ahead to hike his land.

The only problem—Seth didn't hike.

He looked down at his sneakers, purchased over a month ago. He kicked them off and pulled on a pair of work boots he'd bought at a flea market on a whim instead. He also packed his backpack with a few essentials.

Daisy rubbed up against his legs as he strode toward the door. "Not now, girl." He gave her a gentle push, grabbed a hat and his keys. Already the sun made him squint. He should have gotten an earlier start but had gotten tangled in his research of Earl and his brother David. Seth wanted to know everything he could about that family before he slammed them on page one.

After a few wrong turns, he finally parked his Jeep near the rundown cabin. The property was overgrown like the cemetery he'd visited but manageable. He hoisted his supplies onto his back, slung a pair of binoculars around his neck, and took off.

If Earl was hiding anything, he'd find it.

A hoard of questions peppered his brain.

Why would Earl try to shut down every means of entertainment in the

Bend? What was driving him to pressure women to leave their husbands and quit their jobs? He'd heard rumors about several incidences where wives had up and left, with their children in tow, only to show up a few months later dressed in outdated garb, their hair grown long. Was Earl housing these women? When he tried to question a few, they turned mute. He'd tracked down their husbands, but they had refused to speak to him, too.

Was Earl brainwashing the women of the Bend?

This time he'd printed off a better map than the one he used before. After dousing himself with bug spray, he headed toward the pines, clambering along the faint path beneath his feet. Several times he tripped from jagged stones protruding from the dirt. Once he caught himself on a branch that claimed his hat. A few feet down the trail, he sloshed across a bubbling creek. The longer he walked, the more the ground rose. Soon the path inclined at a crazy angle making him rethink his plans. He pulled out a Tootsie Pop and shoved it between his lips.

No turning back now.

The last time he hiked anyplace, he'd been eleven. His older sister, Marie, and he had gone to a playground near their house. His mother worked that summer, and his father was deployed overseas. That left his sister to watch him. They'd packed peanut butter sandwiches, swung on the swings for five minutes, and then she announced that she wanted to walk up the hill behind them.

"It'll take all day," he said. Marie threw him one of her long-suffering looks before pulling on his arm.

"Stop being a wimp. It won't take long."

It had taken hours. By the time they reached the summit, it was almost dark. He could see the lights coming on in the houses and he was shivering from the cooler air. His smarty pants sister acted as though she was a queen surveying her kingdom until he told her that their mother would beat her butt if she didn't get him down. She did, but both ended up with no dinner and a mountain of chores to do the next day.

His sister died when she turned eighteen. Why he thought about her as he pushed his way through brush made no sense to him. She'd run away from home when she turned seventeen. The man she lived with had promised her the world. Instead, she lost her life living like an animal in the hills of Kentucky. The police said she hadn't eaten in weeks.

She was also five months pregnant.

20

The auto shop mechanic showed Kate where a roofing nail had punctured her tire. He applied a $22 fix to her original tire and asked for her number. She politely declined.

Didn't need to go there.

She slipped into the Mom and Pop diner near the theater where she could have an unobstructed view of town. Famished, she ordered a ham and cheese omelet and home fries.

"New here? I don't think I've seen you before, and I know everyone in the Bend." A willowy waitress with the darkest hair Kate had ever seen slid her order in front of her. "I'm Becky Place." Becky's eyes were rimmed with black mascara and a hummingbird tattoo peeked from her neckline.

"Kate Song. I just started at the paper."

Becky took the seat across from her. "Then you work with that cute reporter, Seth. I can't seem to get him to even take notice of me. He's a hard case for sure. What's he like?" She propped her elbows beneath her chin as though Kate were going to tell her a long story.

"Sorry. I hardly know him. He's quiet. Say, maybe you know David Foreman. Can you tell me what he's like?"

Becky's smile flattened. She glanced over her shoulder. "He's one I tried to set my sights on, but it went no place. He's polite, but I can't get him to bite. I heard he moved away to college and returned about a year ago. An accountant or something." She glanced to the street. "Speaking of the devil." Her eyes flickered.

Kate followed her gaze. David was striding across Main Street headed in their direction.

###

"We meet again. May I?" He dropped across from her in the seat vacated by Becky and raised a finger toward the waitress. Becky set a cup of steaming coffee in front of him as though she did it every day. She shot Kate a pointed look from behind David's back before shuffling over to the counter.

"Running errands?" Kate asked, although she preferred to ask about his brother.

"A few. And you? Isn't it early for someone as attractive as you to be out and about?"

She choked on her water. Attractive? No wonder Becky had set her sights on him. The man oozed personality.

"Thank you, but no."

His smile grew. Kate found herself staring into his dark brown eyes. What was his appeal? She hadn't been this attracted to anyone in awhile. She pulled her gaze away.

"It's true you know. You're going to have a line out the door of men wanting to ask you out. We don't get that many pretty girls here in the Bend. For that matter, we don't get that many outsiders. Kind of town where you've lived here all your life, and everyone knows everyone." He took a long sip of his coffee, keeping his sight fixed on her face.

"Outsiders. Is that what you call me?"

He had the grace to blush. "It's a term. Nothing more."

"Is that how your brother feels as well?" She pushed her plate away, her appetite gone.

He looked down. "I see you've heard the nasty rumors. My brother means well. He just gets a little passionate about saving the town. I don't always agree but that's not new."

"Why doesn't he run for mayor, if he's so adamant to prevent change?"

"Have you met our mayor? He'll die in the position. Earl can get more done with his rallies than the mayor can in his entire term. But that's not why I sat with you." He reached across the space and grasped her hand in his. Kate inhaled.

"Why *did* you sit with me?"

"How else am I going to ask you out?" He squeezed gently. So gently she wondered if she'd imagined it.

She swallowed and then glanced at Becky who swooped past with a tray. "I'd love to go out with you," she said in a voice unlike herself. It wasn't until David promised to pick her up tomorrow for dinner that she found herself wondering why she'd agreed so quickly.

21

Seth stopped to catch his breath. Would he ever get to the top? He'd been hiking for over an hour. Maybe longer. Why hadn't he brought two bottles of water instead of one? He kicked a nearby tree, angry that he'd rushed out of his cabin ill-prepared. First thing he'd do when he got back to town would be buy a thermos. Who knew when he'd need one again? He pushed forward into a slight clearing. Finally, the top. He propped his backpack against a stump. Then he dropped to the ground himself, taking in the expansive view.

The owner told him he would be able to see for miles once he gained the crest. He hadn't lied. Squinting in the bright sunlight, Seth scanned the horizon to get his bearings. If his map was correct, due south would be Earl's land. He put the binoculars to his eyes.

Trees and more trees. A speck of white and then his gaze caught on something. What was that? He adjusted the lens. He should have brought a high-powered telescope, but lugging that all the way up here would have been a joke. Instead, he blinked and tried again.

What were those buildings? Cabins? One, two, three… He stopped counting. From what he could tell, someone had built a regular village behind the main house. The trees blocked most of them, but definitely there were cleared patches in front of each cabin. From this distance he couldn't make out much more. Were they sheds for storage? Why so many?

And were there people?

His binoculars fell to his chest.

Why did Earl need that many buildings behind a funeral home? What did it have to do with the Bend, if anything? Seth raised his binoculars again. He stumbled backward.

Women. Women dressed in long garbs.

His gut twisted.

What were they doing on Earl's property? He lowered the binoculars and took a swig from his water bottle.

The only way he'd find out what Earl was doing was to get closer.

And the only way he'd manage that was by using Kate. She already had been invited to dinner once. With a little encouragement, maybe she could arrange a second visit.

With him as her escort.

22

Kate waved Becky over as she left the restaurant. The waitress dropped her stack of menus and met her at the exit. "I saw the way David looked at you. He'd be a real catch."

"I'm not looking for a catch. He's an acquaintance. That's all."

"Tell *him* that. Drop back in and let me know how it goes, okay?" She gave Kate a warm smile, patted her arm and left her at the door.

Was she that transparent? Romance. Fat chance. She'd be more vigilant. Guard her emotions. Especially with David. One date. That would be all.

She set off to her car, thoughts of Debbie prodding her.

In no time at all, she pulled up in front of the yellow cottage, proud of finding it without getting lost, and without Seth's help. The place still looked deserted. She cut across the littered yard rethinking her decision to check on a woman she hardly knew.

Buster's picture intruded on her thoughts. She'd owned a dog, too. Sheena. When she died, Kate had died a little too. The least she could do was offer Debbie condolences again.

She rapped her knuckles on the door. The latch popped free—swinging the door open. Kate stuck her head inside. "Debbie? Hello? It's Kate from the paper." She stepped over the threshold hoping she wouldn't scare the poor woman.

The living room was empty.

Her gaze dropped to the chair where Debbie had interviewed with Seth. A light green sweater dangled from the arm.

Stepping further into the room, she called again. "Hello?" No answer. A few more steps.

A nasty odor rushed at her from the next room. She pinched her nose. Despite all her senses warning her to leave, she followed the smell into the kitchen.

Thawed burger sat open on the counter. It looked as though Debbie had planned to cook a meatloaf. Why had she stopped? Kate scooped up the platter and thrust the meat into a nearby trash can.

"Debbie? Are you home?" An intruder. That's what she felt like.

Her pulse quickened as her courage strengthened. She scanned the room again knowing she should leave but couldn't.

Her sight landed on the kitchen table. Debbie's purse lay next to an open newspaper. What woman leaves her purse behind?

"Debbie, are you in your room? Are you sick?" She turned the doorknob of a room leading off the kitchen and peeked inside. Debbie's unmade double bed greeted her. The rest of the room appeared untouched.

She returned to the kitchen with the decision to leave a note. Maybe Debbie would phone her later tonight, and then she could apologize for the intrusion. She scribbled a few words on a napkin with a pen she found near the purse. As quickly as she could, she left the cottage for the fresh air outside, shutting the door behind her.

Still, something didn't feel right. Her grandmother often told her to follow her instincts. With her curiosity still piqued, she peered around the side of the house.

An older model Chevy was parked next to a rusted water tank. The driver's side door was ajar.

"Debbie?" Kate steeled herself for the worst. She dashed over to the car. Empty.

Instead of finding Debbie on the driver's seat, she found women's sunglasses and a silver cross necklace. The same necklace Debbie had played with while Seth spoke with her. A size twelve pair of jeans had also been neatly folded and left on the passenger's seat. Along with the broken picture of Buster.

23

The Trainer never liked people who asked too many questions. Not even as a child. Nosing into his life. Wanting to know why he moved around so much. Why he changed jobs. Why he wasn't married yet. Just today, he was almost forced to make a major change to his plans. But then it all worked out.

It always did.

He stepped outside his house into the back yard. Inhaled the fresh air.

He had been doing this a long time. Finding women to train. He was quite good at it, indeed. Some might say he was an expert. Everyone needed to be an expert at something. Otherwise what was the point in living? Everyone needed to find what they're good at.

God didn't create people to waste their talents.

The Trainer never wasted his.

That's why he selected his women carefully. The ones with the most potential. The ones who molded easily. Harlots who would turn to righteousness.

The Trainer squatted—plucked a weed from the crack in the patio.

He had his eye on another one who would fit perfectly. She might take a little work getting her to warm up, but he wasn't too worried. After all, he had this talent. They never knew what hit them. That was the joy in all of this. He reeled them in like a fighting bass. They flopped around a little, and then snag, they were his. Hook, line, and sinker.

He tossed the weed onto his garbage heap.

Someday the world would follow his lead. They would finally see their errors and do exactly what he did to these women. Train them.

A smile tugged his lips.

Too bad he wouldn't be around to see it.

24

"Get over here right away. Something's wrong." Kate tried to sound calm but the rocketing feeling that Debbie was in trouble made it difficult. "Do you hear me, Seth?"

"I'm a little busy right now."

She stopped her pacing. "Get unbusy and get over to Debbie's right now. I need to show you something." Her rising panic fueled her tone. Why had she chosen to call Seth? Maybe because he was the other last other person besides her to see Debbie. Maybe between the two of them they could figure out if they needed to call the police.

A long sigh filled her ear. "Give me a half hour."

"I'll be waiting." She clicked off and stuffed her phone back into her pocket. The view from her car gave her little insight into why Debbie was missing. She could sit here all day, and the woman might not return. Besides that, the memory of the aura scared her.

Something had happened. She was sure of it. Like she was sure of it with all the other people over the years. If she called the police and tried to explain her hunch to them, she'd sound crazy. Of course there were a dozen other possibilities. Debbie could be out with a friend. Her car might not run, and she walked someplace.

All the scenarios sounded plausible—but not likely. Not after seeing that death sentence around her head.

The rising heat in the car forced her to return to the attached porch. Two patio chairs sat next to the railing. Kate chose the one closest to the sidewalk and waited. What was taking Seth so long?

She heard his Jeep before she saw it. Seth rounded the corner and blasted into a space behind her car. She let out her breath when he leaped out and hurried toward her. He was puffing by the time he reached her.

"This better be good." He wiped a stream of sweat from his face with the back of his hand.

"It is. Follow me. The door was open when I arrived."

"Good to know I'm not associating with a burglar." He followed her into

Debbie's living room where a lingering odor from the hamburger still clung to the air. He made a gagging sound. "What is that?"

"Thank me later. I found rotting meat on the counter." She nodded toward Debbie's vacant chair. Then led him into the kitchen. She pointed to the purse. "No woman leaves her purse when she goes out."

Seth frowned. Obviously unimpressed with her discoveries.

She waved him toward the bedroom. "What woman leaves without taking her medication?" She showed him a prescription for pain she'd noticed when she was in her room earlier. "She could be ill and need these."

"She might have another purse and another bottle of meds. You're overreacting. You brought me out here for nothing." He turned and headed for the door. "When you develop better reporting skills, call me. In the meantime, let me write the stories. You take the pictures."

She gripped the medication tighter. Arrogant man. "You haven't seen everything yet." She brushed past him into the living room. "Follow me." She opened the sliders, not waiting for his answer. Instead, she headed directly to the partially-opened car. Seth followed but at a slower pace. Why had she called him? He was no good to her at all.

She pointed to the open door.

"Look inside," she ordered.

He made a face but did as she asked.

"Do you see that necklace? It's the one she wore yesterday. She fondled it the entire time we spoke to her. And that's the picture of her dog. It's busted. It wasn't yesterday."

Seth withdrew his head from the car's interior. He rested his elbow on the top of the door frame. "I don't know what it means. She's mad and took off?" His eyebrows waggled.

Kate fumed. "You're no help. I thought someone like you had a nose for news. Anyone can see that she's not here and she left in a hurry. Probably not on her own terms."

Seth gave a slow whistle. "Someone has read one too many mysteries. What did you do in your prior life?"

So now he was going to make fun of her. "Forget it. When we hear on the news that she's been found dead in a creek somewhere, then you can mock my skills." She left him standing by the car. She couldn't tell him her greatest concern, that she'd seen the death curse in Debbie's picture. He'd lock her up if she did. She'd have to hope that Debbie was all right and let it go.

"Are you coming or not?" She turned back to find him scanning the backyard. He bent down in the dirt. Fingered something. "What are you doing?" Her curiosity surged. "I asked you a question."

"Come back here and look at this."

Kate joined him near the front tires. "What? I don't see anything." He pointed downward but all she saw was mud.

"Don't you see? Someone has been here who wears shoes both our feet could fit into."

They met back at Kate's house. Seth suggested using the office, but she didn't want to alert anyone nearby that they were working on a Saturday. She didn't want to go to his place, so that left hers. She scooped up a pile of clothing from the kitchen chair and motioned for him to sit.

"Water or water?" she asked.

"That's it? Water or water?" He shook his head. "Water it is then."

Kate poured each of them a glass from the pitcher she kept in the refrigerator. She joined him at the table. "What should we do? Report her missing?"

"And tell the sheriff we were snooping around her place uninvited? That's a smart way to lose our jobs."

The Bend didn't employ a regular police department. A sheriff who worked part time took the calls.

"What then? Wait for her to return—*if*—she returns?"

He nodded. "We can take turns driving out there to check on her. Give it a week. She might be with relatives. In the meantime, I think we ought to find out if Brother Earl knows anything about this. She did say he threatened her. And there were those prints."

"Are you suggesting that Brother Earl could be responsible? He asked her to stop running a daycare. He didn't say he'd kill her. Now who needs to get a grip." She grabbed his glass and took it to the sink. "You can go that route, but not me. I enjoyed myself at dinner there the other night. He can be quite social in his own environment."

Seth leaned forward. "Maybe you're right. I doubt it. I'd like to see him like that myself. Why don't you invite me to go with you the next time? I could see what his real plans are. Maybe he'd change my mind." He gave her a thin smile.

"I don't know when I'll be going back. He didn't invite me." It rattled her that he had abruptly said goodnight to her that evening, but she wasn't going to tell Seth that part of the story. "I'm having dinner with his brother tomorrow. Maybe I can ask him."

Seth's jaw tightened. "David? You're going out with that guy?" He snorted, crossing his arms over his chest. "Now that's a story."

She gritted her teeth. Maybe she shouldn't have revealed her plans for tomorrow. "He seemed nice, and I thought it would be a way to learn more about the Bend. Like you said, his brother practically runs the town. If there is something more sinister going on as you like to suggest, I'll find out. Besides, you haven't told me you've done anymore digging—other than dragging me to that cemetery."

The sneer left his face.

"I've got to go. It's been a long day." He pushed back from the table and stood, prompting her to join him. "If your reporter skills do pick up on anything, let me know on Monday. I'll take my turn and check on Debbie tomorrow." He narrowed his eyes. "Does that work for you?"

What choice did she have? "That works. I'll see you Monday."

He steered past her out the back door. Seconds later, she heard his Jeep roar out of her driveway. Kate wasted no time pulling up her pictures of Debbie again.

The aura had grown brighter.

25

Whenever Seth's frustrations kicked in, he couldn't stop himself from buying an entire pizza and devouring it in one night. Tonight he grabbed a large pepperoni and sausage, ate it alone in his house, washing it down with a bottle of soda he'd saved for this occasion.

What was Kate thinking by agreeing to go out with Earl's brother? Was she crazy or plain stupid? He wished he'd asked where they were going. He thought about calling her. But didn't. Yeah, that would have been nice and creepy. Checking up on the new photographer like he owned her or something. Sounded like something Earl might do.

Instead, he sat on his back deck nursing an achy gut. Something was strange about Earl and his clan, but he couldn't figure it out. Those cabins behind his home. The way the women dressed who attended his functions. He was certain they weren't all Earl's wives. Girlfriends? Maybe David owned a few of them. And then those kids. Sure, they were polite but— He couldn't put his finger on it.

Then there was the theater. It hadn't been open in weeks. Last he heard, it was closing. For personal reasons the sign on the door said. Personal reasons, or Earl reasons?

He fisted his hand. How was he to get the story of the century if he couldn't get on Earl's property and look around?

Daisy purred next to him and leaped onto his lap. He stroked her neck a few times before returning to his troubling thoughts. Tomorrow was Sunday. Maybe he'd take a little trip. Get a little sermonizing in him. He'd heard Brother Earl packed a crowd on the Sundays the pastor let him preach. Kind of like those rallies.

With his plans set, he nudged the cat to the floor and grabbed his keys. Another trip to Debbie's house wouldn't hurt. By now she would have returned. He could get a few more questions answered. If not, he could find answers himself.

A poor plan was better than no plan.

He grabbed a flashlight from the laundry room thinking it might come in handy at Debbie's. He'd parked his Jeep twenty feet from his back door. Ten feet out, he heard movement behind him. He froze. Cocked his head. A bear? The landlord had warned him. Had he covered his trash? He listened again.

Nothing but katydids.

But just in case, he dug for his keys. Turned toward the area where he stored his garbage cans.

More rustling—closer.

Seth froze. Was he supposed to yell or play dead? His brain screamed to remember. Better to make a run for it to his vehicle.

He turned to his right when something hard slammed into him.

Seth collapsed to the ground. His shoulder seared from the brutal impact. What happened? He scrambled to his feet and lurched toward the side of his Jeep, swerving to remain standing. He must get inside, but his feet wouldn't cooperate.

Another sound from the right. Louder.

Seth steeled himself for impact.

26

The hard knock on her front door later that evening ripped through Kate's chest. She dropped her spoon into her soup and reached for the nearby can of Mace. The only person who knew where she lived was her landlord and Seth. Hadn't she and Seth seen enough of each other today?

She left her chair and crossed into the living room. Since she'd yet to hang curtains, she could see her visitor. Her heart slowed as she set the Mace aside.

Kate opened the door with a smile. "Doc. What brings you here?"

Her new neighbor held a covered dish in his two hands. He, too, was smiling and cocked his head to the side. "When I told my wife about you she jumped right in and baked a treat. Once you taste it, you'll understand why I've stayed married to her for forty years."

"How nice. Come in, please." She opened the door wider as Doc crossed the threshold into the room. He smelled like apples.

Doc passed her the dish and patted his belly. "You can also see what her good cooking has done to me. But I don't think it will hurt someone as tiny as you."

Kate raised the pan to her nose and inhaled. "Apple pie?" She sure hoped it was. Her grandmother had made the best in the town. She won a blue ribbon every year at the county fair.

"Have a piece." He waved her toward the kitchen.

Kate took the pie to her kitchen table. She lifted the lid to find a still-warm, golden-crusted apple pie. She inhaled the sugary aroma. "I think I've died and gone to heaven."

"Go ahead. I promised Mary I wouldn't leave until I was sure you liked it."

Kate grabbed two plates and two forks and motioned for him to sit. After a little back and forth banter, she convinced her new friend that he should partake as well. It didn't take that much convincing before the doctor was shoveling a forkful into his mouth. When she'd eaten half of her slice of the delicious dessert, she set her fork down.

"I couldn't help but notice that you don't think much of Brother Earl. Am I right?"

"Now why would you think that? He and I have known each other since we were kids. Went to the same school, dated some of the same girls. I fell for Mary hard though by tenth grade, and Earl played the field a little longer."

"So you knew his wife?" Maybe she'd get more information for her story. Someone like Doc Brown would know everything in the Bend.

"*Knew* his wife is right. She left him a few years ago. Up and disappeared. Earl said she high-tailed it back to California where her parents lived. Probably a good thing. He was getting a little more radical then. Guess she didn't want to put up with it." He rubbed his chin with his palm. "Seems to me she left right around the time his parents died. No, maybe a few years later. Hard to remember anymore. So much goes on."

An image of the family plot rose to her mind. She must remember to tell Seth. "Can you explain to me what you mean by radical? I attended one of his rallies. Seems he has good plans for the town."

Doc coughed and glanced away for a moment. "If that's what you want to call them. He and his brother seem to think they know what's best for the rest of us."

"David? How well do you know him?" She fingered her fork, wishing she could gulp down another slice of pie but didn't want to appear rude.

"He's a bit younger than the rest of us. Went off to college to become an accountant. Moved around a lot. He works with Earl doing his books. I also heard he's quite the lady's man. You aren't falling under his spell too, are you?" His eyes twinkled. "He hasn't ever married, and I don't know if he ever plans to. He implied as much one time when I treated him for a horrible bruise on his arm awhile back. I think he's more interested in having a good time. Just a friendly warning."

"Thank you, I'll keep that in mind. Can I get you water or make coffee to wash down the pie?"

He pushed his empty plate to the center of the table. "No, no. But you can tell me where you got that nasty limp from, and don't give me your old injury story." His gaze traveled down to her bad leg. Kate tucked it beneath the table.

"It is an old injury. I wasn't lying. I was twelve when it happened. I try not to think about it."

"Sometimes thinking about things can do a world of good. Also talking about it." His expression softened. He was a good doctor if this was his bedside manner. How much did she dare tell him?

She glanced at her camera.

"I was injured in a blast. My folks were killed but I lived." She wouldn't tell him that she was the only person to live from her entire sixth grade class, including the teachers and other parents. He might call the media, and that would be her signal to run.

Doc folded his hand over hers. "I'm sorry. Your life must not have been easy after that. Who raised you?"

"I was blessed with a set of fantastic grandparents. They took me into their home, and the rest is history. In fact, my limp makes me think of them sometimes. Both have passed."

"You're alone in the world? No siblings?"

She felt like he was doing a family history for a medical chart. "I have friends here and there. And you?"

They chatted about his life for a few more minutes until he announced he had to get back home. His wife would be wondering what happened. "Stop by one day to meet Miss Mary. She doesn't get out as much as before. Likes to stay put."

"I'd love to meet her. I'll finish this pie this week and drop off the dish." She walked him to the door and watched him hobble to his truck as though he had nothing on his mind but the pie he ate.

Would she ever be so carefree?

As she readied herself for bed, her phone rang.

Seth.

Kate answered, "Did you find Debbie?" Her heart galloped with hope. Maybe they'd been wrong to worry about the daycare lady.

"I'm not calling about Debbie. I called to warn you. Someone stole my laptop."

She dropped into a nearby chair. "What? How did that happen?"

"I was cold-cocked from behind. Let's say my normally handsome face isn't as handsome anymore, and I'm running out of frozen peas for the lump on the back of my head."

Kate tightened her grip on the phone. "You're kidding, right? Are you all right? Do you need to see to a doctor?"

"No joke, Red. I'll live but someone wanted what was on my computer and they got it. Lucky for me I backup my work in the cloud. Lousy for me is I've written some pretty nasty things about a lot of people."

"The Bend?"

"Bingo."

27

Sometimes the Trainer was forced to take action he would rather avoid. No one was going to ruin his plans for the future. No one. He'd been observing the reporter for a while now. Nosy. Too many questions. Wrote measly articles that did nothing for the town. Or him.

Normally, he opposed violence (unless it was his own brand). A recourse for the weak. Violence made him sick. Last night, his unfortunate actions made him quite sick to his stomach. On his trip home, he threw up twice.

A nasty habit from the past he couldn't overcome. Yet.

He took Seth's computer to his office. Set it on his pristine desk. Cleanliness was a blessing, he thought, as he settled in front of the lit screen.

Finding the password took seconds. After his mother was gone, his father and he delved into electronics. He remembered the machines they built—ones Microsoft would envy. He wiped his hair back from his sweating forehead. *Focus.*

He stroked the keyboard.

KEEPAWAY. The Trainer shook his head and punched several more keys.

His fingers stopped. Hovered over the keyboard.

The reporter was too close. He needed to find a way to disillusion him. Make him think about his choices. Persuade him to see the benefits of his grander plan. If only he had more time.

Men like him never got it right. They preferred their women as equals. Didn't they understand what the good Lord wanted? Women were made to breed. They weren't made to run a corporation. They weren't created to wear dresses showing too much skin. They were made to be mothers. Sound mothers. They were made to bear children and train them up in the way they should go.

His way.

The Trainer opened another document. He scanned the short paper. His breathing increased.

So the reporter called her *Red*.

28

Kate slipped a silky blouse over her head. She tugged it over her hips, spreading away any stray wrinkles. David would arrive in under a half hour. She'd put off dressing as long as she could. After Seth assured her again this morning that he didn't need her help, she'd taken a drive through the back roads, snapping photos of the scenery—a broken-down barn, a pond filled with ducks, an apple orchard.

On her way back through town, she passed a country church with a parking lot filled with cars. She slowed down, memories taking shape inside of her. She'd spent hours attending church with her parents and brother. Then the bombing. Everything changed. Even God. She still believed He existed—she just didn't trust Him.

She studied the families that gathered near the entrance. Women in prairie dresses. Children dressed like their parents. Their fashions seemed out of place in today's world.

But this was the Bend, she reminded herself. A place that set itself apart.

She looped around the block. Parked across the street. Focusing her camera, she snapped a few pictures of the church. She might need them for her article. That's when she noticed the signage announcing the special speaker.

Brother Earl.

She lowered her camera.

David was waving at her.

When she saw David wave, she started her car and drove away pretending she hadn't seen him walking toward her. Would he bring up his sighting of her tonight?

She chastised herself for not waiting for him to speak with her. But he might have invited her inside. And the last place she wanted to be was in a church service. Instead, she fled like a startled rabbit.

Of course he'd bring it up when he saw her. She would make up another story. One so convincing that even she would believe it.

She didn't have to wait too long. David knocked on her front door at 5 p.m. Dressed in fitted jeans and a plaid button-down shirt, he reminded her of a cowboy. Boots included. He smiled as he stepped over the threshold.

"Not going to run from me now?"

Her breath caught. "I'm sorry. I was on a mission. I figured I could apologize tonight." She reached for her purse, ducking her head.

"Apology accepted. I don't want to ruin my chances with the prettiest girl in the Bend tonight."

He shut the door behind them, stepping onto the porch with her.

"Flattery will get you everywhere." Kate climbed into his truck. The interior smelled like him. Peaches. "Where are we going? You never did tell me." She snapped on her seat belt.

David put the truck in gear and drove out of her driveway, turning right. The opposite direction of town. "A little place I know. Sit back and be surprised."

She didn't like surprises. Least of all from a stranger. She was tempted to put a call into Seth, but then realized he had his own problems. Besides, he'd think she was ditsy if she called him on a date to say she was worried where this guy was taking her. She'd heard enough warnings from him. Seth didn't want her in the Bend and that was all there was to it. Competition. That's what she was to him.

Just in case, she studied the direction David drove.

He turned on the radio. Tuned it to a familiar country tune. "Like country?" he asked.

"I'm learning. This is the north, but I'm surprised how many places play country music here."

"It doesn't matter whether you're in the north or south—country music is real music. The way all music should be. Easy on the ear. Tells a story. God-fearing people everywhere listen to it." He shot her another toe-curling smile.

He *was* cute. The physical attraction she felt for him was difficult to dismiss.

She wanted to remain vigilant, though. David was Earl's brother. Perhaps tonight he would shed light on his brother's plans for the Bend. She needed to uncover a story that Tim would print besides the little league games and the county fair blue-ribbon winners he assigned her.

"Here we are." He turned down a dirt road that dead-ended next to a field of daisies. Kate wished she'd brought her camera. "It's beautiful."

David slid out and came around her side to open the door. "It's my favorite place in the county."

He helped her down before reaching into the back for a wicker picnic basket.

"Is that a creek ahead?" She followed behind as David led her past a dozen or more old oaks that spread out to a clearing. A rustic picnic table faced the field while a small creek ran along beside it. He propped the basket on the table and patted the bench.

"Have a seat. I hope you like fried chicken and potato salad. That's all I could find on a Sunday." He unwrapped fresh-smelling rolls then handed her a fork and a napkin with a bottle of cold water.

"This is so nice. Thanks for bringing me here." She settled across from him facing the field. "Do you own this property or are we trespassing?"

"My brother owns it. This and another few thousand acres in the Bend. He hopes to buy more."

"Whatever for? He's an undertaker." The chicken melted in her mouth. David was doing equal damage to his plate as well.

He shrugged. "He has important plans for this area. You know how I was telling you about country music? He believes doing things the real old-fashioned way works better. If he can get the community on board with his beliefs, the Bend might be the best place in the country to live."

She swallowed the last part of her roll. "On board with what? Can you be more specific?"

Another shrug. "My brother always did things differently. It's the way my folks raised us. I came along later so I didn't have as many restrictions."

"The baby in the family." She passed him the salad.

"That's right. And you? The baby too?" He stopped chewing. Gazed directly at her.

A shiver wriggled through her belly. "The oldest."

"Brothers, sisters?" He gripped his water bottle and jolted back a slug.

"One brother. He died when he was younger. So did my folks." She needed to change the topic. Get it back on Brother Earl. David was a master of directing the conversation away from himself. "What about your parents? How did they die?"

David lifted one brow. "What makes you think they're dead?" He laughed. A nice laugh. "They moved to Arizona a few years back. My mother had enough of the cold weather and funerals. Earl bought them out while I was in college. He'd made good money with some land transactions."

"They're alive?"

"Sure." He tipped his head back, raising his brow.

"I thought someone told me they had died. I must be mistaken. Do you see them often?" she asked instead of the question burning in her chest. Why the tombstone?

"Now and then. When we can." He busied himself by packing the remaining food into the basket. He took it to the truck, returning with his phone. Within minutes, soft music filtered through the speaker. All planned steps to create a romantic date. Yes, she was impressed.

"Dance?" He held out his hand.

She hesitated. The last time she'd danced had been at the wedding of a coworker from one of her short-lived jobs.

David tugged her fingers. Pulled her to her feet.

She let him. How could she resist a slow dance with a cowboy? David pulled her into his arms as the sun set around them. She shut her eyes. Let her body sway with his.

Where was her willpower? It was as though David had cast a spell on her, and she had no power to break loose.

They stopped moving when the song ended.

He ran one finger down her cheek. "You're beautiful, Kate. Absolutely beautiful." His voice turned silvery soft. She leaned into him, struck by the amount of passion that rose in her.

No one had made her feel this attractive.

Ever.

29

Tim called for a staff meeting Monday morning. Kate didn't have time to ask Seth how he felt or comment on the nasty bruise on his cheek. Instead, she thought about David and how he had kissed her last night.

She'd practically danced into her house afterward.

She also forgot to check her phone messages until that morning. Two calls. One from a number she didn't recognize.

The other call from Jackie. Her heart skipped when she listened to that one. Trevor started chemo this week.

She turned her attention back to Tim. He looked like he'd been awake all night. Dark circles rimmed his eyes. He stooped when he paced. His chest heaved a long sigh when he finally collapsed into his chair.

"We need a story. Not your usual ones about dance recitals and bowling leagues. I'm talking a story. Word on the street is the theater closed. The story is what's coming in its place."

Seth shoved a pen behind his ear. "I haven't heard about anything coming in. Didn't realize it closed for good for that matter. I thought he had temporarily shut down."

Tim slammed his fist on his desk. Maybe he wasn't so tired. "That's why I'm the editor and you work for me. I did a little digging. Seems there is to be a health clinic or food store taking it over. A woman from New York City. Supposed to get all remodeled fancy-like. That's what Harry told me last night. He wants the job. Not that he'll do it the way anyone from the city will want it done, but when has Harry cared about that. It's work." Tim sighed. Kate thought he'd fallen asleep until he hopped from his seat and plucked up the last published paper.

"I want the story. I want her name, what she plans to do, and her background. Get me anything. Plenty of pictures. Get down there and get a story. The Bend needs to know who its new neighbors are and what changes are coming."

He pointed to Seth. "And you with the fancy face today. Go see Doc Brown. You look like crap."

Seth rubbed the bruise and lowered his gaze.

"Do you still want to run the story about the upcoming fair?" Kate had already gone to the fairgrounds and interviewed the organizer.

Tim rolled his eyes. "It's news, isn't it? Have it on my desk by three." He shooed them out of the office and slammed his door.

Seth made for his desk. Kate followed. "Why didn't you tell him about the break-in? That's news. And for that matter, why didn't you call the sheriff?"

He stopped stacking note cards. "You haven't learned yet, have you, Red? There is no law in the Bend except Earl's law. Didn't your David tell you that last night?" He scowled before grabbing his briefcase.

Her David?

"Where are you going?" Kate grabbed her camera bag and purse. She followed him through to the front office, bid a quick good-bye to Rhonda and ducked when Seth let the door swing back. "I'm coming with you, you know," she called as she raced behind him to his Jeep.

Seth stopped, his shoulders sinking. "Then get in and quit talking." He threw his briefcase into the back seat. Kate scrambled into the passenger seat before he changed his mind. She had hardly buckled up when he floored the gas pedal.

They pulled up in front of the theater minutes later.

A woman in tight, black yoga pants, a skimpy tank showing fit biceps, and a string of pearls around her neck was barking orders to several men. None of the trucks read Harry's Construction.

She crossed the sidewalk and came up to Seth's open window. "Oh good. Maybe you can make sense of this town for me. You're the press, aren't you?" She nodded toward the magnetic sign on Seth's door. "I'm renting this building in hopes of bringing not only health to the area but a little more culture. Now some bully named Earl says I needed to run my ideas through him first. Is everyone crazy here? This is America. I can build anything I want, and some old coot isn't going to stop me."

She swiped imaginary dirt off her hands and stalked into the building.

Kate looked at Seth's profile. He was beaming.

30

She said her name was Amy Anderson.

She'd lived her entire life in New York, except for a year in Paris where she studied art. She also dipped her toe (her words, not his) into politics when she returned but decided men could be nasty in that field. Instead she studied healthy lifestyle alternatives.

The Bend needed her, she said.

Seth decided he needed her.

The woman mesmerized him. Of all times to have Kate sitting next to him taking in every word as though her entire career hinged on this one woman's story. Amy invited them into the theater once she understood they were there to help, not hinder. She offered chai tea and cookies made from gluten-free products. Kate tore into them like she'd never eaten before. He nibbled on one to be polite but in all honestly thought they tasted more like cat food.

"You say you want to open in a month? Is that possible?" Kate asked.

Of course it wasn't possible. Not with Earl breathing down her neck. He controlled all the comings and goings. It wouldn't surprise Seth if he had the lumber store in his pocket as well.

Amy smiled for the umpteenth time. "That's the plan, but as you see they need to tear out the screen and all these useless chairs. Then I need new walls, and paint and so much more. It all depends on the help I find here. Please put in your story that I'm also looking to employ at least two people who want to learn healthy habits and share them with others." Her teeth gleamed. Seth ran his tongue over his, finding multiple food particles. He closed his lips.

"Do you mind if I take your picture?" Kate then directed Amy to sit and pose for several shots. Afterward, she wandered off to take pictures of the building, leaving Seth alone with Amy.

"What brought you all the way from New York to a place like the Bend?" She pulled her chair closer. Deep, blue eyes.

"My daddy used to fish with his father along this river when he was a boy. He always told me about this place. How special it was back then." Her eyes took on a faraway look. "I always promised myself that someday I would visit. I did last year for a week. I fell in love with the area. Since then I have been working on finding the right building to start a business here." She smiled and looked at him with raised brows. "Good enough reason?"

Seth clicked off his recorder. "I hope you know what you're doing."

"Well, aren't you sweet. Of course I do. I always do." She leaned closer to inspect his face. "Looks like I need to give you lessons."

###

"Okay, Romeo, are we going back to the office or take a ride past Debbie's? Neither of us checked on her yesterday." Kate wrestled with her seat belt after they left the theater.

"I was predisposed yesterday because I had to drive into the city for a new laptop. And if you recall, you were romancing Earl's brother." He shot her what he hoped was a pointed smirk.

Her cheeks turned pink. "I wasn't romancing him any more than you were that woman just now. I probably should have left you two alone."

Had he been that obvious? He was out of practice. Well, to be truthful he was never *in* practice. Something about Amy, though, hit him hard. Her looks? Her determination? He gripped the steering wheel with one hand and rammed the gear shift into drive. "We're going to Debbie's." Seth turned left and drove over the river bridge. His decision seemed to appease Kate. She strummed her fingers lightly on her knee as though plucking a tune.

The back of his head still ached. A stop at Doc Brown's might not be a bad idea, too. They could swing in on their way back.

Debbie's cottage came into view.

The first change he noticed as they approached was the car in the driveway. It was gone.

"Where's her car?" Kate pointed as he pulled into the empty driveway.

"Stay here." He got out of the Jeep and surveyed the ground in front of him. It hadn't rained in a few days, so the mud was dried and hard.

"Are you Sherlock Holmes as well?" She stood next to him.

"Didn't I tell you to stay put?" He led them to the front door. Jiggled the knob. It wouldn't budge. Someone had locked the house.

"Maybe she came back, packed up and left again."

Her suggestions sounded plausible if it weren't for the way they had seen her house before. No, he'd more likely think someone else returned to do a clean-up.

"There's nothing more we can do here. If we hang around, someone will catch us and turn us in for trespassing. I don't know about you, but I'd like some fresh air." He noted her sullen expression. "You don't agree?"

She nodded. "I do. It's just hard to let it go. Something happened here and now we're supposed to walk away?" Her eyes hardened. He should drag her back to the Jeep, but his head pounded. He had better things to do, like write his story, rather than stand around debating the what ifs of nothing.

Seth ground his jaw, stepped around her, and trekked toward his vehicle. Either Kate would come with him or walk back to town.

She followed.

Guess she wasn't quite clueless.

Once settled in the Jeep, Seth told her he wanted to stop at Doctor Brown's before returning to the office. Hearing Doc's name made her smile. "You've met him?"

"He changed my flat tire this past week. He's charming. I want to meet his wife."

She wanted to meet Mary? Now that might be a memorable moment.

31

Seth could be such a mule at times. Kate nibbled on her bottom lip and watched the passing scenery. He'd taken to the new owner of the theater—like a boy to a dog. Amy had seemed nice—almost too nice—to both of them. She hoped the woman realized how different life was in the Bend. It hadn't taken Kate very many days to figure out that Brother Earl kept his fingers in everything. David had alluded to that last night, too.

David told her he would call her later to arrange another date. Another date meant a future. Could she afford to do that here? Her forehead creased.

"Good, he's home." Seth swerved into the driveway. Doc's pickup was parked near the whitewashed barn.

Doc answered the door immediately. He took one look at Seth's face and whistled. "Get in here. I hope the other guy looks worse." He clamped his hand on Kate's shoulder. "Good to see you again so soon. Mary will be pleased to have a chance to meet you."

"I was hoping she'd be home." Kate gave a once-over to the old farm house as they passed through. It was neatly decorated and so clean it looked as though no one lived there. Doc led them to his office off to the right of the front room. This area looked a little more lived in. Stacks of paper lined the ancient oak desk. An examining table filled the rest of the area. Seth sat on the edge of it while she dropped into a nearby chair.

"Tell me what happened."

Seth told him the truth. Someone broke into his house.

Kate met his gaze. So he trusted the doctor.

They spent the next fifteen minutes listening to Doc Brown spout off about what the world had come to. Thugs everywhere—for what—a computer? He clicked his tongue as he examined the bruise on Seth's face and the lump on his head.

"You'll live. I'm going to give you something for the pain, but take it only if you must." He scribbled a prescription on a pad he pulled from a nearby drawer. The inside of the drawer looked as jumbled as the top of his desk. Kate spotted a dozen pens, earplugs, and a gold ring.

A gold ring?

Both their backs were turned to her as Seth and Doc chatted about the upcoming fireman's parade.

She must know.

She leaned to her right. If only she could see the front of the ring. She shot a sideways glance toward Doc. He was checking Seth's shoulder now. Talking about fishing.

She stretched one finger into the drawer—enough to flip the ring.

Kate straightened like a rocket.

Doc owned the exact same hawk ring as Brother Earl and the bowler. What did that mean?

"You must be our new neighbor. I'm Mary."

Kate's gaze shot to the doorway.

"I've been hoping to meet you." A woman with powdery white hair pulled up into a bun extended her hand in greeting.

She was dressed exactly like one of Brother Earl's followers.

###

Once they arrived back to the office, Seth typed his story. He told her it would be about the problems that the Bend gave new businesses. How they were stopping progress with their stupid requirements. Kate plugged her camera into the computer. She hoped to be able to give Seth at least four good photos for the story.

The pictures of the front portion of the theater came in nice and clear. No adjustments needed. The one with the workmen ripping out the chairs would work too. She clicked through a couple more and then came to the batch she'd taken of Amy.

Her fingers froze. No. This couldn't be happening. Not again.

What was wrong with the people in the Bend?

A faint aura surrounded the new owner of the downtown theater.

###

Fresh air, that's what she needed. No, a fresh life. She pushed back from her desk. "I'm going over to the diner for something to eat. Do you want me to bring you back something?"

Seth didn't raise his head. "I'm good. You go. I'll get something later."

She grabbed her purse. Almost ran to the front area where Rhonda was painting her nails for the third time that week.

Two minutes later, she parked in front of the restaurant. Kate took several deep breaths. She needed to calm herself before she went in. Another deep breath. Why were so many of her pictures showing auras? Had her curse changed? Was everyone going to die here? No, that couldn't be it. It had to mean something else. She wasn't an expert on her curse. She could only go on what had occurred in the past.

But this was the Bend.

Nothing was normal here. Absolutely nothing.

32

There were moments when the Trainer chose a different course. He didn't mean for tragedy to happen to anyone. He tried to stick to his original plans. But sometimes plans didn't always go their best way.

Like today.

If only she had listened to him. If only she had accepted the wisdom of his counsel. She was a strong-willed woman—the kind he admired. The kind he preferred. Yet that kind was also the most difficult to bend. Her will was exceptionally strong. So strong he had to break it another way.

Permanently.

Their offspring would have been so perfect. If he hadn't upped the timing of his plan.

He hammered the last nail in the coffin. Already the pungent odor of death seeped through the cracks. He'd have to hurry. Bury her before someone noticed. He washed his hands in a nearby bucket. Dried blood. Always hard to remove.

Like his mother—she had fought to the bitter end. No, he didn't like to go there. His father told him that sometimes force became a necessary option. He glanced down at his hands—still dripping with water and blood.

He understood options.

He glanced at the woman's final resting place. He'd built this box out of oak. It would be heavy to move. Unlike the last one—pine. He'd wait until the cover of darkness.

The Trainer gave a final kick to the box, sighed. Harlot.

33

The cafe overflowed with customers. Kate slid into a booth in the far corner. After several minutes, a pretty waitress placed a well-worn menu in front of her. "We're busy today. Give me a few minutes and I'll be back to take your order."

Kate studied the menu for only a moment. She already knew what she wanted. A huge burger, fries, and a chocolate shake. Comfort food.

The waitress returned as promised, took her order, and left Kate to watch the other diners.

A teen wearing a baseball cap sat at the counter. A worn-out mother with a crying child sulked in a corner booth. Two elderly women, dressed in long garb, talked at a nearby table while sipping soda from straws.

She didn't know anyone.

They didn't know her.

That's the way her life had mostly gone for her the past twenty years until Jackie.

She scanned the area again. It would have been nice to run into Becky again. They seemed to have made a connection the other day. Hadn't they? Becky was outgoing and determined. Like the new owner of the theater. Confident.

Unlike herself.

She considered that picture of Amy. The aura. It had been years since the bombing. Surely whatever happened to her brain would return to normal. Wouldn't it?

Then there was the doctor's wife. Mary had been friendly, giving her a quick tour of their home. The tidy den. The cozy kitchen. The antiquated parlor. She had started by showing Kate the pictures. An entire wall covered with photos of children at various ages. Mary said she gave birth to ten children. Seven survived. She wanted more, but her body didn't.

She had fingered each frame gently. Reverently.

"Where are they now?" Kate asked.

Mary dabbed her eyes with an embroidered handkerchief she pulled from her apron pocket. "They left the Bend."

Kate hadn't known how to answer, so she had kept silent. She waited for Mary to compose herself, raise her chin and continue the tour. Like a trooper.

Kate didn't believe it though. Something seemed off.

She drew in a mouthful of chocolate shake. All seven of Mary's children had left the Bend. That seemed unusual considering the large farm and family history. Mary had stopped talking when Doc and Seth joined them. Lowered her head. Like she'd discovered a spec of dirt on the floor. Unlikely.

"Can I get you anything else?" Her waitress swayed near her table.

"Can you tell Becky I stopped by to see her?"

The waitress's smile slipped. "She don't work here no more. Up and left a day or so ago and hasn't showed up for any of her shifts." She leaned down. "I think she ran away with a man. I don't blame her. If there was some way for me to get out of this town, I'd run too."

Ran away? After the way she spoke about Seth and David?

"Do you happen to know where she lives? Maybe I can stop by and leave a note." Kate flashed a quick smile hoping the waitress thought she and Becky were more than acquaintances.

The girl scribbled on the back of a blank check. "If you find her, tell her thanks a lot. She stuck me with the late shift." She dropped the paper on the table.

After Kate paid, she studied the directions to Becky's house. Another place in the country. She checked her watch. Still time to run out there and make it back to the office in time to finish her story.

Fifteen minutes later, she pulled up in front of a rundown shack. A couple of bare-boned hounds sniffed the perimeter. A scruffy, yellow cat perched on the porch railing licking her paw.

Kate considered honking her horn.

Instead, she pulled out her phone to call Seth. He might be interested in knowing another woman in the Bend appeared to have left town suddenly. Her fingers hung over the pad. She put her phone away. He would tell her she was overreacting.

With renewed determination, she left her car. "Here puppy, here puppy . . ." she called to the dogs. They ignored her and continued pushing their noses into the earth in pursuit of dinner. The porch floorboards were bare and groaned when she stepped on them. Someone had set up two folding chairs with a rusty table between them to her left. A wilted rose drooped in a cheap vase.

She knocked on the door.

She knocked again.

The mangy cat circled her legs. Mewed up at her.

She twisted the knob like Seth had Debbie's.

It didn't budge.

The windows. She took two steps, cupped her hands and peered inside. A couch. Outdated TV and a TV tray with a coffee mug. Becky was short on designing skills. And Kate was short on detective skills. Better to leave this sleuthing to Seth. She turned to leave.

"Looking for someone?"

Her heart shot to her throat. The guy from the bowling alley. Mole stood in front of her. Cradling a rifle.

"Becky. We're friends, but I see she's not here." She nibbled on her bottom lip, hoping her voice sounded more confident than her legs felt right then. What was he doing here? She clasped her hands together.

Mole rubbed his scraggly chin with the back of his free hand. "She ain't home. A little nosy, aren't you? Peeking in the window like some kind of pervert?" His voice held a sneer to it. His eyes flicked from right to left. He looked a lot uglier in daylight.

"She didn't show up for her shifts at the cafe. I was checking to be sure she was okay."

He spit a wad of brown goop into the dirt by the porch. "She's fine. You aren't."

Kate inhaled. "I'm glad she's fine." Sweat built beneath her pits. "Are you related?"

Mole shifted his weight. Leaned against the porch rail. "Not sure that's your business either. What you should be concerning yourself about is keeping your nose clean around the Bend." He leered closer. "We don't appreciate outsiders like you." He nodded toward the locked door.

"I was concerned. Now I have to get back to my office before they wonder about me." She glanced at her car. Glanced back at him. Could she run faster? Did she want to find out?

Mole motioned with his head. "Be my guest. Just remember this conversation the next time you think about breaking and entering."

"I wasn't—" She started to protest but changed her mind when he shifted his rifle. She nodded, and strode past Mole with as much poise as she could muster.

That's when she noticed the mailbox.

Stuffed.

34

Seth had covered for Kate long enough. Tim wanted the theater story by the end of the day. He'd tried her cell, but she didn't pick up. What was it with that woman? She'd lose her job if she kept this act up. But then what did he care? She'd leave, and he'd get the cover story on Earl. No competition.

He popped another handful of pretzels into his mouth. Lunch. It would have to do since it was already late, and he needed to finish.

He moved over to her desk. She'd pulled up the photos before she left for lunch so it was only a matter of choosing what he needed and sending them to his computer. Fortunately, he knew the passwords to all the computers. A couple of clicks later and he found her folder.

He scrolled down. Selected one he thought might bring life to the story. He opened her email and uploaded a few. He returned to the rest and continued his scrolling.

Maybe he'd blow the one up of Amy in her pearls to twice the usual size. Tim wouldn't mind. Might even increase their sales.

"What are you doing on my computer?"

Seth's fingers froze. He spun around. The color had drained out of Kate's face. He rose out of her chair and waved his hand. "It's all yours. I was getting the pictures you should have given me by now. We have a deadline."

She dumped a bag of Tootsie Pops on his desk. "Lunch."

With one click, she shut her computer down. Faced him. "Becky's missing, too."

"Becky who?"

Her eyes widened with impatience. "The waitress at the cafe. She and I talked the other day. Today she wasn't there. I got her address and ventured out to her place. She's gone. Just like Debbie. Something's going on in the Bend, Seth. Something strange with the women."

"Whoa. Slow down."

"I can't slow down. Something is going on here. I didn't believe it at first, but now I'm sure. Her mailbox was full. And then Mole wouldn't let me get into the house, even when I tried to—"

"—Mole? What are you talking about?" Seth glanced over his shoulder. Tim was still busy in his office.

"Mole was there. With a rifle. On her front porch. The man is disgusting. I might have suspected it before, but now I am certain." Her face twisted.

"Why would Mole be there unless it's his house? Was it?"

Kate sniffed. "I don't know. I was too scared to stand around and chitchat." She frowned.

Before he could open his mouth to respond, Tim walked into the room carrying a stack of papers. "What are you two jabbering about out here? Where's my story about the theater? Do you see the time?" He pointed to the wall clock. "Time is money, so let's get it into gear. Kate, I want you to cover the hardware store's fiftieth anniversary celebration tomorrow morning. Get me several decent shots of the place. I need more filler for the paper this week. Lost another contributor." He shook his head and left the same way he came into the room, carrying a stack of papers.

Seth waited for Kate to say something.

Instead, she blew her nose and fired up her computer. Her cell phone vibrated a few seconds later. She slipped it out of her purse and put her back toward him.

"Hello? Me too. Sure, that would be great. I'll put it on my calendar. Thank you."

He couldn't squelch the question that rose in his throat. Blame it on being a reporter.

"David?"

The look she gave him said it all. It was none of his business.

But he'd make it his business.

35

Kate couldn't believe Seth had gone through her photos. Of course he wouldn't see the auras, but she couldn't be certain. Just because her grandmother never did when Kate told her, meant nothing. Seth recently sustained a blow to his head. What if he could now see what she did? Kate never told anyone or asked anyone to check her pictures after her grandmother looked at them. She couldn't stand the humiliation she would receive.

But what if her grandmother had bad eyesight? She'd never thought of that possibility until now. If she knew for certain that she wasn't the only freak who saw the auras, it could change her life. Or maybe it was the pictures and not her.

Right now, she had plenty to think about. Mole showing up and scaring her half to death was only part of her worry. Since coming to the Bend, she hadn't impressed her boss much. She needed to write a great story and show him her worth, or she would be moving again. She was so tired of leaving. The Bend was a perfect hiding place from the media, and besides that, there was David.

His call earlier that day had helped calm her.

She couldn't wait to see him at the parade on Thursday. He promised to treat her to pork barbecue and attend the fireworks display with her. Yes, she told herself not to get involved again. Told herself—warned herself—if she had to move again it would be hard to break it off.

Something about David swept all the warning bells out of her head.

Once she turned in her story, she left for home without another word to Seth.

He hadn't seemed too impressed with her details about Becky anyway. Perhaps she was over-dramatizing it. Worrying when she shouldn't. Though Mole had given her a scare. Had he meant to threaten her, or was he like that with everyone? An outsider. When would she stop being an outsider anywhere?

After a toasted cheese sandwich and a cup of tea, she loaded her personal pictures onto her computer. She held her breath. Counted the shots. Would another person's imminent death jump onto her shoulders? Sometimes the burden was too enormous. She should work in a grocery store where she didn't take photos. Maybe get a job as a school secretary.

Who was she kidding? Photography kept her alive. She could no more give it up than breathing.

She waited for the pictures to focus. The church came into view. She'd snapped that one while people were milling around out front, before she saw David.

No . . . No! She bent over her computer. She couldn't tear her eyes away from the scene in front of her. The entire church glowed.

Kate couldn't sleep. She finally called Seth at midnight. He answered on the first ring.

"What's the matter?"

"Nothing earth shattering. I just wanted to run some things by you. We didn't get a chance to finish our discussion about Becky."

She could hear him groaning, sitting up in bed.

"Did you hear me?"

She's probably on vacation with Debbie."

Kate moved to her open bedroom window. "I also remembered something Doc Brown told me the day he stopped by. He said Brother Earl's parents moved to Arizona or something. They aren't dead. David said the same thing."

"They're alive?" His normally flat voice elevated.

Good. Maybe he would take her seriously now.

"Yes. And if they are, who's buried in that cemetery plot? I also think something happened to Becky. Women—*people*—just don't disappear without telling anyone." As soon as she said the words, she thought of herself. She disappeared all the time. But then she had a good reason. Did these women? "And her mailbox was jammed full. Who leaves town without stopping their mail, or at the very least, emptying it?"

"Maybe that's what Mole was doing until you interrupted him." Again his snide tone. Why did she bother with him? She pulled back her curtain. Studied the black outside.

"Another thing. Several men in the Bend wear the same gold ring. It has a hawk emblem on it. Have you ever noticed it before?"

A lengthy silence answered her.

Finally. "Who?"

"Brother Earl, Mole and Doc Brown. Doc had one hidden in his desk drawer." She flinched at telling him about how she saw it. "What does the ring mean, Seth?"

Another silence.

She let the curtain drop back into place.

"Seth? What does it mean?"

"Where are you right now?"

"At home. In my bedroom."

"Is your window open?"

"Of course."

"Shut it. Turn your light off. Now. Do it, Red."

She stalked over to her bedside lamp. Clicked the switch. The room vanished into darkness. "Light's off. But I'm leaving my window open. What is it? What's going on?" She lowered herself to the bed. "What do the rings mean?"

Another sigh before Seth finally spoke.

"It means the Bend is worse than I thought."

36

After his mother failed both he and his father, they worked to improve their skills each night after school. He practiced on rats, local cats, and an occasional stray dog. His father dubbed him the Trainer when he successfully controlled a pit bull they found.

Eventually, he needed a human candidate.

The girls at his school were too risky. Their parents watched them like hawks. Besides, the pretty girls didn't like him much. Snobs. Stuck on themselves. He blamed his mother for that too. She was the reason he missed so much school. Taking care of her needs. Cleaning up her messes. Making him miss . . . No! He would not remember that day. Not like that anyway.

He had spent years creating a solution.

He'd have to bide his time. Besides, he wasn't ready to put his entire plan into action.

When he turned eighteen, though, he did what he'd been planning to do for years. Tried his skill on his father. Called it a birthday present to himself. He found his father that day in the basement tinkering on the furnace. He'd been sick, coughing all night so much that the Trainer had been unable to sleep.

"Hand me that wrench." His father pointed to his nearby toolbox.

Forget the wrench—his knife would do.

He'd graduated from whips to knives. Sharp knives. For the non-compliant. Quick and painless. At least for him. He also loved the feel of the handle—how it fit his palm. He couldn't speak for his father, or the countless other candidates over the years, but when he brought his knife out, they behaved. Much better than with a whip. Did as he said. Eventually all women would obey his commands. Especially the one he wanted most.

He never got caught. Either he was too smart or the world around him was plain stupid. Maybe a little of both. And his property choices. Always perfect. Trees. Buildings. Everything he needed to execute his plan. Just as he had written about it in the eighth grade.

Ms. Hibbard. What a fool. Thinking she could change his thinking about women. She'd made him read a book about women in America—how they had evolved into CEOs and worked outside the home. He'd burned the book. Burned it with the cat that had given him such a hard time until he sliced it beneath the chin.

He knew what a woman's role should be. Breeder. Nothing more. Except for one woman. Only she was worthy of joining him in his final plan.

37

Another nightmare. Running. Falling. Trying to breathe. Kate awoke with slick sweat coating her body. She slid out of bed, pulled on her bathrobe. The room had cooled considerably during the night. She slammed the window shut.

Seth and his nonsense.

Just because someone broke into his house didn't mean they would break into hers. If they did, they would get nothing.

She fumbled with the belt at her waist, shuffled into the kitchen. Coffee. That would help wake her up to meet with Seth at the cafe this morning. He said he would tell her what he knew about the men in the Bend—for her own protection he said. She would listen, but she didn't need protection. Besides that, Seth was the last person in the Bend who would protect her from anything. If she lost her job, he would celebrate in the street.

She bit into a stale banana muffin.

Summer in the Bend wasn't so bad. She looked forward to the carnival and parade on Thursday. With David.

As she pushed her mug away, a hard knock came on her front door. Kate reached for the nearby Mace and checked her robe. Doc again? Maybe he'd brought more of Mary's treats. It was a little early though.

Another knock.

She peeked through the living room to the front door.

The delivery man.

She set her Mace aside. Last week she'd ordered a file cabinet. The same guy had delivered a new lens from Amazon when she first arrived.

She threw open the door.

"Good morning. You're early." Her gaze caught on the large box next to him.

The guy gave a half-smile. "Sorry, Miss Song. Couldn't get this out to you last night, so I'm out early today. Can I carry it in for you?"

She stepped to the side. "Thank you so much. Is it heavy? I can get it from here."

"No problem. Let me put it inside for you." He hefted the package, setting it next to her couch.

"Thank you so much. Have a good day."

He tipped his head, smiling. "Sure thing, Miss."

If only the other men in the Bend were as polite.

When she was alone again, she pulled the top file drawer open. Here is where she would start. Here is where she would place the printed photographs of people she saw with an aura. Maybe she'd see a pattern. Maybe she'd finally figure out how to turn her curse into a gift.

###

The cafe was empty except for Seth, Kate, and an older man at the counter. Seth ordered another cup of black coffee for himself. Kate nursed the one in front of her.

"Tell me about the rings. What do they mean?"

He rubbed his forehead. "Nothing like getting straight to the point."

"You're the one who's trying to scare me."

"You're the one who asked."

"Are we going to play games or are you going to tell me what you know about the Bend?" She checked her watch. "We'll be late for work. Talk fast."

"Doesn't matter. Tim is out for a few days. Called me last night."

She dumped a packet of sugar into her coffee. "Again? What does he do with all this time off? Is he sick?"

Seth lifted one eyebrow. "He owns a ring, too."

She dropped the packet. "What? How do you know?"

"Saw it when I stopped by his place once. It was sitting on a table by his couch. Like he took it off before I came in."

She considered his news. Tim didn't act like the other men in the Bend. He was sweet for the most part and treated women as equals. "Do you think he's involved in a secret society? Is Brother Earl in charge of it? And the hawk? What about that symbol?"

Seth waved his hand. "Slow down." He glanced to the entry where two men dressed in identical work pants entered the cafe. He lowered his voice, leaned across the table. "I think it has to do with their women. I think they train them."

"Train them?" She thought of the local zoo where she grew up. "Like with animals?"

He nodded. "More like dog training 101."

38

Seth wasn't stupid. He wasn't going to confess all he knew about Brother Earl and his sect, who somehow convinced their wives to dress like peasants and follow them like slaves. But never before had women disappeared from the Bend like they were now. Three women in under a year? Couldn't be coincidental. There had to be a connection. Getting smashed over the head also made him realize Kate might be in danger herself. A target. Another reporter who could blow their secrets right out of the county into bigger headlines.

He absently rubbed the back of his head.

"Still hurt?" Kate stared at him with huge green eyes. If things were different...

"I'll live. But if I were you I would lock my doors and keep watch. Whoever took my computer wanted to stop me from writing about them. What else could they want?"

"Or they could have wanted a computer." She raised her perfectly contoured eyebrows.

"That too."

"But what about Debbie and Becky? How do they fit in?"

He had never gone back to check on either of them.

"I haven't figured that one out yet. I have an idea though," he paused, hoping he might be able to convince her of the importance of what he was going to say next. "We need to get inside Earl's home."

A crease formed on her forehead. Figured. She was more skeptical than anyone he knew.

"I'm not asking anything you haven't done before. Just take me there. I want to know what's behind that property."

"I looked out into the back when I used the bathroom. There's nothing but a path into the woods."

"A path that leads to cabins. Dozens of them."

As Kate opened her mouth to respond, a terrifying boom exploded outside. Behind them, the cafe door slammed open. A bearded man thrust his head through the opening. "The theater just blew up!"

39

Seth's eyes widened. "Amy."

He bolted from his seat.

Kate scrambled to follow, grabbing her camera. Already the street was pulsing with onlookers. She lost sight of Seth as she limped to keep up.

"Sounded like a bomb," a voice next to her said. Kate glanced to the speaker. A mere child—sixteen at the most—dressed in prairie garb. "Maybe they'll blow up the school next."

Kate ground to a stop in the middle of the packed street. The child sounded almost wishful.

She swallowed bile that rose to the back of her throat suffocating her windpipe.

How could someone wish for that? How could anyone suggest such a travesty? She glanced at the faces around her. Masks of anticipation. Macabre smiles tugging at the corners of their lips.

A man whistled. Whipped his arm in a large arc.

Kate peered ahead of her where the theater glowed from the arching flames.

She hobbled closer. The pain in her leg radiating deeper with each step. Reminding her. Piercing her. Flashing horrifying scenes that she had tried to forget.

She moved closer.

Closer to the fiery furnace that was once the theater. She remembered her school. Blown up. A twelve-year old. A mere child herself.

Her pulse raced.

She could do this. She must. But her past threatened to roar into her face.

Not now! She must find Seth.

She pressed forward. Heard the faraway sirens.

Kate pushed around two women who stared at the flames as though they were diamonds. Was everyone crazy here?

She gripped her camera to her eye. Felt for the switch. The memories of her school bombing refused to leave. Bright lights, rocketing blasts, falling to her back, torturing pain as her head and legs took the entire impact of a shredded wall.

She gave up and lurched to the curb, clutched the lamp post. Drew deep breaths. She must focus on the scene. Do her job. Try again. Her trembling hands pulled the camera to her eyes, steeled her sight on the hell in front of her—not the hell that was her past.

That's when she saw it. Him. Seth.

Staggering through the theater opening. Covered in soot. Gasping for oxygen.

Carrying a limp woman in his arms.

Kate snapped the photo.

40

The Trainer stood next to his truck, appalled at the sight before him. What happened? He pressed his lips together. She was supposed to be his next candidate. Her grandfather grew up here, she told him yesterday. She was perfect. Perfect!

He slammed his fist against the hood. Quickly straightened, reined in his anger.

No one noticed him. They were too busy watching a woman die.

More sirens. The whole dumb county wanted in on this fiasco.

This wouldn't happen again. No one would interfere with his plans. He had been willing to take a risk with a city girl. Now he would have to start the selection process all over.

He scanned the crowd. The air hummed with speculation and excitement. These people would probably stay through lunch until every inch of ground had been sifted through. They'd find the cause. Then he would know who was responsible.

A woman to his right on the sidewalk spoke to him. "Can you believe this? Brother Earl said God would take care of those who broke the rules." She shook her head.

"Some rules aren't meant to be broken," he said.

She sighed. "Some people need to learn the hard way."

The Trainer took a closer look at the speaker. She was old—too old for his plan—but she might be good practice. The woman disappeared into the crowd. His breathing evened. No, he had someone else in mind. Someone who also needed to learn about rules.

He leveled his gaze on her.

41

Heavy, dark smoke swept through the street, burning Kate's eyes. The crackling of the fire roared in her ears. Within minutes, the local volunteer fire department was hosing down the building, ordering the gawkers to move back. Kate found Seth at the ambulance where the paramedics still worked on Amy.

She placed a hand on his arm. Seth turned to her with a closed-up expression.

"Let's go. I'll drive you home."

He pushed away from her grasp and tore through the crowd.

Kate squeezed her eyes shut.

Could she take more death? Or sadness. She opened her eyes and surveyed the people around her. Smiles. Like they were happy with the building's demise.

And Amy's.

She needed to get out of there before she threw up.

As she wormed her way through the tangle of people, a voice called from behind.

"Kate?"

David closed the gap between them. He tugged her into his chest with one arm. "Are you okay?"

She forced a smile although her legs were jittery and all she wanted to do was get to her car. "I'm fine. I need to get to work."

His smile faded. "What about tonight? Are we still on?"

Tonight. The fireman's carnival. How could he ask? Now?

"I have to cancel. My heart's not into it." Or you right now, she wanted to say. Instead, she gave him a lopsided grin and stepped away. Not even David could take away the gruesome reactions she'd seen from the townsfolk.

A muscle twitched in his handsome jaw.

"I'll call you." She spun around, pushing her way down the street to where she parked her car. Seth would be devastated if Amy died. He had feelings for the woman. A moron could tell.

She would find him.

###

Seth was typing at his computer when she entered the newsroom.

"I made coffee." She heard the now-familiar chugging of the coffeemaker.

"Thanks. Can I get you a cup?" She stopped at his desk. Waited.

Seth raised his face to her. "Don't play nurse with me, okay? Get your pictures up. I need to turn in this story for tomorrow's paper."

Her cheeks warmed. So much for compassion. "Sure. You're in charge." She straightened her spine, stalked up to the coffee bar.

Once settled into her seat, she took a sip. Strong. Almost too strong. She bet he did that on purpose.

"Any word on Amy?" Her question fell between them.

"DOA. Earl is taking care of it." He swiveled his chair toward her. "You and I will be there." His eyes blazed with heavy emotion.

She gasped. Looked away. "I'm sorry. But I can't attend her funeral."

"You don't have a choice. It's your job. Besides, it's our in."

She met his gaze. "Our in?"

"Someone did this to her. I want to know who." His words came out hard and flat.

"Surely not Brother Earl? He might be crazy—but a murderer?"

Seth's face darkened. "Give me your pictures." He turned away, once more intent on writing his story.

Kate reached for her camera and started the download. Her breath caught as she stared at the last picture she'd taken. Seth carrying Amy in his arms.

How far would Brother Earl go to save this community?

How far would Seth go to stop him?

42

The article was handed in on schedule, but Tim made last minute changes, choosing a different heading and photo than the one Seth wanted to use. And a different cause.

REPORTER'S HEROIC EFFORT TO SAVE WOMAN FROM BURNING THEATER. GAS WATER HEATER BLAMED.

Below that, Tim used Kate's picture of him carrying Amy through the front doors.

Seth had argued with his editor, but Tim's decision proved final. Everyone loved a hero in their community.

Even if Amy died?

Some hero.

He slammed the paper onto his kitchen table. Daisy jumped off his lap, her tail twitching.

The funeral was set for two o'clock today. Terrific way to spend his Saturday. He raked his fingers through his hair, studied the weather through the window. Summer still barreled down on them. The humidity would be heavy. People would be packed into the funeral parlor. Even if Earl cranked up the air, the place would be stuffy.

Good excuse for him to step outside.

And nose around.

He'd almost spilled all his information about the Bend to Kate that day in the cafe. How he was sure there was a club of men who used women like toys. Brainwashed them. Held them prisoner. If he discovered that everything he thought was true, he'd contact the *New York Times*. Blow them out of the water.

Then he'd pack his belongings and leave this place.

And her.

Hesitant to admit it, something about Kate drew him. He'd searched her profile online but found nothing. Zilch. It was like she had no past. No social media whatever. Highly unlikely in this day and age. He reached for his coffee, downed the remaining cold liquid.

She looked shaken when she approached him by the ambulance. More than he expected a seasoned photographer to be because of a fire or death. He scratched his day-old beard. Was she hiding something too?

Seth left his thoughts of Kate at the table and shoved off to change. He would study her reaction at the funeral today. Along with Earl's. All he needed was one break. One woman to come forward and tell him what she knew. One disgruntled follower to shake up the group he was positive had been formed. More and more the women in the Bend dressed in similar outfits. Grew their hair long and pulled it into a bun. Teenagers were following suit. Dressing like the outside world had no influence in the Bend. A few days ago, Selma hired a guy to cart away her video machines. She wouldn't talk when he approached. Said she had better things to do than waste her breath on a reporter.

He handed her his card.

Encouraged her to call him if she needed him.

From the corner of his eye, he watched as she tore the business card into tiny pieces, letting the shreds flutter into a nearby trash bin.

####

Seth ducked beneath the onslaught of rain as he left his car and sprinted toward Kate's porch. He'd tried to get her to meet him at Earl's, but she insisted they ride together. Safety in numbers.

He checked the darkening clouds. It wasn't supposed to storm, but when did forecasters ever get anything right? He rapped on the front door.

She answered on his second round.

"I'm ready," she said, as she pulled on a light raincoat. She raced him to the Jeep, jumping in as he shut his door. "Anyone ever teach you manners?" She brushed her hair back from her cheeks with a swat.

"Such as?" He turned the key, looked over his shoulder as backed out.

She groaned. "We're going to be early."

"I did that on purpose. I might get a chance to look around."

"Snoop around. Really? You think you're going to uncover something about Brother Earl at a funeral? The best you might find is he gets a little carried away like he did at that rally."

Seth tightened his grip on the steering wheel as they crossed a bridge covered in puddles.

"That won't surprise me. I'm actually hoping I might talk to his wife. One of his many wives."

"I thought you said he didn't marry them."

He shrugged. "I don't know what I believe."

She didn't say another word until they drove up to the gate. It was open. Several cars filled the parking area already. "So much for early," she said as she unbuckled.

A funeral for a stranger could bring out the whole town. Especially if Earl was going to speak. Seth was positive Earl would point out that Amy had been an outsider—bringing in unwanted devices.

Kate grabbed her purse. "Ready or not." Her shoulders firmed.

"Are you going to be okay? You don't look well." The color had drained from her cheeks. Maybe he shouldn't have pushed her to go with him. Maybe she had a fear of funerals.

A look of pure terror passed over her face before she spoke. "I'll be fine. You worry about staying out of trouble."

His thoughts teetered. "I can take you home if you want."

"Let's get it over." She rushed out of the car and hurried to the front porch. Overhead a clap of thunder sounded. Seth joined her after glancing one more time around the parking lot. Two more cars had arrived. He stomped his feet and followed her through the door marked *Visitors*.

43

Kate searched the half-full room for David. Once she was certain he wasn't present, she allowed herself to breathe. She had ignored his calls yesterday and the day before, not ready to delve into a deeper relationship with him right now. Not after what happened to Amy. Or the way the townsfolk reacted to the disaster.

She took the lead and found two empty seats toward the back. Seth shuffled in next to her, loosening his tie as he did. Only then did she dare to look toward the front again. Dozens of pink carnations surrounded a simple coffin. The odor found her nose. She sneezed wishing she had taken an allergy pill before coming. Since her grandfather's funeral, she harbored an aversion to enclosed spaces filled with flower arrangements. Her grandmother told her it was all in her head. It wasn't. She hated the sight of bouquets.

"Does she have family?" she whispered to Seth who plucked at the cuff of his jacket.

"I couldn't find any. Neither could Earl from what I was told. An only child. Her folks passed away a few years back. This was her new beginning according to friends."

He pointed to a couple near the front. "That might be them. I'm going to ask." He left her side and worked his way to the couple who huddled in two arm chairs nearest the coffin.

His absence gave Kate time to compose herself. She listened to the soothing music that played through the overhead speakers. Several more people converged in front of the coffin, touching the flowers, shaking their heads.

If only she could hear what they were saying. No one looked or acted particularly grieved except the couple Seth was speaking to in hushed tones. She watched how his lips twisted and how he pressed his fingers against his forehead several times. Like her, he didn't go up to the coffin, merely offered a quick glance. After a lengthy five or ten minutes, he returned to her side.

When she could no longer stand his silence, she touched his arm.

"She lost a child and husband last year." His voice came out strangled. "In a house fire."

Kate removed her hand. Her fingers trembled as she clutched them together. Had Amy planned her own death? No, she was starting over. They said it was a faulty gas water heater. Still, would someone try to stop her from reclaiming her life? And why?

She shushed her crazy thoughts. She was getting as paranoid as Seth.

From the back of the room, a door banged.

Followed by another clap of thunder from outside.

Kate twisted in her seat to see Brother Earl. He was working the crowd much like a politician. Shaking hands. Patting shoulders. Nodding and smiling. Smiling? Her stomach lurched. Beside her, she noticed Seth's eyes bore into Brother Earl's back. She should calm him but doubted she had the energy. Already her pulse raced as images from her parents' and brother's funeral pounced into her mind. The local funeral home had held off the spectacle to allow time for her to be well enough to attend.

And the reporters.

She blinked remembering the flashes of light from the photographers' cameras.

That's the moment she decided to become a photographer, promising herself she would never do to others what they did to her.

Brother Earl tapped the mike. He checked his watch, took a sip of water from a paper cup behind the podium. Cleared his throat.

A flash of lightening bolted across the coffin.

Kate straightened in her chair, tugging her skirt closer to her legs.

Another flash followed by booming thunder.

"Don't worry folks. A little storm." Brother Earl picked up his Bible, flipped open to the middle. He set aside a bookmark.

More rumbles of thunder. Deafening.

Kate covered her ears. She hated storms. They reminded her too much of the blast.

"It'll pass." Seth. Trying to comfort her.

Then the entire room flickered into darkness.

44

Seth slipped into the dark foyer midst the gasps of people around him. He hated leaving Kate alone when she was upset but what better opportunity than a power failure? He opened the front door and peered into the angry clouds. Instead of two o'clock, it was as dark as midnight.

Earl's generator would kick on any minute. He didn't have much time.

He left the porch and turned left following the lines of the house. He stumbled through bushes and stumps. Twice he flattened himself against the wood siding as lightening shattered around him. His clothing soon grew heavy with moisture. His shoes took in fast-rising water. How would he see anything in this sheet of driving rain?

He reached the backyard minutes later. Tearing across the expanse, he followed a path that led into a cluster of pine trees.

A metal fence identical to the one out front greeted him.

Seth glanced upward. Could he climb it? But the gate was topped with pointed spears every six inches. He slammed his fist against it—pushing his face as close to the opening as he could. In front of him he could make out the same cabins he'd seen from above. A clothesline. A wheelbarrow. A child's toy.

Then movement.

Seth slid behind a tree and watched as a woman dressed as an extra in *Little House on the Prairie* rushed from one cabin porch to the next.

Was that screaming?

Another round of thunder exploded over his head.

He would learn nothing more today.

Seth left the fence and raced across the backyard against a wall of rain. When he reached the corner of the building, a light flicked on. He froze.

"Thought you might need this."

David stepped off the back porch with an umbrella over his head. "Every hero needs a little help now and then."

###

"We must believe her death was for a reason. The good Lord would not take his child for any other purpose. And that purpose, Brothers and Sisters, is sin. Yes, sin! This woman was a scab on our community. Refusing to follow the rules. Refusing to honor those who know what's best for the Bend."

Kate's chest froze. She glanced at Amy's friends in the front row. They sat ramrod straight. How could Brother Earl speak like this at a funeral? About a woman he didn't know? Her jaw tightened.

And where was Seth? The generator had kicked on right after he left the room. She should leave to find him. She clutched her purse and slid past the people on the end of the row.

As she did, Brother Earl stopped speaking. Kate remained still, hunched over at the end of the row.

"When we refuse to listen, we bring trouble into our lives." His voice grew nearer.

She dared to look toward the front. Brother Earl stood three feet from her.

Seth took the proffered umbrella. "Thanks. But I'm not a hero."

David tipped his head toward the gates where Seth had come from. "Curiosity killed the cat, you know. If Earl caught you back here he wouldn't be happy. Come on." He sprinted toward the gate, punched in a few numbers and waited while they opened.

Seth followed but took his time. He wasn't about to let David think he controlled him. Even if he was trespassing. Let him wait, although strolling in a thunderstorm didn't make a lot of sense.

He caught up with his benefactor right as the gates closed behind them. The slight click reverberated through Seth's chest. David ignored him and headed in the direction of the cabins. When they stood in front of the first one, he waved his hand. "You first."

Since the storm was letting up, Seth lowered his umbrella but hung on to it. The cabin was constructed from bare wood. One story. A front door. Someone cared more about function than style when they built them. He opened the door and stepped into a dimly lit room. Once his eyes adjusted, he saw a cot, a sink, and a toilet. A counter hung from the back wall with several bowls and cups stacked on it.

It looked like a hunting cabin one might rent in the mountains.

"We rent them to people who want to get away from the rat race. Nothing fancy. Functional."

So he agreed. Seth tapped the rocking chair that faced the only window setting the chair in motion.

"Who rents them?"

David joined him. A smile lifted the corners of his mouth. "Whoever feels the need. Mostly women. Women who want to get back to basics. Earl's wife offers classes. Those who choose to take them leave with a new sense of worth. A purpose. Their families thank us."

He was talking crazy. What woman would want to stay in a place like this for any length of time? Seth took another glance around the dingy quarters. He might as well ask.

"Mind if I write a story about it? Human interest. Maybe interview some of the women who are here taking the course?"

David's smile grew broader. "Now that's a question for my brother, seeing how he's in charge. Why don't you return to the funeral that you came here for and ask him before you leave?" He pulled the door open.

Seth had no choice but to exit the cabin. As he did, he studied the other buildings, hoping the prairie woman he saw earlier would reappear. She didn't. Instead, he was forced to follow David through the back entrance of the funeral home, through a maze of hallways until they entered the back of the parlor. His clothes were dripping, and his shoes squished when he walked. David paid him no more attention than to point to an empty chair in the back of the room.

Brother Earl was praying.

He searched for Kate. She was nowhere in sight.

45

The Trainer stood in the pouring rain. Digging exhausted him. He needed to find a better way to remove the candidates when they let him down. He had considered burning the bodies but didn't want the smoke to alert anyone. He could bury them without a box but that wasn't civilized.

He could also cut them into pieces.

Like he did to his mother.

He let the muddy shovel drop to his feet.

His mother never understood him. If only she would have loved him the way other mothers loved his friends. They baked cookies. Arranged sleepovers. Became Den mothers. His mother sought the inside of the bottle.

He blamed his father. He married his mother, after all. He saw what he was getting when he did. The Trainer would never make that same mistake. If he had time left to choose a wife she would be disciplined in all the homemaking skills she needed. She would breed and raise his children the way he taught her.

His thoughts turned to the woman called Red. He knew her real name, but he preferred the term the reporter used in his notes. More fitting with her flaming red hair. His breathing surged.

And her eyes. He couldn't wait to see those green gems submit to him.

He licked his bottom lip.

Time was running out. He needed to train his next candidate before the final day.

46

Kate used the excuse that she needed to find the bathroom. Brother Earl pointed and then resumed his sermon. He didn't look very happy with her. Well, she wasn't any happier with him. If she hadn't gotten out of there she might have thrown up. Poor Amy. To be buried with a eulogy like that one. Someone needed to stop that man.

She hoped Seth wasn't the person. His extended disappearance concerned her. She passed the bathroom, an office, and two rooms filled with coffins to find an exit. It led out to a porch that overlooked an open space.

It also led to David and Seth.

She ducked behind a chaise lounge.

What was David doing with Seth? Seth couldn't stand him. He'd told her so on many occasions. She peered around the furniture and tried to overhear their conversation.

Nothing.

Instead, they headed her way. Kate bit down on her lip. Held her breath. If David found her like this—.

They mounted the porch, passed by her and entered the same door she came out.

She exhaled. Now to get back inside without anyone noticing.

Her bad leg ached from being in the crouched position. She'd regret this adventure tomorrow. Standing, she took a long look at the area behind the house. The swing sat in one corner. A gate similar to the one surrounding the house blocked the path into the woods.

Tiny log cabins showed through.

Seth had been right. It looked like more than one.

She stepped from the porch, and quickly closed the gap between her and the gate. She poked her head near the bars. Looked up at the key pad.

Maybe.

She studied the number pad longer.

Punched it three times.

The gate creaked—swung open.

Her hunch had been right. 666.

###

If she didn't hurry, the service would be over, and Seth would come after her. They would both be in trouble for trespassing. Kate ducked behind a tree, surveying the scene in front of her. Several women dressed in traditional Bend garb left the cabins and gathered around an old-fashioned pump. Two young children tugged at their skirts. One held a dirty doll. A woman pumped water into the buckets, saying little to the others. Another woman, older than the rest, traipsed up beside them, pulling up her skirts as she stepped over the puddles. Her one striking feature—blonde hair.

Kate froze. Her mouth fell open.

Debbie?

She narrowed her eyes for a better look, but the woman turned away.

She could be Debbie's twin.

Kate edged closer, debating the risk of marching up to the woman. A great reporter would. Seth certainly wouldn't hesitate. She took a deep breath.

"You shouldn't be here."

Kate spun around to come face-to-face with Earl's wife, Adriana.

"If someone discovers you, there could be serious repercussions. Follow me."

Follow her? Kate nearly toppled in the mud as she forced her unsteady legs to work. She glanced one more time over her shoulder toward the woman she had been certain was Debbie. No one remained near the pump.

They passed through the gates as she kept a close pace with Adriana. The petite woman moved swiftly like a bird. "Wait. Those women. What are they doing here?"

Adriana stopped her trek to the house. "It isn't your business. Don't make it yours."

"But one woman. I think I know her. I've been worried."

"It will all work out in the end. Trust Earl's word. He has heard from the High One."

"The High One? Do you mean God?"

Adriana's face paled. "Call Him what you want. But His word is final."

"But those women . . . do they believe as you do?"

"They will." She mounted the steps and opened the door. Kate had no choice but to follow. There was no use pushing Adriana or she might call her husband, dear Earl, who thinks he's heard from God or is God.

At least she had her story. A cult right here in the Bend. Her mind flashed on memories, but she buried them twice as fast. This could be her chance to right a wrong.

47

Seth grabbed Kate by the hand. "Where have you been?" He led her out of the funeral home toward his Jeep like he might a child, especially after seeing her appearance. She looked worse than he felt. Her lips were almost white, and she was soaked like him. "You didn't leave to find the bathroom, did you?"

With a tug, she pulled her hand from his. "Neither did you. We need to talk."

He'd done enough talking with David to last a life time. No more needed. "At the office."

"No. I have a better place." She pointed for him to turn left when they pulled through the gates.

The clearer skies made him blink after being cooped inside that funeral home. "This better be good."

She picked at her fingers, occasionally giving him directions. "Stop here."

He pulled next to a stream and a picnic table. "Who owns this place?"

She didn't answer him immediately. Instead, she got out and limped toward the table. Her limp seemed more pronounced than before. Did she hurt herself at Earl's? If he was considerate enough to ask, which he wasn't, she'd bust his chops and tell him to mind his own business. He joined her at the table.

"I might have uncovered the biggest story the Bend has ever seen. The country for that matter." Her green eyes sparked flames. "Brother Earl started a cult. I spoke with his wife. I saw women in the cabins out back. I think I saw Debbie. We have to bust this wide open before others get sucked in."

He swallowed hard. His story and she found it.

Now what? Let her run with it? His story? The one he has been working on since arriving in the Bend? The one that would make or break his career?

Or should he convince her she was crazy?

Her face turned scarlet as she gasped to finish her tale. "Earl is ruining the town. He thinks he's God."

He chose the crazy route.

"Slow down. How do you know all this? Did you see the cabins?"

She leaned forward. "I got into the compound myself."

Okay. Now she hooked him. "You got inside that gate? What did you do, climb over it?" No bloody hands. No bruises that he could see. She wasn't an athlete. With that bum leg, it's a miracle she made it across that vast lawn in all that rain.

She rolled her eyes. "I punched in the code."

"Like you knew it. What are you, a mind reader?" He rolled his eyes.

"Are you finished?" She struggled to her feet and headed toward the car. When she reached it, she turned back to him. "I'm done by the way. No more talking."

He'd pushed her too far. "I have something to show you, but since we are no longer colleagues sharing our leads..." He paused. Waited for it.

She traipsed back to the bench. "It had better be good. I just shared everything with you."

"Not how you knew the code. Did David whisper it into your ear on your date?" Her nostrils flared. Would he ever learn to keep his big mouth shut?

"666. The Mark of the Beast. It made sense that Earl would see himself as rooting out evil. Satan's evil in the Bend."

He gave her credit. Why didn't he think of it?

"What do you have?" She tapped his arm.

Seth reached into his shirt pocket and pulled out a folded paper. He flattened it in front of them. "The next rally is in three weeks. Brother Earl is promising a huge surprise."

48

The Trainer rarely made mistakes. He shoved his hands into his pockets, watching the crew of men by the river's edge. They were wasting their time. Whoever sent them on this fruitless chase deserved nothing less than his wrath. Missing women? He spat. He was surprised anyone cared that much in the Bend.

Did the simple-minded folks think they could outsmart him? The Trainer? The one who had been overcoming the evil through his huge purification act? No one could stop him. He had been practicing for years. He might not have time to finish, but look at the difference he'd made already.

He returned to his truck with sweat building on his upper lip. He wiped it with the back of his hand. They were all idiots. He was the one with all the power. No one else. He turned the ignition key and pulled away from the area where he'd been hiding. He needed a diversion. A new candidate perhaps. Someone to take his mind off the one he was preparing. Someone who he could practice with until the final moment.

He headed toward the fairgrounds.

A horse show.

Plenty of likely candidates hung around horses. Tight jeans. Wide hips. Healthy cowgirls. The thought made him thirsty. He pulled the cap off a bottle of water and brought it to his lips. He sucked down the cool liquid until he emptied it.

He set the container to the floor next to his supplies. What do they say? Never leave home without them.

49

The flyer showed a picture of the church. The same church where Kate took a photo. The church that showed the aura. Bile from her stomach rose to her throat. She gagged and covered her mouth. Was this what Earl planned to do? Was this his big surprise? Kill everyone who came to the rally?

"Are you okay? You look sick. Listen, I don't do sick women, so if you're going to barf, find a tree."

Ever-so-special, Seth. She shot him a glare. "Try listening to yourself. Really."

She turned her attention back to the flyer. There had to be a mistake. But toward the bottom, it clearly apprised the visitors of a planned surprise. "We must stop this."

Seth grabbed the paper and stuffed it into his soggy suit jacket. "Anyone ever tell you you're delusional? We can't stop anything in the Bend. My job is to write stories. Your job is to take pictures. If we can by some stroke of luck make a difference, then we get a bonus. Besides, Tim will never go for your story. If we write it, we need to take it elsewhere."

"*We* write it? It's my story. I'm the one who figured out what he's up to." Of course. That was why Seth never liked her. He had been afraid of her uncovering his story.

He marched to the Jeep.

"Are you coming? Looks like another storm. We can hash this out later. I need dry clothes."

She glanced upward. A dark cloud rode the sky. Was rain all it did in the Bend? It was downright depressing. A sudden weariness overcame her. Maybe she wasn't cut out for this sleuthing around. Seth was right. What could she do?

He dropped her off at her house with little fanfare. She flipped on her kitchen light and tried to put her mind to the task of making dinner. Instead, she couldn't stop worrying about the church and the upcoming rally. Maybe she was wrong.

She snorted. When was she ever wrong about her auras?

Until Trevor. She reached for her phone and punched in her friend's number. It had been a few weeks since they last spoke. Jackie answered on the first ring. "It's me, Kate. I've been thinking about you and Trevor. How is he doing?"

"Kate? I wanted to call . . . but I couldn't." She sniffed.

Kate's hand gripped her phone tighter. She dropped to the couch. "What's the matter? Is it Trevor?"

"I wish you were here. I wish . . ."

"Tell me what's going on. Please." A shiver snaked down her back.

"The doctor performed more tests. Trevor won't make it. Months," she said, choking on a sob. "All I have is months."

50

The sounds of the rodeo penetrated his head. Hooting and hollering. Applause. The thump of hoofs on the packed earth. The Trainer chose a seat close to the bottom row. He munched on a bag of popcorn as he surveyed the fans around him. Horses had never been his thing. Dirty animals. Nothing like the lions at the circus. Nothing like his women.

"Mind if I sit here? Doesn't look like there are any other seats this close." A young woman slid her tight jean-clad legs onto the bench next to him, gripping a can of soda in one hand and her cell in the other. "My best friend is barrel racing tonight. I don't want to miss her."

The Trainer smiled. "Wouldn't want you to miss your friend's performance. Be my guest." He shifted over six inches. "You like rodeos?"

"First time here. I'm visiting from Albany. You like them?" Her red lips flirted with him. Teased his brain. Another outsider. His hand trembled.

"Not particularly. Actually, I know a better place for a good time." He raised his brows. "Great music. Chicken like your mamma makes."

She returned his smile. Oh, she was so easy. Already he envisioned the fun he would have with her. Maybe this time, he would perfect his act. Then he could move on to the woman he desired most.

"Sounds like a plan. Is it far?"

"Not far at all. My truck is right over there." He tipped his head and waited.

She sucked on her bottom lip. Glanced back at the arena. "I don't know. I promised my friend . . ."

"These events go on all night. We could take a run, get some chicken, and be back before you're missed."

The deafening roar of the crowd surrounded them. A rush of fear that she wouldn't give in rose, but he shook it off. No one ever said no to him. No one. He pumped up his charm, touched her hand. "What do you think?"

Her resolve melted away like the bloody flesh from his last candidate. "Sure. Sounds like fun. I'm actually kind of bored." She tucked her hand inside his as they left.

51

Unbelievable. Seth played the day's events through his head. The funeral. David catching him. The cabins. And then Kate said she's going to write the story he'd been working on for over a year. He opened his refrigerator and took out the leftover pizza.

His cat meowed at his feet. "You don't like it either, do you?" He threw Daisy a piece of pepperoni.

The Bend was in more trouble than he first suspected. Kate said Earl was running a cult. People joined thinking they would find the answer to their problems. In reality, the cults expanded their problems. He tried to remember what Kate said at the picnic table. He hadn't been in the best state of mind to listen but now he ran her comments through his brain.

He took a bite of the cold pizza.

Did she say she saw Debbie?

As he reached for his soda, a knock sounded on his back door. With a quick glance out the side window, he grabbed a nearby knife and made his way through the laundry room. Another knock. Lighter.

"Who is it?" Seth called. No one visited him. Only the mailman.

"It's me. Can I come in?"

"Red?" He yanked the door open. She stood in front of him trembling. Her eyes reddened and her arms hugging her sides. Seth stepped back. "How did you find this place?"

"I'm a reporter, remember?" She stepped past him and bent down to pet his cat.

"Great cat. Totally not you."

"Daisy. Her name is Daisy."

"Like the flower. Because she's got yellow eyes. I get it." She stood back up and faced him. "I need to talk to you."

Now wasn't the time to play twenty questions. He nodded and led her into his kitchen. "Pizza?"

She took the one other seat at the table and reached into the box. She pulled the biggest piece to her mouth and bit. "It's cold."

Shrugging, he joined her at the table. "I prefer it that way."

He watched her look around his place, take in his bare walls and sparse furnishings. "I don't decorate either."

"I get that." She chewed again. By now the swelling around her eyes had toned down.

"So did you want to talk about what happened today again? You mentioned Debbie. Did you see her?" He waited for her to swallow.

She shook her head no. "Yes, I think it was her—but no that's not what I want to talk about. Something else." She set the remaining crust on the table. Seth eyed it.

"Something worse." She lowered her lids. Was she going to cry again? He scanned his counters for a tissue box. Nothing. Maybe she could use a dish towel. He started to rise but she spoke again.

"It's what I saw. Not today but before. I see it often but nothing like this." She met his gaze. Seth found himself falling into her eyes. He looked away. Not now. Not ever.

"I have never told anyone else what I'm going to tell you. Well, except for my grandmother."

He wished he hadn't opened his door. Her revelation sounded like the kind of thing a woman should hear. Not him. He didn't do personal testimonies. He took a gulp of his soda. "Sorry, want a can?"

Once again, she shook her head no. "Let me get to the point. Something dreadful is going to happen to the Bend. Really horrible. Hundreds of people will die. That's the only reason I'm going to tell you what I am. Because only you can help stop it."

His skin prickled. Now she worried him. "What are you talking about? Hundreds of people are going to die?"

"I said I would sound crazy but trust me, I'm not." She drew her feet up onto the chair. Propped her chin on her knees. "A terrible thing happened to me when I was twelve. Before that, I was a normal kid. I had a brother and a mother and father. I attended a private school, loved my friends, and planned to be a veterinarian someday." She paused. Took a long breath. "Then it happened. This really horrible thing. There was this guy. He belonged to a cult. At the time, no one knew it was a cult. We found that out later." Her voice shook now. Seth renewed his search around the room for a tissue.

"It was a Friday night. My school was having a choral concert. I couldn't sing, so I helped with the stage crew. I remember a packed audience. My family sat toward the back, but I could still see them from behind the curtains. I also remember a man arriving late and sitting next to my mother.

He carried a backpack with him. I remember thinking how ugly a color it was. Maybe dark green. Not cool at all. When the concert drew to an end, I had to go to the bathroom. My teacher let me slip out." She swallowed hard. Tears rimmed her eyes again.

Seth pushed his soda toward her. She shook her head. "I need to get through this." She changed her mind and took a sip. Settled her gaze back on his. Seth saw strength grow in in her eyes. The fear gone.

"Then the blast happened. The bomb killed everyone in the school." Tears rolled down her cheeks. "Except me."

"The Miracle Girl." Seth's mouth dropped open. He'd heard the story his whole life. How a bomber had taken out an entire school, but one child lived. She shouldn't have but did. "The whole country is looking for you."

Kate held out both arms. "In the flesh."

52

She told the Trainer her name. Shelly. She added that she turned eighteen on her last birthday and liked country western music. He tuned the truck radio to a channel that blasted the stuff. She leaned back in the seat and pulled out a cigarette. Offered him one.

The Trainer shook his head no. He didn't partake in anything that would hurt his body. He needed it to be healthy and strong to do his work. He watched her draw the smoke into her lungs and blow lazy rings into the space in front of her.

"You really are beautiful," he said.

She turned in the truck toward him. "You told me that already." She flashed a smile. "Tell me something I don't know."

A flirt. Good. That was the easiest kind.

He started the engine and drove south. Back toward his place. Time for the party to begin. He had a guest. What more did he need?

"You're from around here, huh? It looks pretty desolate to me. Farms and more farms."

"I like it that way. Gives you more freedom."

She shifted closer to him. The scent of roses drifted up to him.

His breathing increased. He scolded himself to keep it under control. Wait for the best moment.

"Where is this place you told me about? The place with the great chicken. I'm starving and it's getting dark. Do you think it'll still be open?" She checked her cell phone.

"It'll be open. Don't worry. I'll get you back on time."

She settled closer, humming some country jock's song. When he thought he couldn't stand the music anymore, she snapped it off.

"I'm starting to think this place is too far for me to go and make it back in time to see the show. Maybe you should take me back now. We can grab a hot dog or something."

"It's just around the bend. Hang on, darling. You won't regret it at all."

She might. But he certainly wouldn't.

The lights from his house showed through the trees. In minutes, they would be in his driveway. He pulled the truck to the side of the road.

"Why are you stopping?" Her voice rose as she slid across the seat toward the door.

The Trainer snaked his arm around her and pulled her closer. "One kiss before we go in. I'm kind of shy but you are driving me wild." He used his best suitor's voice.

It worked.

The rest of the night—easy.

She never got the chicken, but she got something better.

53

Seth stared at her like she had a green head. Of course he would have heard of her. Back then, bombings were unheard of. Every newsman in the country had been trying to get her twenty year-anniversary story. What has your life been like? What do you remember most? Especially with the recent bombings in the country. She'd never given any interview. Her grandmother had kept her away from the reporters. Now and then, one slipped passed but got nothing.

"I'm not done. There's more."

"More?" His voice sounded strangled. Not at all the confident Seth she knew.

"I was injured in the blast but survived, obviously. My grandparents took me in and raised me. I had good days and bad. But when the bad ones came, my grandma and I invented a signal." She held up two fingers horizontally. "It's the sign for H. It was our personal signal for help. My aunt had been deaf, so Grandma showed me how to sign. In case I needed her anywhere."

Seth signed the letter H to her. "One of those times now?"

She nodded. "Shortly after the blast, I took a picture of my grandfather. I loved my new camera and was always trying out different poses. Grandpa played along." She pulled a strand of hair behind her ear. This was the hardest part. Would Seth judge her? Would he call her crazy or a liar?

Could she trust him with her curse?

She thought of Trevor. And the church photo. A sickening fear burned in her gut.

With no other choice before her, she continued her story. "One day, I brought home pictures I'd taken of Grandpa. I noticed a funny aura around him. A faint white glow. I showed it to Grandma, but she couldn't see it. My grandfather was killed two days later. That's when Grandma asked me to look at the picture again. The aura was gone."

"A fluke? Maybe you imagined it."

"I sustained a head injury in the blast. We think that's why it happened. From that day forward, I see auras around a lot of different people in their photos." She paused. Watched for something. Rejection. Fear. She didn't know what. "They all died."

His reaction came slow but soon spread over his entire face. "You've seen your auras here? In the Bend."

"Over the church where the next rally will be held."

Kate dropped her feet to the floor, exhausted from the telling of her story. A pounding headache sliced into her temples. Daisy jumped to her lap, meowed until she petted her. "I know it sounds crazy. It does to me too. My grandma thinks God blessed me with this gift, but I think it's a curse. Do you know how awful it is to see an aura around your best friend's kid?" Her voice broke at the thought of Trevor. "I've never been wrong. I wish I was, but I haven't been."

He rose from his chair and paced the small room. "You know that picture you took of me carrying Amy . . ."

"She was already dead. And no, in answer to your other question, I haven't seen any rings around you." He gave her a half-smile and returned to his seat.

"Where do we go from here?" she asked, uncertain he believed her.

What story did he believe? The one about her being the Miracle Girl, or that she saw stuff around people in pictures. Both blew his mind. He raked his fingers through his hair. Kate looked like she expected him to absolve her of some horrific crime. He didn't know what to feel. Crazy. That's what her story was, but something about the way she told it . . .

"You're telling me the truth. Aren't you?" He retook his chair across from her.

Kate frowned as fresh tears filled those green eyes. Too blunt. He should have played along until he got more proof.

"Do you want to see my scars?" Sarcasm. Yes, she was good at that too.

"What do you want me to say? You come over her and share this crazy story about being able to predict death. Give me time to process it. It isn't every day I'm handed front page news."

She scowled. "Who said I gave you the story? I'm trusting you, Seth. The least you can do is play along. If you go public with this, I will deny everything." Her lips pressed into a straight line.

She looked serious.

"Okay, so let's say what happens to you is true. For the sake of argument. If you saw this aura," he waved his hand in the air, "around the church, that means you think everyone in there is going to die. Probably at one time. You think a bomb? He's strange, and I believe he's got a cult going, but a bomb?"

"A crazy cultist killed everyone I loved. It happens. Think about Jim Jones. David Koresh. Leaders of cults and their followers will do anything if threatened. It happens all the time. The bomber who blew up my school had only been with the cult a few months. It doesn't take long to control the mind. I've done the research. We think it's crazy when thousands of people follow a man to the ends of the earth and then feed poison to their babies, but they do it. So a bomb in the Bend is not out of the realm of possibility."

"When do you think this bomb is going to go off?"

"At the next rally."

The flyer that Seth snagged from Amy's funeral lay between them on the table. He looked at the date. Two weeks.

54

As Seth reached for the flyer, his cell rang. "What's up?" His brows knitted together as he listened to the speaker. Kate waited, wishing she could go home and crawl into her bed. Shut out the evil in the world, but now she'd included Seth, and she needed to be sure of his commitment.

"I'll be right there. Thanks."

"They found a body." His lips pulled at the corners. "I've got to go, so . . ." He stood and scooped his keys from the nearby counter.

"I'll drive." He wasn't going to do this story by himself. She sidestepped him and darted to the door she came in.

"I can drive myself."

Kate spun around. "We're a team now. We go together." A prickly feeling pulsed at her neck while she waited for him to make up his mind. He could be so stubborn. But then so could she. His decision didn't take long.

"Fine. The body's at Doc's. He's also the Bend's one and only coroner."

While he locked the house, she started her car and peeled out as soon as he hit the seat. Why didn't she know Doc was the coroner as well? The scenario fit, though. Tied up the town nice and tidy. She took the next curve a little fast but relished the pleasure of watching Seth dig his fingernails into the dash. "Sorry."

The night had grown blacker, and with no street lights on the back roads, she half-worried that she might smack into an unsuspecting deer. Thankfully, Seth didn't live that far out of town, and a moment later they rolled into Doc's driveway.

Seth led the way up the sidewalk, rapped twice on the door. When Mary opened it, he said a few short words and brushed by her leaving Kate to offer further pleasantries. She caught up with Seth in Doc's brightly lit office.

On the table lay a woman clothed in a muddy waitress uniform.

Kate covered her mouth.

Becky.

Mary set the steaming cup of tea in front of Kate and patted her shoulder with a soft murmur. "It took me quite a long time to get used to seeing dead bodies in my house. I finally had Doc put that side door on the office so I wouldn't have a front row seat to the comings and goings."

She wiped a dribble of tea from the table with a clean dishcloth. Then with a faint rustle of her long skirts, she settled next to Kate. "Feeling any better now? You looked like you wanted to faint. Good thing Seth caught you, or I would be nursing more than your queasy stomach."

"I'm fine now." Kate didn't tell her that the sight of Becky's dead body brought up the memory of her school's bombing. It was bad enough she told Seth who was now in the room with Doc getting the scoop. "I better get back in there. It's my job. I should be with Seth."

When she stood, a dizzying wave overcame her, and she slouched back into the chair. "Maybe I better wait here for him to finish." Finish discovering why Becky had wound up in the river.

"Maybe so. Molasses cookie?" Mary rose and brought a chunky cow cookie jar to the center of the table.

The smell of fresh baked cookies crept into Kate's nose. She dipped her hand inside the ceramic jar and grabbed two. Seth might be in there all night and she hadn't eaten dinner. She bit down on the soft morsel. "Oh, Mary, these are heavenly."

Her compliment made Mary sit straighter. "That goes to show you what being a good wife is all about. If it weren't for Doc and his training, I would be sitting alone somewhere." Her expression took on a faraway look. Was she remembering life before the Doc?

Another swallow. Kate wiped her mouth with the mint-green napkin Mary had given her. "What sort of training did you get?"

"The best." She tipped her head closer. She tendered the ghost of a smile. "The best training the Bend offers."

Her answer didn't give Kate enough information. If she pushed, would Mary open up or retreat back into that puritan head of hers? She'd take the risk. "Who exactly trained you? Doc?"

A blush grew in her cheeks. "Oh, no. No. I went to the Club. Where women who care about their husbands go. Haven't you heard about it?"

"The Club?" She trod carefully. Mary reminded her of a sparrow that would take off if spooked. "Who runs this club?"

The woman looked over her shoulder as though she expected to see Doc hoofing it down the hall. He wasn't. Nor was Seth. Kate would push a little harder.

"I'm not supposed to talk about it, but you seem sweet. Maybe if you went to the Club you could find yourself a good husband. The men who send their future wives and girlfriends end up happier than those who don't. I'm so blessed that I was given the chance. If not, I don't know if my marriage would have survived. Now I know how to take care of Doc the best way I can."

"Did any of your children go there when they reached the age?" She glanced toward the room with the photos of her eight children.

Mary gripped her fingers together. Had she hit a nerve?

Kate pushed her tea aside. "You can tell me. I won't tell anyone."

"Doc sent our sixteen-year old. Liz. She was a tiny thing. She didn't . . ." Mary glanced over her shoulder again. Her bottom lip protruded out.

"Didn't what? Want to go?"

"She fought hard. But we knew it was best for her. She needed to learn how to be a good wife someday. Like her friends had. Brother Earl said he had refined the Club to include much more than when I went there. She would learn how to please her husband in many more ways." Her face reddened.

"How long was she gone, Mary?" A nagging thought pressed against a nerve in Kate's forehead. A sixteen-year-old teen sent to camp she didn't want to attend. A camp for errant women. What must it have been like for her to live in Brother's Earl's cabins? Trained by who? For what? Her thoughts spun into a troubling arc.

Mary blinked hard. "Can't say." Her hands fluttered in front of her face then she stood abruptly nearly knocking over the teapot. "More cookies, dear? You look like you could use a pound or two."

So that's how it would go. Kate exhaled. She finished her cookie then excused herself to find Seth. She found him talking with Doc outside of his office. A wave of relief shot through her at the realization she would not have to see the body again.

Seth glanced at her, his eyes asking if she was okay. "Sorry about my dizzy spell. Mary fixed me up with cookies."

"Mary's molasses cookies will do the trick." Doc nodded. "Told you what a good cook she is."

Kate didn't want to hear about his wife's attributes, in fact, it made her slightly nauseous when she considered how Mary learned her culinary skills. "What's the cause of death?" Might as well get to the point. It was late, and she wasn't sure how long she could stand being there.

"Drowning. Probably accidental or suicide. Can't be sure. She had some good-sized cuts on her. Probably done by the rocks. Surprised she washed up the way the current is going."

"Why would a young woman be out in the river alone?" She almost said Becky but wasn't positive that either Seth or Doc knew her identity yet. She would tell Seth later.

Doc shrugged. "She could have gotten separated from friends. Who knows. I'll get Earl to pick up the body in the morning. He'll take care of the details. Like always."

Like always.

"Let's go, Kate. It's been a long day." Seth tugged on her arm, and they left through the front door after saying goodnight. She pulled her keys from her purse. Seth grabbed them from her hand.

"I'll drive. I'm not taking a chance that you nose-dive while I'm in the car with you."

"Fraidy-cat. I'm better. I promise. Besides, you need to get home and that means I'd be driving anyway." She held up her open palm. Seth dropped the key ring onto it.

After they were settled in her car, she waited to turn on the headlights.

"Forget something?"

"What are you going to write in your story?"

"Body of woman found dead in the river. What else?"

Although she could barely make out his face in the darkness, she met his gaze.

"I know who she is . . . was. It's Becky. The waitress I told you about from the diner. She and I talked."

A throbbing silence enveloped them.

"Did you see that thing around her?"

"No. I didn't see that thing. It's called an aura. Why would I have taken her photo? She seemed happy. Alive. Now she's dead. By her own hand or stupidity? I don't think so. I think it's more than that. Worse."

Seth tapped the car door.

She wanted to scream at him to stop.

Didn't.

"It's all connected." His voice came out dead.

55

"The sheriff verified the identity of the body early this morning. They found her purse near the edge of the river. She left a note." Seth rolled his chair near hers.

Kate stretched, trying to fully wake up. By the time she'd fallen asleep, half the night had passed. "A note? What did it say?"

"Sheriff said she apologized for what she was going to do but her life stunk. Something like that." He unwrapped a Tootsie Pop. "So much for your theory."

"I still don't believe it." The sugary smell of his candy floated over to her. She reached for a stick of gum from her desk drawer. "She seemed happy. Excited about life. I think her death is connected to Earl somehow or Mole." She remembered the full mailbox. The veiled threat.

About the time she decided to dig a little deeper into Becky's background, Tim rounded the corner. "Got someone who wants to see you, Seth. Says she has a story needs getting out."

A young woman stepped into the room. The toe of her cowboy boots tapped on the hardwood floor as she pulled her hands out of her jeans pocket. She looked like she just stepped out of the rodeo.

###

Another fiery redhead. Seth wasn't sure he could take another one this early in the morning. He rose and maneuvered around the desks until he joined them. She was a knock out yet looked like the hard-to-please kind of woman. Not his type. And young. "How can I help you?"

Tim excused himself. The woman dropped into a nearby chair. Seth did the same.

"It's my best friend. Shelly. She's missing."

"What happened?" Seth glanced over his shoulder toward Kate. She saw his look because she picked up a tablet and pen and hustled over. "This is my assistant." Kate snorted but settled into the chair next to him.

The other redhead, Mandy Baker, had invited her out-of-town friend to visit her for the week. Last night, Mandy barrel raced at the rodeo on the outskirts of town. Shelly was supposed to watch. But when the rodeo ended, Mandy couldn't find her friend anywhere. "I told her to wait by my car, but she never showed up. When I called the sheriff, he told me to settle down. People walk off all the time. He said give it time. I gave it time. Now I want help and figured the newspaper will do something since the law won't."

"How old is Shelly?" Kate spoke softly. Very unlike her. Now *he* wanted to snort.

"We're both eighteen. Old enough to know better, if you get my drift. No way on this here earth would Shelly take off with someone. But she hasn't called, hasn't come back for her suitcase. Nothing. I called her cell, and it's turned off. I called her mother and she said Shelly hadn't called her either. Something isn't right." The girl's voice trembled.

Seth exchanged glances with Kate. Another missing woman?

"Do you mind if my assistant takes your picture? We can put it in the paper with your story. It might help catch a readers' eye. Do you have a picture of your friend?"

With a swift movement, she dug into her leather bag and produced her phone. She scrolled through her apps using one of her pink nails. "Right here. Can I send it to you?"

Kate gave her the paper's email and left. She returned with her camera. "Do you mind standing against that wall for me?"

It didn't take much to get Mandy to pose. He suggested several shots so that Kate could choose the one that looked best for the paper. Seth doubted her story about knowing better. Mandy looked like an easy mark herself. She preened like she was in a dog show.

"Thanks, Mandy. Seth will get the rest of your information while I work on this." She winked at him before returning to her desk.

After asking Mandy a few more questions, he promised to run the story in this week's paper. Then he herded her out to Rhonda at the front office where she recounted her story.

Seth headed for Tim's office.

He found an empty room. Next, he checked the men's room, then interrupted Rhonda to ask where Tim had gone. She shrugged. Her usual response. All she was good for was greeting people. Oh, and painting her dumb nails. Seth stepped outside. Another summer storm brewed overhead. He double-timed it to the parking lot to check that he'd closed his windows, and to see if Tim's truck was still parked there. No on both accounts.

Where did Tim run off to all the time?

Seth jogged toward town and scanned the main street. Nothing. In fact, the

Bend looked like a funeral itself. Few businesses remained open as Earl had closed most of them. The burned-out theater still waited for someone to tear it down. His heart sank when he remembered Amy and her excitement to enlighten the Bend. No one could do that. Only Earl with his plans to get everyone to submit to his authority.

A bolt of lightning snapped overhead.

He hoofed back to the office where Rhonda was still deep in conversation with Mandy. Seth stopped next to her. "Did you ever attend one of Brother Earl's rallies?"

She winced. "One time with my parents. They tried to get me to go to the Club for training. I threatened to run away if they did. Only reason I didn't get forced to go was because David sided with me."

"Earl's brother?"

A smile snaked across her lips. "The one and only."

Seth squatted next to her. "Listen to me, Mandy. Did you tell David that your friend was coming to town?"

"He's the one who suggested I invite her. Said everyone likes a rodeo. Especially outsiders."

"And have you and David ever gone out together, like on a date?"

That same smile reappeared. "Give me time."

###

The picture of Mandy blew up her screen.

"Anything?" Seth's warm breath fluttered against her ear. His idea to take a photo of Mandy had been smart. Fortunately, the aura they feared didn't appear.

"Nothing." She clicked out of the program. "I'm glad you suggested it though. Wait . . ." She spun back around. "I didn't upload the photo she sent me of Shelly."

Another few clicks.

Her email sputtered.

Finally opened.

She clicked on the photo link.

Kate inhaled as the photo of Shelly materialized in front of them.

Seth's hand dropped onto her shoulder. "It's there. Isn't it?"

She scrubbed her eyes with the back of her hand.

Nodded.

"It's fading."

56

The room lacked windows. He had chosen this place on purpose. Why look out when all the Trainer needed to see lay right before him? The walls—oh yes, he loved the extra touch he'd added to them.

"Do you like the wallpaper, darling? I hung it myself. Got a little sticky at times but nothing I couldn't get myself out of." He chuckled as he stroked the embossed crimson roses in the design. His mother had used a similar pattern in their living room. A fitting tribute. He liked to think that her last view on earth was of those roses. Before she became fertilizer for them.

After the freezer, he and his father finally dug up the trellis on the back of their property. That's where the Trainer got his first hard lesson in digging. It was also when he first hated his father who sat on a rock and watched as sweat dripped from the Trainer's brow.

"Good practice for you. Learn life the hard way like I did," his father said between puffs of his newly formed cigarette habit. He tossed the butt at the Trainer when he finished. "Bury her deep. Don't want wild animals digging her back up."

His father changed once his courage returned. No longer did he act meek and mild. No, he strutted around like a rooster with a new hen. His business improved. He seemed like a new man. Even went out on a date with a local woman.

"Let me go, please . . ." The Trainer's new candidate roused. Time to teach her the next lesson.

She lay in the box with her wrists secure against the sides. Maybe this time he would use his longer knife like his father did with his mother. The reaction was always more pronounced.

"How are you feeling? Get a good rest?" He stood over the makeshift coffin, staring down at Shelly's tear-streaked face. Too bad her mascara ran. She had looked so nice when he chose her. And now the part of his training he enjoyed most—the first slice.

57

Congealed grease covered the pizza. Kate bit into it anyway. The only other food choice in her fridge was an overripe banana and a carton of yogurt. Neither appealed to her taste buds and she had been too tired after work to grocery shop. She almost suggested to Seth that they stop at the cafe for something, but after she told him about Shelly, he looked green.

Tim had finally returned with a string of stories for them to follow up on the next day. A canoe contest down the river, a fishing derby, and the ladies' sewing group was having a quilt raffle for the library.

Seth, on the other hand, was following up on Shelly. He planned to go to the rodeo and talk with the set-up people, check their video feed if they let him, and nose around. What real reporters did on the job.

Kate sipped her water.

None of what either did would make a difference to Shelly's life. Whatever was happening to her was already happening. Seth knew as well as Kate did there was only one place they needed to nose around. They just had to figure out how to get there.

As she brushed the pizza crumbs into her hands, her cell rang.

"You missed pizza," she said. "I could have warmed it up for you."

"I bet. Listen," his voice held that familiar edge. "I have an idea for tomorrow night."

"Dinner? Because that would be great since my choices have dramatically diminished with this last piece of pepperoni." She tossed the chunk into her mouth.

"A better plan. I vote we go to the Club again. Only this time through the back door."

A cutting pain twisted her stomach. She slumped down into the chair. "You're not serious." Trespass onto Earl's property? She remembered the mountains and trees behind the cabins. "At night?"

"If we go late at night, we arrive early in the morning at first light. When everyone is sleeping. I think we could find out who is there and who isn't."

And she thought he was a wimp.

"You know I limp, right?" She rubbed her leg where the pain never left. "It will take me time."

"I can go alone, but two would be better. Another eye-witness. Pack your smallest camera, too."

His argument made sense. If they discovered women were being held captive, or heaven forbid, injured or killed—she didn't want to say that word—two of them would be safer.

"All right. I'll go. I don't have a better plan."

"Good. I'll fill you in tomorrow at work. Lock your doors and close your blinds."

Her house looked like a dungeon already. What little sunlight that remained filtered through the kitchen window.

"Sure." She touched the front pocket of the khakis she wore. The familiar shape of the pocketknife reassured her. More than the closed blinds.

"And don't answer your door to anyone. Not even lover boy."

Bringing up David did not help Seth's case. "He isn't my lover boy and besides that, I haven't seen him since the fire. I hate to say this out loud, and especially to you, but something about him gives me the creeps."

A too long pause.

"I got to run. Remember what I said."

Her cell died.

She wandered into her bedroom where she'd set up her file cabinet next to her computer. After the deliveryman brought it, she had printed off pictures of everyone she remembered that had an aura. A pack rat trying to make sense of a senseless situation. She dropped to her knees and pulled open the top drawer. Sort of like making sense of God and how He let that bomber into her school. Probably impossible.

The papers called him a martyr for his faith. His crazy faith. But then she had been crazy in love with God before that blast. Was there a difference?

As soon as she asked the question, she knew the answer. Her cheeks heated. Of course, there was a difference. She tightened her jaw and pulled out the first file folder. Maybe she could find a pattern.

Drew.

They attended college together. Met the first day in Sociology. He died nine months later in a car accident on icy roads. She placed the picture of him, in his gym shorts and T-shirt, aside.

Mr. Bigalow, her twelfth-grade science teacher. Her favorite teacher. She'd clipped this picture from the yearbook, taken by her. When she first saw the aura, panic filled her. Mr. Bigalow had two children. One required full-time care. His wife depended on his income. When he drowned at a class picnic that following summer, she cried for days. Her grandmother knew why but couldn't console her. If only he had been struck by a car or a building had fallen on him. Something where his wife could have collected a big settlement.

Bad thinking. Always bad thinking.

She pushed the file away and went to her computer, opened a blank Word document. Her mind sifted through the facts about the Bend. Facts she had discovered since coming there at the beginning of the summer.

Two women were dead. Two had gone missing.

Brother Earl built a settlement behind his funeral home surrounded by a huge gate. Mary said she went there to learn to become a better wife. Her daughter refused to go and no longer lived in the Bend. Several men in the area wore similar rings. A good old-boys' club? And then there were the women who dressed in long outdated garb, wore their hair in braids or buns, and attended the rallies as though God himself spoke in the form of Brother Earl. A new Jerusalem he declared that night. Utopia for all. A place where everyone helped everyone.

Socialism? Fanatical thinking?

And then there were the Bend businesses that didn't agree with Earl. Forced out. Burned down. Is that how he meant to accomplish his reign?

Finally, there was David. She sighed. How to explain him?

Something about the way he looked at her the day of the fire. She had tried to push that strange feeling from her mind when he asked her out again, but today the thoughts would not leave her alone.

With a couple of clicks, she pulled up her internet browser. Typed *David Foreman* in the search bar. She poured over the web for an hour, adding to her document any information she could find on him. When he graduated from high school, what sports he played—football. The captain. Went to college in Texas, moved from there to Ohio, then Michigan, and finally back here.

Her fingers stopped typing. Wasn't Texas where that huge cult was located? The one where people blindly followed their leader? What if David had gotten mixed up with them? What if he was the one who pulled Earl's strings?

Her theory sounded crazy on all accounts. What had he done but be kind to her? She remembered his kiss. Soft. Sweet.

She blinked. She remembered his comment afterward. "You are perfect. The kind of woman the Bend needs."

She'd laughed it off as foolishness. But why would he say that unless he was unsatisfied with the women here? Maybe he wanted to change her like Earl tried with the rest of the female population.

A light breeze blew in her window feathering her shoulders. She rose from the desk and crossed the room. Hadn't she closed the window earlier? She slid it down, fiddled with the antiquated lock.

That's when she thought about her mail. In her rush to get fed, she'd forgotten to check it tonight. She left her bedroom and headed toward the front room. She flipped on the front porch light switch.

Nothing.

She bit her lower lip. She should have checked if the landlord replaced the bulbs on day one. Now she would have to worry about tripping on the front walk. Or she could wait until morning. It wasn't like she got that much mail anyway. But still, when she did, it made her day.

She slipped on her sandals. Opened the door. Strode across the front porch, down the three steps toward the mailbox.

A few bills.

A package.

She hurried back inside. She hadn't ordered anything.

She set the small box on her kitchen table for a closer inspection.

No return address. Just her name printed with a red marker.

The troublesome idea that nothing was as it seemed in the Bend rose in front of her. She winced. When had she ever been frightened by a package?

She inspected the duct tape used to seal the edges. Who used duct tape? Why not regular clear packaging tape? And red ink? Caps for her full name?

Her inspection grew dull. Kate dug her hand into her pocket and drew out her knife. She sliced away the tape. Whoever wrapped it had been detailed. The corners matched. She pulled off the brown wrapping paper. Another strip of tape greeted her. She dug her nail beneath it. Lifted it up.

The lid popped open.

58

The Trainer chose tonight to study his next candidate—his *last* candidate. The only one he ever wanted or cared about. He glanced upward to the clouds covering the moon. Then he zipped his jacket as the cooler late-summer air circulated through him.

It wouldn't take long.

A peek. That's all he needed.

His breathing escalated as he raised his binoculars to his eyes. She had left her kitchen light on. Good. He could see her clearly. Her long red hair curling around her shoulders. The way she limped across the room. Much differently than how she walked around others. Her leg must still be causing her pain today.

Of course it would. That blast she survived would always follow her. Like her fears that no one would find out. What would she say when he told her he knew? That he understood her fears.

As he took another deep breath, an owl hooted. The Trainer glanced upward, cursing the bird. He glanced toward the house. His candidate had opened the package. Ran a finger over its softness. An agonizing shiver shot through his gut. Soon. Soon she would belong to him. After one more longing glance, he lowered his binoculars. Time enough to judge her reaction to his gift tomorrow. Besides, he hated to ruin his surprise by watching. No bridegroom would watch his future wife in such an intimate situation.

With his breathing under control, he slipped out of the trees, and trailed back to his truck that he parked down the road. Besides, he had more pressing work at home. His current candidate was being uncooperative. And that meant more work for him.

59

Daisy craved more than her usual attention tonight from Seth. He refilled her dish twice and petted her on his lap after his call to Kate. But still she meowed. Finally, he opened his back door and tossed her outside. Let her cry out there. He had more to think about than a miserable feline.

Like a woman named Kate.

He poured a second glass of soda and sank down in front of the darkened TV screen. He should be in bed but couldn't sleep. Especially after the plans he made for tomorrow night. Who did he think he was? Superman? The two of them might well make it over that mountain, but then what? Snoop around undetected for how long? And what if Kate was wrong about Debbie or Shelly? What if neither were in the compound and Earl decided he had enough of him? Jail time? Lost job?

Tim hadn't been too helpful either about the whole missing person article. He had balked about suggesting foul play. Said kids her age always took off but finally agreed to run the story. Lately, it seemed like his editor's brain was elsewhere. Not on news in the Bend where it should be. And then all those days he left town. What was he up to? He was single, no kids. Said he lived in the Bend his entire life and knew everyone—that's why he was good at his job. Of course, whenever he said that, he stared down his nose through his glasses as though Seth wasn't doing his.

Seth needed this job. There was a story in the Bend. A big story.

He thought of Kate again. Now there were two big stories.

The possibility of exposing her cover and connection to the bomber—the fact that she was the Miracle Girl—skidded through his brain. Everyone who was any kind of reporter wanted the story. Seth clenched his fingers together. And he had it. Plus, he knew about her power. *If* she was telling the truth. His story would blow all the others out of the water.

He was sitting on his future. A bomb of his own. Expose Kate and pull out of this horse-and-pony town forever. He trembled at the mere idea. His dream. Surely there was a way he could do it without hurting her. He hoisted himself off the couch and paced the narrow room. A rush of euphoria overtook him as a plan emerged.

He reached for his cell phone to call her. Then changed his mind. It could wait another day.

60

Kate lifted the loose flap and raised the opposite side.

A smaller box rested in a pool of confetti. She reached in and pulled the blue velvety box from its container.

Her mouth formed an O. Who would send her jewelry? She dropped into the chair, the jeweler's box resting in the palm of her hand. She raised the lid.

Her heart roiled inside her chest as she dropped the case onto her kitchen table. She lurched from her chair, her hand splayed against her stomach. How could it be? Kate sucked for air as she wheeled into her bedroom and scrambled for her cell phone.

"Please answer, please answer . . ." she begged, waiting for Seth to pick up.

She peered over her shoulder, fear slewing all reasonable thought.

"I'm headed to bed."

"Come over here. Now." Her voice came out in a gargled whisper. She gripped her phone tighter. Eyed her bedroom door.

"Do you know what time it is? It's—"

"I don't care what time it is. Something happened. I need you here to verify I've not gone crazy. Please Seth. Now."

"All right. All right. Give me time to pull on my clothes. Leave the light on. I'll be there in ten."

"The light doesn't work," she said, but Seth had already hung up.

Kate curled onto her bed. She would not return to the kitchen until Seth arrived.

When Seth pulled into Kate's driveway, he noticed her kitchen light shone through the open blinds. He gritted his teeth. Hadn't he told her to shut all her windows and that included the curtains? Anyone could stand outside the house under the cover of those trees and watch whatever she did. He got out of his car and looked around. The silence shrouded him with menace. He shrugged his nagging fears away and hiked toward her front door. When he rapped, the door moved beneath his knuckles. Great. She left her door unlocked as well. He stepped inside. "Kate?"

Kate rushed out to him from a room to his left. She looked like she wanted to cry but forced a smile. "I know it's late, but you have to see this." She tipped her chin toward her kitchen where he saw the overhead light.

He wanted to grumble. Instead he followed her into the next room. A jeweler's box lay in the middle of the table. "You called me all the way over here for this?" He pointed to the box. "David?" He raked his fingers through his hair. He tried not to yawn or drop down on her floor and sleep.

"Look inside." Her voice shook.

Why would a box freak her out so much? He reached for the container.

"Prepare yourself," she said, as she stepped back. "I almost threw up."

He raised his brows. "You have a nasty habit."

"Just look at it." She pointed, then stepped back.

He eyed the box. Pushed it open with his thumb.

A smaller version of the hawk ring stared up at him. He raised his gaze to Kate's. "And you're worried because?"

"It's the ring! Don't you get it? Someone sent me the same kind of ring the men in the Bend wear. A match. Made for a female. You know what that means, don't you?" Her eyes widened.

Was she going to stroke out on him? "Mary wears one."

She stepped closer. "So did Debbie."

61

Kate stumbled into work the next morning. She made coffee, dropped into her chair, and turned on her computer. Seth hadn't arrived yet. By the time he left her house last night, both were dead-tired. However were they going to hike down the mountain tonight? But they had no choice. From what she learned from Rhonda, the sheriff still hadn't found Shelly.

She clicked through her pictures.

She let her breath out. The photo had not changed at all.

Meaning they still might have time to find her. Maybe Shelly lay injured someplace. Maybe in one of those cabins.

"Headed out to the sewing circle today? I want full-color photos of those quilts." Tim shuffled up to her desk. He smelled smoky. Funny. He didn't smoke. It was too hot for a wood-burner.

"You'll have them. I need to finish up the last article." She smiled up at him. So far, they got along fine. Hopefully, he liked her work enough to keep her.

"Who's that a picture of?" He pointed to the one she had opened of Shelly.

Her cheeks burned. "The missing girl. Her friend gave it to me. It's supposed to run with the story." Tim should have seen it by now. The paper came out tomorrow.

"She looks awfully young. Too pretty." He shook his head. "Too bad about outsiders. Coming here and stirring up trouble."

"Stirring up trouble? She was visiting her friend."

"Doesn't matter. Look at that outfit. Nothing but trouble." With a final shake of his head, he left her side and closed himself in his office.

Every molecule in her blood screamed. She grabbed her mug and marched up to the coffee counter. Banged her cup down. *Nothing but trouble?* Before his comment, she had believed her editor to be open-minded. Now she wasn't so sure.

"Make enough for me?" Seth stood beside her. She'd been so angry she hadn't heard him come in.

"Help yourself." She brushed by him.

"Looks like I'm not the only one who couldn't sleep."

"I might take a snooze under one of the quilts I have to go photograph."
She checked her watch. "I'm late. I'll touch base with you later." She
grabbed her purse and camera, hurried out to her car. The last thing she
wanted to do was attend the quilt raffle. She drove through town, eyeing the
closed signs in the windows. The Bend had looked rather pathetic when she
arrived a few months back—now it resembled a ghost town. Earl had been
busy.

She braked in front of the library.

Several women in their drab prairie dresses mingled at the front door. Each
carried large packages under their arms. Quilts, no doubt. The last time Kate
slept under a quilt was at her grandmother's house before she graduated.
Grandma insisted she take one with her to college, but Kate thought it would
label her as outdated. She refused the blue and white one offered.

Foolish youth.

As she got out, she recognized Adriana near the doorway. Earl's young
wife nodded, then turned away. Could she be angry at Kate still for her
behavior at the funeral? Not every guest sneaked into private property.
Unless they were named Seth or Kate.

She thought of what they planned for tonight.

Kate moved faster to catch up. When she reached the door, Adriana held it
open for her. "Thanks. Are you donating a quilt or here to bid on one?" A
little friendly banter couldn't hurt.

"We need new ones. Winter is coming." Her voice sounded flat.
Emotionless as usual.

Adriana left Kate by the entrance and hustled to the front area where the
ladies were draping the colorful quilts.

Okay. Clearly, Adriana didn't want to talk with her. Maybe afterward.
Maybe she could catch her before she left. She wanted to ask her a few more
questions about the compound. Maybe it would save her and Seth a lot of
aggravation if Adriana would tell her that Shelly and Debbie were fine. That
they had gone to the Club of their own free will.

Or maybe she would share something more with Kate. Earl's supposed
wife carried a look of fear in her eyes. Was that normal? She doubted it.
Unless the poor woman felt trapped—afraid to leave the man. Afraid she
would end up in one of those cabins. Maybe she needed someone like Kate, a
friend, to share her concerns with.

Her thoughts were cut short when another woman charged into the room
and took over. Within minutes, the organizer had instructed the women on

how to lay out the quilts. Kate snapped photos as the room filled with townspeople who were looking and buying. The bidding soon started, and within an hour, they had sold everything.

Kate packed away her camera, keeping her eye on Adriana. When she noticed her head to the door, Kate lurched after her. "Adriana. May I buy you a cup of coffee at the diner?"

Adriana froze. A deer at the end of a barrel.

"I don't have any friends here. Also, I want to apologize for my rude behavior the other day. Just a cup. I promise not to keep you long."

The woman's cheeks colored a pretty pink. "I don't drink coffee. But thank you for the invitation." She looked over her shoulder. Returned her gaze to Kate. "Please leave me alone. Leave the Bend alone. You don't know what you are getting into."

Kate hooked her by the arm and gently guided her into a private corner. "What are you saying? What's happening to the women in this town? Do you know some have gone missing? Are you aware that one woman was found dead, and I believe another is dying?"

Adriana's eyes widened. She shook her head viciously. "Earl is a righteous man. He is our Messiah. He would not hurt anyone."

"He's not a Messiah. He's just a man. That's all. Not God. Please." She glanced at the women coming their way. "Please let me talk with you."

"You're wrong. You will see. He is building a New Jerusalem. Please stay out of the way." She pushed past Kate and lunged out the door.

62

The Trainer watched Kate leave the library. She seemed angry. Frustrated. He studied the way she packed her camera into her car. Slammed the trunk lid.

She might take more training than he thought.

He viewed her hands as they waggled her keys. The ring. She hadn't worn it. Was something wrong with it? Didn't it fit?

His hands fisted at his sides. He had gone to extra lengths to get it for her—convinced the old doctor to order one for him once he learned the meaning. A symbol. A symbol of her upcoming Utopia.

With him.

"Excuse me." An old man hobbled past him into the barber shop. The Trainer stepped aside, annoyed by the intrusion. He didn't appreciate interruptions. He climbed back into his truck.

She couldn't see him.

But soon she would. Up close. Like old times.

He fondled the quilt on the seat next to him. A blue and white one. Like the one she used to lie beneath when he watched her through her bedroom window.

He would line her box with it.

His breathing increased. So many years of tracking her. So many years of moving around the country or paying people to watch her. When she took this final job, he hadn't felt so much joy since the day his mother died. Because the Bend was perfect for what he planned to do.

Kate and he would finally finish what should have ended that day.

63

Seth stuffed two flashlights into his backpack. He'd already filled it with water and other essentials someone who was breaking into private property might need. He dropped it by the back door. Then he turned back into his kitchen for a final bite of his roast beef sandwich. Kate wanted to drive so now all he had to do was wait.

2 a.m. He could barely keep his eyes open. The nap after work had helped, but not much. He glanced out his kitchen window, watching for car lights. She said she wouldn't be late. What if she overslept? He could call. Should call. He reached for his phone. No. She'd think he didn't trust her.

Should she trust him? He flinched at the direction his thoughts took him. A while ago, he had considered selling her story. It was his best chance to finally make it out of this town into a bigger paper. But now . . . what a slime that would make him. He'd done some low things in life, but that would be the lowest.

Headlights flashed against the garage.

He switched off the light, grabbed his backpack. When he stepped outside, he heard only crickets and the low rumbling of her car. Mist clung to his shoulders as he hurried to the passenger side.

"Ready?" he asked her, as he buckled in.

"Certainly not. Are you?" She yanked on the zipper of the hooded sweatshirt she wore with jeans.

"Got a better plan?" He stuffed his backpack at his feet. She barely missed hitting a tree in his driveway as she pulled out onto the foggy road. Great. They would be lucky to arrive alive. Let alone worry about the hike.

"No. But I wish I did. We still don't know what to do if we get there and find Shelly or Debbie. Drag them out with us? Back up the mountain or through the front gates?" She bit her nail. "Are we crazy, Seth? Is this entire town crazy? I should have looked for a job on the west coast."

He'd better calm her down, or she'd blow what little chance they had to succeed tonight. "Listen to me. We are all they have. Sorry you had to get mixed up in this mess but for whatever reason, you are. The local authorities have turned their eyes away from the truth of what Earl is doing. He's dangerous. He's taking over the town, one person at a time. If he has resorted to something worse, then someone must stop him."

"What about calling in the state police? The FBI? Someone who will listen."

He snorted. "Right. What are they going to listen to? The sheriff will cover everything up, and the way Earl is so sneaky about his tactics, no one will listen."

She turned to him. Her cheeks glowed from the dash light. "What makes you think anyone will listen to us?"

Her question was the same one he had asked himself a dozen times since discovering what the Bend meant. "Because we are going to show the world people who have been brainwashed. It takes only one. We find that one."

"Debbie?"

He nodded. "Or Shelly. We only need one."

She parked the car where Seth told her to park it. He promised that the owner of the cabin knew nothing about the compound or their plans. Already the night air had crept inside her sweatshirt making her shiver. How would she get through the rest of the night? She tugged her backpack from behind the rear seat. Her hand touched something soft.

Another jacket. The one she threw in a week ago on that cooler morning. She grabbed that too and stuffed it into her bag. Better to be prepared.

The light from Seth's flashlight bit into the dark space around the car. He aimed it to his left. "That's where the path is. I brought my compass in case but doubt we'll need it. It's a straight shot right down over that bank. Parking up here helps. I climbed above last time before I found this other road. What time do you have?"

She held up her wrist. Almost three. She drove slower at night, and the deer in the road had slowed them down even more.

"Let's go. Now or never." He started ahead of her.

She shivered again. "Never sounds good to me." She turned on her own flashlight.

Seth took off into the trees without another comment. With no choice but to follow, she hoisted her pack onto her back and caught up with him. "Remember my leg. I'm not racing down there."

"Heard you before. Neither am I. Anyone ever tell you that you whine a lot?"

"Never. Actually, the opposite. You must bring the worst out in me."

She heard him chuckle. A smiled tugged at her lips. Then a branch smacked her in the face. "Ouch! Watch it, please." He slowed and waited for her to catch up. Already her breathing had increased. What kind of shape would she be in when they reached the compound? "I'm still not convinced this is the best way in. We are going to be exhausted when we get there. Then what? Find an empty cabin to lie down in?" She didn't make sense, but then neither did any of this.

"Keep up, will you? Watch your footing ahead. It gets steeper soon."

"What about a bathroom break? Are you open to those?" she called to his receding back. She aimed her flashlight closer to the ground, trying to avoid roots.

She continued like that for another fifteen minutes. Seth not saying a word, only a groan now and then when his feet tangled in ground cover. Already her leg burned with increasing pain. She doubted her ability to get back up the mountain but tried not to think about that now.

"Look." Seth stopped and pointed upward.

"It's getting light already. How can that be?"She could see him better in the early morning dawn.

"It does that every morning. Ever get up early before?"

"Not if I can help it. I hope it stays dark enough so no one sees us. Isn't that the plan?"

"It's not going to get light that fast and besides, we're almost there. Stay close." He turned the way he had been headed, leaving her to once again to follow.

The ground leveled off and the brush began to thin. Seth kept a steady pace for another ten minutes. When he stopped, she nearly ran into his back.

He raised his finger to his lips. "We're here."

Her legs shook. Next her hands.

She opened her mouth and spoke, "Lord, please have mercy on us."

64

The Trainer knew it was time. Time to complete his purpose in life. Might as well end his charade with all these other women. The ones who would never match up to Kate.

He left his home and crossed the yard to the building where he kept his candidates until they passed or failed his training.

So far, no one had passed.

It wasn't that he was picky or difficult to work with. Rather, the memory of a particular girl-turned-woman intruded upon his thoughts. He had hoped for the day they would be together, and now that Kate lived in the Bend, the timing was ordained. He couldn't concentrate. He woke early and fumbled through his chores. Once he dropped his knife during practice—his hands shaking from expectations. Quite unlike him. At first, he considered seeing Doc, but then decided his concerns were nothing. Just excitement over the thought of getting so close to Kate. So close.

He opened the door. A dim light from a low-burning candle outlined the coffin sitting in the middle of the room. A groan escaped him. Low, guttural. The end would come fast. Shelly lacked the strength and endurance he saw in her when he first chose her. Instead she cried non-stop, complained and threatened. The hips he thought perfect for bearing his children were bruised from lashing against the sides of her box. She didn't understand that the more she struggled, the more he would need to train her. He checked his supplies that lay out on a long table nearby. Picked up the shortest knife and tested the blade with his thumb.

Sharp.

He stepped closer to the coffin. Peered down at the woman who now turned his stomach. "It's time lovely girl. Time for you to say goodbye."

Her eyes widened. Oh, he should remove the gag he had added after the last session—allow her one final scream. Sadly, she might curse him instead, and he didn't need to hear those words today. Not today. The day he planned to acquire his final candidate.

His one and only beloved. The one he had loved since he turned twelve.

65

"Wait. We need a plan." Kate grabbed him by the sleeve. A death grip almost. He frowned.

"I told you. We check every cabin. The women should still be sleeping. If we find someone who looks like Debbie or Shelly, we wake them and take them with us. Back up the mountain."

"What if we don't find anyone? What if they find us instead?"

"We'll think of something."

"That's your answer? We'll think of something? How about we do that now?" She clamped her hands on her hips like a stern school teacher. Great. This far and now she wanted to argue. He sighed.

"It's getting lighter. The fog will be rising, and we'll be bigger targets. I honestly don't think anyone will be around this early." He watched her sift through his words. Finally she nodded.

"Let's do this. My feet are wet."

His were too, but he wasn't going to tell her that. He pushed forward a few more yards until they came upon a clearing. No fence. He let out a deep breath. Part of him had feared a gate like in front of the compound. Probably no one ran once they let them roam free. But that might make it harder to convince someone to leave.

He'd read up on brainwashing. How people were subtly threatened. How cultists warned victims that they could die and go to hell if they didn't believe the group's beliefs were the only way. Quite often they allowed no information, controlled access to the outside world, and acted as though they were the victims' best friends.

How would he convince someone to leave if they had bought the whole pie? Especially Debbie who had lost her entire business? She probably felt accepted here. Maybe they had her caring for the children. Nothing would surprise him. Nothing at all.

He glanced over at Kate who stood next to him. Her teeth chattered. He stretched out his arm and draped it around her shoulder. "It's going to be okay. I promise."

"My parents used to say that to me all the time, too."

He dropped his arm.

What did she want from him? He had his own reasons for taking Earl down. Not only his sister, but now Amy. And future Amys who came to the Bend on a dream. One man shouldn't be able to control an entire town with his promises of a Utopia. One man shouldn't be able to speak words that lulled people into a false life. One man who was as tarnished as the rest of the world.

"This time will be different," he said.

She looked at him with an unreadable expression. Like they were about to march into hell, but couldn't stop if they wanted to. Maybe that was true. For him it was. He had spent most of his life running or chasing a dream. If he made a difference for the good in Bend . . .

"Seth?"

"Yeah?"

She moved closer to him. So close he could smell her shampoo. "You're a good guy. You really are. I wouldn't sneak onto someone's property with anyone else but you." She grinned.

His heart pinged.

Did she have to go all nice on him now? Seth licked his lips. He hiked his bag onto his shoulder and pressed forward. Time was no longer on their side.

When he drew close enough to see the first building, he squatted behind a wide oak tree. He felt, rather than saw, Kate do the same thing next to him. A heavy mist shrouded the compound. He spotted coals burning in an outdoor fire. Probably from the night before. At least he hoped so.

The early morning coiled around them. The only sound was his breathing.

Maybe they *could* do this.

"I'm going in." Kate rushed past him, crouching low among the bushes.

She took him so much by surprise that he didn't immediately follow. What happened to that scared girl he saw further back on the mountain? He flicked off his flashlight. Hurled himself into the foggy mist behind her. When he caught up, she was flattened against the first cabin. She motioned him to peek into the window since she was too short. Would he recognize Debbie? Anyone for that matter?

She beckoned again. This time with a little more urgency.

He stretched up onto his toes. It was hard seeing inside as the rooms were dimly lit with only the morning light. Two women were sleeping in twin beds. Neither looked anything like Debbie. Kate motioned for him to follow her to the next cabin. Empty. They slipped toward one set back into the tree line. This one didn't have any windows. She pointed to the door. Motioned him forward.

Was she crazy? He couldn't walk in like he lived there. He shook his head no.

She raised her brows, pointed again. When he didn't budge, she rolled her eyes and plunged straight for the door. He froze.

The woman had guts.

He gripped the end of his flashlight tighter. Hustled over to the cabin porch behind her. She glanced at him like he was a bug, then slowly turned the knob.

Kate's fingers slipped on the doorknob. Steady. Turn the knob and peek in. Her instructions to herself did little to rid the unbearable fear mounting inside of her. Seth crouched next to her with his flashlight raised over his head. She wanted to laugh but her mouth had stretched into an excruciating grimace.

One turn.

Another.

Push it open.

She felt a flash of surprise at how easily the door cooperated, replaced with more fear as her eyes adjusted to the room's darkness. A dank, dark, musty odor filled the room.

A woman lay on the cot. Her clothed back faced Kate.

Could it be Debbie? She inched closer.

A floor board squeaked. She raised her foot. Set it down softly.

Behind her, deep breathing from Seth.

Or was it her own? Either way, she had to figure out what to do. She made a decision. Maybe her last.

"Debbie?" Her voice came out a notch louder than a whisper. At the same time, Seth's fingers clamped down on her arm.

The woman groaned in her sleep. Rolled over. Her arm splayed across her blonde bangs.

Eureka. They found her.

66

Seth inspected the sleeping woman on the bed. Debbie. No doubt about it with that hair. He slipped past Kate. He was not going to let her surprise a sleeping woman without some protection. He gripped his flashlight tighter, squatted next to the bed.

"Debbie. Debbie." His voice came out in a whisper. He touched her hand, a rush of thanks to God torpedoed through him—she was alive.

He must be losing his mind.

Debbie opened her eyes.

"She's awake." Kate dropped down next to him.

"Not fully. Sh. We don't want to scare her to death." He touched her hand once more. Debbie groaned, blinked her eyes. Then she jolted upward, her lips contorting into a scream.

Seth clamped his free hand over her mouth before she woke the entire compound. "Sh, it's me and Seth. Don't be afraid. We're here to help you."

Seth frantically shushed the woman as he held her in his arms. Her wide eyes darted back and forth between him and Kate until he felt her breathing relax. "I'm going to take my hand off your mouth. Okay? We want to talk with you a minute."

Debbie nodded.

Seth slowly dropped his hand. Kate joined him on the other side.

"We've been so worried about you," Kate said. "We went to your house and saw your car door open and wondered what happened to you."

"I guess you found me."

Kate patted Debbie's arm. "We came to take you home."

Debbie stared at them as though it was they who had been locked away in a compound for crazies. "I don't want to leave. I like it here. They promised to take care of me. Find me a husband of my own."

Seth stopped a groan. Great. Had they gotten to her this fast? "You have a home. Remember how you said Earl was shutting you down?"

"No, no. He was only trying to show me that life could be better with my own family and children. How was I going to find that doing what I was doing?" Tears. Actual tears formed in her eyes. Even though the room was dim, he saw the glitter. His hope sank. They would never convince her.

"It's all a lie. Earl is doing this for himself, not you. Please. Come home with us. We can take you right now." Kate was not giving up. She hooked Debbie's hand to tug her to her feet. But Debbie pulled back, wrapping the blanket around her.

"You better get out of here. I'm not going anyplace with you. Don't you see? I've been given a promise. A promise of a better life. I've left everything behind for this." She inched closer to Kate, who looked like she wanted to cry herself. "You can have that same promise. A home, a family. Kids. Don't tell me you don't want that."

Kate opened her mouth. Looked at Seth.

He had to take charge. Earl might have won with Debbie but he wouldn't let Earl take Kate.

She had been promised a family? Kate probed Debbie's face and found peace there. But for how long? How long would this promise Earl offered give Debbie that peace she needed? How many promises would the man truly keep?

"If you believe what he told you, then come with us tonight. You can always return. Please. Remember Buster." She hated throwing the dead dog into the mix, but she was growing desperate. Seth frowned at her.

"Earl didn't kill Buster. It was the people who wanted to destroy the Bend. He wants only good for the Bend. Can't you see that? Write that in your newspaper. Now get out of here before you wake everyone else up." The old Debbie they met during the interview made a quick appearance as she stood and shuffled toward the door, dragging her blanket.

Kate figured she must have been a good child care supervisor by the way she herded them. But Kate would not leave without one final attempt to persuade Debbie.

She placed both hands on Debbie's upper arms. "You haven't been here that long. How can you believe these lies so quickly? They're empty promises. You were one of those people in the Bend they wanted to stop. Now they have. Are you going to let them?"

Debbie stopped tugging at her blanket.

Had she gotten through? Had she convinced this woman that Earl thought only of himself? That Earl's end game was to uplift himself and he cared nothing about who he hurt along the way?

"It's time you left. I will give you three minutes. If you don't, I will scream so loud that I will wake everyone around me, including Earl."

Ice could have formed on her words.

Seth grabbed Kate's arm. Steered her outside into the early morning light.

"Follow me," he hissed into her ear.

She looked over her shoulder one last time. Debbie—a woman who had been totally duped into a dangerous cult—stared at them from her top step.

Kate took a deep breath, trotted as fast as she could toward the trees.

Earl had not won yet.

67

Seth waited. Kate hadn't been able to keep up with his hurried pace to leave the compound. She lagged behind as though she wasn't going to follow him at all. What was it with her? She heard Debbie say no. The woman refused to leave. She believed Earl was the messiah who was going to solve all her problems even though he was the one who had caused them.

He would take Debbie's advice. He would write the story—but the way he wanted to write it. He would write the piece and force Tim to print it, or he would send it to a bigger paper. Surely someone would care what was happening in the Bend.

His thoughts were stopped as Kate huffed up next to him.

"You don't have to race up this mountain. We have all day."

She looked like she had been crying. Seth glanced to his left to find a large rock. "Come sit down. The sun's almost up. We'll take a break."

She settled next to him, dug a bottle of water from her backpack. After a lengthy gulp, she leaned back with a sigh. "I was afraid this would happen."

Seth took a swig of his bottle of water. "Indoctrinated so quickly?"

"For some people. Like that." She snapped her fingers.

"And you know this how? Read a lot about cults?"

She shook her head. "Not exactly." Kate slid further away on the rock.

"It doesn't matter. I'm going to blow Earl out of the water. Write an article that Tim has to run. Maybe it will open some eyes around here to who the man is."

"Tim will never go for it. He's part of the Bend."

"Then I'll send it to Philadelphia or New York."

"There's something I haven't told you."

Her announcement stopped his tongue around his next word. Instead, he said, "I'm listening."

Kate wiped her hands across her face. "The bomber who destroyed my family—I knew him, sort of. Burke. He hung out with a kid in my class. I saw them together on the street a lot. He was in the tenth grade. Didn't go to my school, though. He was home-schooled."

"That must have made it worse. Knowing him."

She waved her hand at a gnat. "The kid he hung out with was a friend of mine. At least he thought so. He followed me around the halls and came once to my house. I was nice to him but that was it. Nothing more."

"What's this kid have to do with anything? Besides knowing the bomber?"

"He got sick the day of the bombing. Didn't show up for school or the play. Todd." She met his gaze. Her pupils had grown twice their normal size.

"He was also a survivor of the bomber."

"But he wasn't there."

"Todd tried to talk to me about the cult and his friend, but I didn't listen. All I cared about was my lunch choice. Pizza or meatloaf." She paused. "I didn't care about some dumb cult. My parents didn't care either. The whole town didn't care as far as I knew. Hence, the cult grew. Along with its crazy ideas. Even after the bombing, the police didn't investigate this 'holier-than-thou' church. Said the family had only attended a few times and their boy was misguided. Misguided? Enough to kill over a hundred people and himself?" She shook her head, then stood. Paced the ground. "People don't want to see evil in front of them. They prefer to turn away and pretend it doesn't exist. Your story will do nothing. Another back page article."

Seth rose and joined her. "Not if you tell your story."

She froze. There it was. She met Seth's gaze with a hard one of her own. "You have been waiting to ask me, haven't you?"

He had the decency to blush. "If I wanted to write it, I would have. I don't need your permission."

She let out her breath. He was right, of course. He could have gone to the media the moment she left his house. She sat back down, her fear of what confronted them a lump in her stomach. "I have to think about it."

Seth joined her. "I understand. I get your fear, but you also need to think about the others. What's happening here now. Today. The halo around the church. We still don't know what happened to Shelly."

Her heart sank as she considered his warning about the missing waitress. They hadn't found her, nor knew anything more about where she'd gone. At least Debbie was alive. For now. "If I expose who I am, do you believe that knowledge will stop Earl?"

A silence mounted between them. Finally, Seth spoke. "It might bring attention to what's going on here. If we say you recognize the signs, and you don't want to happen again what happened to you. I think I could present it that way."

She pushed aside selfish thoughts. Thoughts about how coming forward would destroy any chance she had for a normal life. Maybe she had been worrying about something that was no longer a big deal. Maybe her memories of the press hounding her grandparents' home had grown as she grew. Maybe no one cared like she imagined. She drew a deep breath.

"But I am never telling anyone about the pictures."

"Of course not. No one would believe you anyway."

"Thanks a lot." She scrutinized the terrain they still needed to cover. "It's almost light. Let's do this and we can talk later. I'm not sure how long my bladder will hold out, and those trees don't look too inviting."

He gave a chuckle, pushed off the rock, and grabbed his backpack. She followed, stopping for quick breaks to catch her breath. His idea to expose Earl and what his plans were for the community rolled through her head with each step.

By the time they reached the summit, she was out of breath and out of arguments.

68

Kate dropped Seth at his house and agreed to meet at the office after a quick shower. She wanted to pull up Shelly's photo once more even though she feared what she might find. She turned onto her road, her brain racing over the details. Were she and Seth imagining what was happening in the Bend? What made them think Earl had anything to do with a girl who had gone missing? Ludicrous. That's what it was when she tried to sort out everything and think clearly. They had nothing to go on except hunches that everything was not as it seemed in the community. Even if there was a decent police force, who would believe them? If Seth wrote his article, he might lose all credibility in the journalistic community. Adding her story and beliefs about cults to it might not change a thing.

Kate steered into her driveway. The rising sun made her wince. Maybe she should run. Leave the Bend and all its craziness. It wasn't her battle. She wasn't some modern-day Goliath who could topple the giant. Earl and the men who followed him held the town in the palm of their hands. They controlled almost everyone and everything.

She left her car and entered her home through the front door. A heavy stuffiness greeted her. She rushed to open several windows, ignoring Seth's warnings. Whoever broke into his cabin wanted electronics. What were the chances someone would bother this old place?

With a banana in one hand, she headed for the shower. As she did, a knock pounded on her front door. Kate's pulse shot up to her throat. Then she chided herself for overreacting. Seth's over-the-top warnings again. She veered toward the living room, dropping her banana on an end table. Already she could see David's familiar smile through the glass.

The last person in her world she wanted to talk to.

Besides that, it was early in the morning. She opened the door. "David. What are you doing here?"

"I was driving past and noticed your car gone earlier. Just checking to see that you're okay."

His concern was sweet but still a sickening feeling tugged at her stomach.

"I'm fine. I'm getting ready for work."

He looked down at her muddy jeans. The sneakers she hardly ever wore. Then his gaze met hers. "Doing a little reconnaissance?"

How did he know? She swallowed. "I need to get ready. Tim's a stickler about being on time." She reached to close the door. David's hand shot up and held it open. His grin turned nasty.

"David, I have to go." Could he hear the tremor in her voice?

He stepped over the threshold. Into her house. Uninvited.

"I want to ask you something. Something important." His voice softened, and he gave her the same tender look he did the day they danced. Was she leery of him because of Earl? Was that fair?

She breathed deeply. Ran her fingers through her messy hair. "I'm sorry I haven't been able to go out with you like I promised. I've been so busy at work and setting up this place." She waved her hand around the sparse furnishings. But her explanation didn't seem to make a difference to David. He moved deeper into the room, like a sleek cat, twisting around her furniture until he landed onto that awful couch. He patted the seat next to him.

She remained standing. Anger growing that she had let him in. Earl might run the town, but his brother was not going to run her. "I can't talk now. Ask your question, and then I must get ready for work."

His boyish smile reappeared on his lips. "You aren't playing nicely. I just want to know why you're avoiding me. Is it that brother of mine? Or is it your cohort in crime? The reporter who doesn't know where to stick his nose?"

Her shoulders tightened. "What I do in my free time, and with whom, isn't your business." She opened the door wider and tipped her head. She could see that her words, no matter how firm they sounded, didn't impress David. In fact, he yawned.

The arrogant man.

What had she seen in him? What had Becky seen in him?

"You need to go. Now."

He leaned forward, resting his elbows on his knees. "You didn't answer my question, and now you're mad." He stood, stretched and crossed the room in three steps, towering down at her. "I thought we had something."

She curled back on her heels. "You thought wrong."

His handsome face clouded. She wasn't sure if it was from anger or pure surprise. Maybe David wasn't used to getting turned down by a woman. Her hand crawled to her pocket and her Dad's pocket knife. Not that she would use it, but it might be enough to scare him if needed.

He put his face close to hers. "You'll regret this."

"I doubt that very much."

David straightened, grabbed the door frame, and left.

Once he cleared her porch, Kate slammed the door, locked it, and flattened herself against it. Breathing hard. Fighting tears.

Kate skirted past Seth's Jeep, jumped from her car, and mounted the porch to the office door. She waved at Rhonda, placing a bag of doughnuts on the front desk that she had stopped to purchase at White's Bakery, giving herself a moment to calm down. After her run-in with David, her banana had all but spoiled in her mouth. Her black pants were speckled with confectionery sugar.

Seth raised his head as she dropped her purse and a half-eaten doughnut on her desk. "Tell me you made coffee."

"Fresh." He eyed her treat. "Got one for me?"

"Sorry. See Rhonda. I dumped the entire bag with her." She hooked her mug and made for the coffee station. As she did, she debated if telling Seth about David would be a bright idea. Maybe David would leave her alone now. He could romance someone else for all she cared.

She returned to her desk. "I'm going to check the picture."

Seth met her gaze. He knew what that meant.

She searched her files for the photo of Shelly. "That's funny." She tried another search, flipped through recent pictures of the carnival and the hardware store opening.

Nothing.

She swiveled her chair toward Seth. "Were you in my computer again?"

"Hardly." He raised both hands in his defense. "Not after the last time you almost throttled me. Why?" He rolled his chair next to hers and peered at the screen.

"It's not here. The picture of Shelly is gone."

"That's not possible." He grabbed her mouse and clicked through folders she already covered. "Are you sure you didn't delete it the last time we looked?"

"Why would I do that?" She was certain she wouldn't accidentally delete the picture. Not when she knew how important it was to track. "Someone else did. I'm sure." She looked toward Tim's office.

Seth followed her gaze. "I don't know about that. Why would he? He was here when her friend came in about her."

"Maybe he doesn't want trouble for Earl. Maybe that's his job here in the

Bend."

Seth rolled back to his desk. His eyes darkened. "We're never going to know what happened to her anyway."

"We are never going to know what happens to anyone here and probably we should accept that fact and move on."

His eyebrows met in the middle. "What are you saying? Are you quitting?"

"Do you think I'd give you that satisfaction? No, I'm saying maybe we better mind our own business." She should have stayed in the hot shower longer, but the fear of David returning had wiped that notion away.

"Our rendezvous did give us some answers. We know they are strongly encouraging the women in the Bend to change their ways and join their cult. Maybe have their babies and turn into the kind of wife Mary is."

When she thought of Mary, poor Mary, she wanted to throw up. Doc seemed so nice. What had driven him to put his lot in with a crazy like Earl? What did Earl have on him? Or David?

"Maybe Doc's our answer. Are you up for another interview?" He grabbed his keys.

"Only if you drive. I have an urge for another doughnut and I'll need both hands." She scooped up the half-eaten one and grabbed another from Rhonda's desk as she hurried out the front door after Seth.

The sun had all but disappeared by the time they crossed the town bridge. She glanced up at the dark clouds. Another storm. As they passed her place, she noted the delivery truck pulling out of her driveway. Funny. She couldn't remember ordering anything else. Maybe he was turning around.

Then she remembered the Amazon order. Rhonda had told her about a shampoo that smelled like pineapple. She'd ordered it because David had mentioned he loved the sweet smell of pineapple.

Dumb.

What was it about David's personality that had seduced Kate like that? She had turned into a woman she didn't recognize when in his presence.

Until today.

"Are you okay?"

Seth's question interrupted her turmoil of thoughts. "I am now."

He threw her a quizzical look and shrugged. Seth was a one-dimensional guy. If he wanted something, he went after it. Like her story. She adjusted her seat belt as he rounded the final curve. Why had she agreed? It would only cause her trouble, not him.

"Looks like Doc has company." Seth pulled in behind a familiar van. Earl's if she remembered correctly from her first night in town.

"Should we keep going?" They needed Doc, not a run-in with one of Earl's men.

He shook his head no. "I'm going in. Wait here if you feel more comfortable. I won't tell anyone that my camera person wimped out on maybe the biggest story of the year." He grinned.

She yanked on the car handle. "Get your pen ready."

69

Time was running out. The Trainer rubbed the rising welt on his right wrist where his newest candidate had bitten into his arm. Shelly. Poor Shelly. She was a fighter. One of his best. But also his last. Kate would not fight him when she discovered his surprise. He had waited years to reunite with her. Years to tell her how he felt about her.

Tonight.

Tonight when she showered.

Tonight when she laid her head on her pillow.

His excitement over the coming event sent shivers coursing through his body. Would he be able to wait that long?

He pulled his truck into the diner parking lot. He'd eat a big lunch. Maybe get take-out for his dinner. A snack for his midnight run. Or should he say rendezvous?

For years, he had planned this. Practiced his skills on countless women. Trained them, and when they failed, he let them go back into the ground where they came from. Dust to dust. It's what his friend had done at school that fateful day. Returned to the dust where he said he belonged. It was what the Master ordered his friend to do. *Rewards*, he had told the Trainer.

Now it was the Trainer's turn to collect his rewards.

Kate's turn, too.

He entered the diner with the air of a conqueror. A king, yes, that's what he would be when he fulfilled his final task.

He recalled that day in the basement of his house. The day his father wiped his mother's blood across his forehead. "You were born to be a leader. Make sure you don't waste your destiny."

The Trainer had told Burke about his father's premonition. Burke said his father was right. It's what the Master taught his family. Everyone has a destiny. Finding it wasn't easy. If Todd had found his already, then he must pursue it.

"What's yours, Burke?"

Burke had grinned. A grown-up grin for a teenager. A macabre grin. "Don't go to school tomorrow."

70

Mary opened the door. "Doc's busy, Seth. Can you come back later?"

"We'll wait." Seth wedged his foot inside the door frame. Hard. Mary's wispy hair bobbed as it seemed she was considering her options. She peered over her right shoulder into the house.

"It's not a good time," she whispered. Was she afraid? Of old Doc? Maybe he had gone over the edge, too.

"We aren't leaving. Besides, Kate's leg is acting up and she needs to see him."

The woman's eyes floated downward to Kate's lower torso. He heard Kate sniff but ignored her. She needed to learn how to do things. Good training for a reporter.

"It hurts. I think I did something last night when I was walking around outside after dark."

Seth eyeballed her. Really? That's the best she could come up with?

"I guess you can wait in the living room." The door opened wider. Seth followed Mary with Kate trailing behind him. "Wait in here. I'll tell him." Mary tucked her head and scooted out of the room leaving him and Kate alone with an antiquated piano and a wall of photographs. Kate limped over to the wall.

"You can stop the act. She's gone."

"It does hurt. Thanks to you dragging me up a mountainside at a no-mercy rate of speed."

"You said you had to go to the bathroom."

She shrugged then pointed to one particular photo. "Doc, with his children. Pity they all left the area."

He shuffled to her side. "They were smart. Don't pity them."

"Maybe. But it can't be easy for either of them."

"They made their choice." His attention was drawn to another photo. "Check this one out."

A younger Doc sitting on a porch swing. Behind him stood a younger version of Earl and a number of other men in the community. "He's going to talk. If I have to camp out here all night, I'm getting his full story." He gritted his teeth and strode to the open doorway. Muffled voices came from the office. He debated barging in and confronting whoever was in there, but something held him back. Maybe it was concern for Mary or Kate. Maybe it wasn't the best strategy.

The office door swung open.

Doc's wife came out first, trailed by Debbie and Adriana.

Debbie froze when she saw Seth. Adriana frowned. Both were dressed in long dark skirts and white blouses. The uniform.

"Debbie." Kate's voice behind him broke the stare down. "Adriana? What's going on?"

Doc came out of his office and stood behind the ladies. He was wiping his hands on a paper towel. "Ah, we have visitors. Seth. Kate." He nodded. "Ladies, I'll see you both later." Adriana took her cue and grabbed Debbie by the hand. They whisked past Seth toward the front door. A part of him wanted to call out for them to stop but he didn't.

Instead, Kate did.

"Wait! Adriana. What are you and Debbie doing here? Is everything okay?" Kate rushed to Debbie and placed her hands on her upper arms. "You don't have to do this. We told you we would take care of you." The girl had guts. Maybe she wouldn't need as much training as he thought.

Her gaze shot between both women. Seth kept one eye firmly planted on Doc. One move. He had him.

"I'm fine. Please let me be." Debbie shook Kate off.

Adriana stepped between them. "Let her go. She's with us now. Like she wants to be."

"With you? What does that mean? You go to her home and terrorize her so she'll join your cult? Brainwash her into believing you'll take care of her? Is that what you've done? And now what?" Kate turned and pointed her finger toward Doc. "What are you doing? Being certain she'll be a good child bearer? Because that's the plan, isn't it? Turn the women in the Bend into your toys. Without brains. Playing by the rules." Her voice grew louder. Seth stepped closer to calm her down, but she kept on with her rant while Doc stood by. His lips turned upward. Did the old man enjoy this?

"Listen, we need to talk, Doc. Do you mind if we go into your office?"

"Sure, sure, Seth. If these women are done . . .?"

Kate stopped talking. Glared at both of them.

Maybe she would get with the program and do what they set out to do. He could tell it took all her willpower to let Adriana and Debbie walk out the front door. She straightened her shoulders and followed him into the office. She dropped down in one chair while he took the other, fire burning in her eyes. The girl was mad. Maybe there was more to her than he knew.

Doc seated himself at his desk and folded his hands in his lap. Like he was doing a consult. Seth wanted to snort. Instead he pulled out his notepad. He motioned to Kate to ready her camera. He wanted a recent photo of the good doctor.

###

If only she hadn't lost it in the hallway. Kate worked to even her breathing as she waited for Seth to begin. Hopefully, she hadn't blown it by blasting Adriana and the doctor. But really? They took Debbie in order to change her into the woman they wanted. The town reminded her of a bad movie. What had she done moving here? Why hadn't she run when she saw what the place looked like? Was there a way out? She would search for a new job tonight. Certainly, she could find another job to support herself.

Her thoughts raced as she waited. She didn't want the doc to see how worked up she was. She exhaled, slowing her breathing.

"We're here to ask a few questions about the Bend, if you don't mind, Doc. You've told me on several occasions you're open to an interview. Now works for me. How about it?"

Doc looked at Kate instead of Seth. "I told this young girl I would love to share the history of the Bend with her one day. What is it you want to know?"

Kate cleared her throat. He was throwing the conversation her way. Seth must be seething. But this was no time for jealousy.

"I'll get to the point. Tell us what you know about Earl. About that compound in his back yard, and don't look so surprised. Mary told us about it too. Plus, we saw it."

"There's nothing to hide." Doc spread his hands palms up. "Earl has done a fine job for the Bend. He has vision. Vision to turn this place into a haven for many. A place we're proud to call home. The women who go to the compound do so willingly—convinced about a better lifestyle for their family. Ask Mary. She was glad to go."

"And your kids? Is that why they don't live around here anymore? You forced them to follow Earl?"

Doc's face reddened. "I don't force anyone, Miss. It seems you have the wrong story about this town. Have you ever considered taking another job? Elsewhere?"

His comment infuriated her. She took another deep breath. "I live here.

This is my town for now. What I want to know is how Earl does it. What is he threatening people with? And why the missing women? Where are they, Doc?" She leaned forward, matching his glare with one of her own.

"What she means to say is we're concerned about the missing women. Becky, a waitress in town; Shelly, a girl at the rodeo: and then Debbie winds up at the compound. Are the other women there, too?

"I don't know what you're talking about. Miss Debbie came willingly. Earl doesn't resort to such scare tactics." His chest puffed out like he was truly offended. Kate perused his hands, his eyes, and then his mouth. If he thought she would believe his nonsense, he was mistaken.

They were getting nowhere.

"I don't agree with you," Seth said. "You, Earl, and your followers are capable of more than you say. Tell me about this upcoming rally. Why all the hoopla about it? What's the purpose?"

"You should be asking Earl about that one. I'll be another attendee like I always am." He turned toward Kate again. Why did she ever think he was this kindly old country doctor? Pure evil radiated from him. For a moment, she couldn't breathe, and she had to shake off a heavy cloak of despair. They were in over their heads.

And Doc knew it.

He picked up a silver paperweight and rolled it around in his meaty palms. Back and forth.

Like their questions. Like his answers.

Seth reached over and grabbed it from his hands. "What about the rings? What do they mean?" He set the paperweight on the floor between them. Doc glanced down for a moment.

"We designed them years ago. A bunch of us went hunting together. Up on Black Mountain. Earl has a cabin there. Mary didn't like me to go, but you know how it is with men. If you don't, you're taunted until the living end. So I went with my shiny new rifle. I shot a few squirrels. Nothing more. The highlight of the weekend was when Earl shot the hawk. A huge one. Almost mistook it for an eagle. Anyway, we got to talking and David suggested the hawk be our symbol. We were young then. Didn't realize how significant that weekend would become."

He stopped and wiped his glasses with his finger. "Changed our lives that weekend. When I went home and told Mary, she wanted to learn more. She agreed to become the kind of wife a man with the power of a hawk should have. That's when we built the cabins."

"You said David was there too? Wasn't he too young?" Kate raised her chin.

"Sure, he was a boy. But a boy becomes a man. Train them up in the way they should go."

Her stomach lurched. "I don't think that verse was meant for your situation. Why the rings for the women?"

"Shows the world who they belong to."

Kate glanced at Seth. Did he remember the ring left at her house? The feeling of darkness inched higher. She didn't want to hear more.

"One more thing. Can Kate take your picture? For the article?"

Doc looked at her. A smile gathered around his cheeks. "More than happy to accommodate you. That's what we men in the Bend aim to do."

71

The Trainer waited in the parking lot as a fresh storm washed cinder into the culverts. He would take the package into the newspaper office when Kate returned. He needed to see her one more time before executing his plan. He wanted to see her at work, doing what she loved. For the last time.

His hand tightened on the steering wheel.

Soon. He had allowed enough time in his plan for them to reacquaint themselves. Share fond memories of a time before the bombing. Before she was taken away from him. Sent to another school. He had a challenging time tracking her those remaining school years. His cousin, Mel, went to the school with her and for a few candy bars, would report what he knew about her.

How many years had he waited?

Twenty. Twenty years too long.

And their anniversary was approaching.

He checked his watch. Where was she? She didn't have any stories to go out on. Rhonda told him that news this morning when he dropped off an order of envelopes. "Do you have a crush on our newest photographer?" she asked, while chomping on her wad of gum. Her question worried him. Made him afraid he'd gone too far with checking.

"Only you, dear. Only you," he said in return. The stupid woman had offered him a stale doughnut. As though that would make him want her.

He checked his rear-view mirror. Was that the Jeep? Sweat built on his brow as he contemplated his next move. Kate got out of the passenger side. His Kate. He groaned as he anticipated the upcoming reunion. It was all he could do to not grab her now and start his plan. But he must be careful. Exercise patience. He had schooled himself how to wait over the years. The golden moment always arrived.

It seemed it had again.

Kate followed Seth inside the office. Her insides still burned with frustration. Rhonda waved as she chatted on the phone. Seth veered for his desk, while Kate made a pit stop in the woman's room. She didn't want Tim to see her like this. Red faced. Angry eyes.

She ran warm water into the sink. Splashed it onto her cheeks.

What could she and Seth do now? Write their story. Hope someone took notice and helped. They couldn't make false accusations. It had to be the truth. The entire truth.

She would also tell her story. She had no further reservations after speaking to the Doc. If one more person fell for Earl's false teachings, and she did nothing to stop it—she would never sleep again.

As for Shelly's disappearance, they had reached a dead end. She thought again about the photo. Had Tim gone into her computer?

She wiped her hands on a paper towel. Paused.

There was only one way to find out.

72

Kate left the bathroom. She turned right into Tim's office. Forget knocking. She didn't care.

He looked up at her and frowned, his glasses slipping down his nose. "This better be good."

"I hope you think so, because I do."

Tim took off his glasses and set them carefully to the side. He pushed up the cuffs of his white dress shirt. Dark circles hung below his eyes. She glanced at his fingers. No ring today. Must be a holiday for cultists.

"You were in my computer." She raised her voice. Enough so he knew she meant business.

"Last I remember, I own those computers."

"Last I remember, I took those pictures. Why did you delete Shelly's?"

Tim sighed. She gave him credit. He managed to look bored and irritated with her all at one time.

"The case was closed. We aren't the police. You and Seth seem to think there is a big bogey man in the Bend. You're chasing your own fears. That girl, Shelly, or whatever her name was, is long gone. Probably in the next state with a new boyfriend. You were hired to complete the assignments I give. Not chase your own."

"I didn't chase Shelly. Her friend came to us. I wanted to see her picture, so I could send it out to other newspapers."

He waved his hand toward the doorway. "Get back to what you were hired for, Kate. I don't remember detective being on your job description."

His arrogance made her chest boil. She was more than certain he was part of Earl's band of brothers. Maybe Debbie would become his bride after she transformed. She gritted her teeth. Should she quit? Walk out of there and ignore the strange goings-ons? Then she remembered the flyer. Could she leave knowing she had always been right? Hundreds of people could die soon.

She raised her face and met Tim's glare. "What do you know about the upcoming rally?"

He shrugged. "Same as all of them. A good place to meet your neighbors. I expect you and Seth to cover it. From what I hear, Earl has big news to share."

"Big news? And you don't know what it is?"

He narrowed his eyes. "Don't you think you should go back to your desk and mind your own business?"

Mind her business. The Bend had become her business the day she drove into town. She left her chair, closed the door behind her. Seth was waiting for her at his desk. "Did you get your answer?"

She sunk into her chair. "More than I wanted."

"Before you go all dramatic on me, I want you to read what I've written. Sending it now."

She faced her computer. Fired it up. Read his opening paragraphs without blinking. His story was good. Even before he added her story to it. Maybe, just maybe he wouldn't need her part.

"Don't say it. I'm adding your story next."

"It's good, Seth. Really good. If no one sits up and takes notice with this story, they never will. I sure hope there are enough decent people left who care. It seems like Earl has his thumb on anyone who is anyone in this town."

"You're right. But there is one person he doesn't control."

She watched his eyes light. "Tell me."

"Better yet, I'll introduce you."

He grabbed his pen and notebook and shot for the door. Kate reached for her camera and fought to catch up with him in the foyer. "Who?" she asked when she found her breath, bumping into Seth who had stopped his mad rush. The local delivery guy was holding out a clipboard for a signature. Rhonda usually signed but was nowhere around.

"Thanks. Looks like you're headed out. Short day?" The driver looked past Seth toward Kate. Something about him . . . Sure, the guy who brought her filing cabinet.

"Always news to chase." Seth handed back the clipboard. He took the square package and placed in on Rhonda's desk.

As they left the building, the guy tagged along. "Shame it's raining again. Hate the stuff." She was in no mood for idle conversation. Seth had piqued her curiosity, and this man seemed intent to slow her down.

"I hear you. I prefer blue skies." She flashed a quick smile before cutting the corner toward the Jeep. She caught up to the passenger side and opened the door. Seth already had the engine running.

"Did the guy ask you out or what?" He gave her a smirk before peeling out of the parking lot.

"I think he wanted to." She smiled and glanced over to where the delivery truck was still parked. After David, she was not taking any more chances. Good looks or not.

73

The white clapboard church standing in front of them shook Kate's insides. The resemblance to the one she attended as a teen could not be denied. She unlatched her seat belt. The storm had resumed and driving rain pelted the stained-glass windows, sending cold shivers through her.

"How did you find this place?" They had driven for miles, yet they weren't that far from the Bend. A few hills. A few switchbacks. Kate had considered begging Seth to turn around, but he wore such a determined look she didn't dare.

"*He* found me."

"He?"

"Pastor Ruel. Rick. I don't go for the title stuff. Came into the office one day. He told me about a woman who had stopped to see him, asked for help. She was disheveled, dressed in a dirty skirt that touched the ground. She took off when he questioned her like she was scared someone would hear."

"Then what? Did he give up on her?"

Seth shook his head. "Rick never gives up on anyone."

Kate opened her door. "I want to meet him." She ducked her head and sprinted to the overhang above the double doors. Seth raced up behind her. He pushed on the right door, opening it with a loud creak.

The interior smelled like her grandmother's attic. She counted ten rows of wooden pews filling the sanctuary. A gold cross at the front drew them further into the darkened room. Seth led the way. Kate sneezed, twice. Dust. Coating everything. She ran her fingers on the edge of one pew. Didn't anyone use them?

When they reached the front, Seth paused. "He lives in the rooms behind the sanctuary. Let me go first. I don't want to scare him."

"Scare him? He's a pastor." She glanced upward to where a chandelier hung. Unlit. Unused for a long time.

"He's also somewhat of a hermit. It took a lot for him to seek me out at the paper."

She would wait. Seth stepped forward toward a door on his right. He knocked twice and slipped inside.

Kate disliked being left alone in this forsaken church. The rain pelted the roof. Why hadn't they had waited to come once it passed? A crack of lightning sent her diving for a nearby pew. Dust or no dust, she sat and wished Seth would hurry up.

As she waited, she scoured the scene in front of her. A lonely lectern. A few song books, six unlit candles. How long ago was this church filled with people? People who worshiped the real God, not Earl? After the bombing at her school, Kate had refused to attend church. Packed places caused her to remember. Her grandmother finally found them a church frequented by less crowds. Like this one. She attended, but her heart stayed put at her parents' and brother's graves.

The door Seth had disappeared through opened. A slightly bent older gentleman hobbled toward her. Wisps of white hair that fell into his eyes bounced along with him. Kate rose and held out her hand. "Pastor Ruel?"

He took her hand into his gentle ones. Squeezed it slightly before releasing it. "My friends call me Rick. Please, sit back down. We'll talk."

Kate glanced at Seth who stood behind him. He nodded and joined them on the front pew. "You know about Brother Earl?"

"Brother Earl has been around for a long time. His influence grew with him. Unfortunately. I will tell you a secret." Rick leaned close. His breath smelled like peppermint. "When Earl was a child, his parents brought him to this church. I was not the pastor yet, but soon after. Earl knows right from wrong. He was taught like I'm sure you were at one time." His strong gaze met hers.

Rick continued, telling a story about a determined young man who wanted to prove himself to others. "Earl left the church shortly after he married his wife. It seemed she could not live up to his standards. Consequently, he devised a plan that would teach her and the wives of his friends. His personality convinced others as much as his transformed wife." He paused. Looked away for a moment. "He proposed the same plan to my wife, Helena."

"What happened to your wife, Pastor?" Kate wasn't sure she wanted to hear this part of the story.

Rick stood and shuffled over to the lectern. An old-man shuffle. How did Seth think Pastor Ruel would be able to help them?

"She joined. Convinced that Earl was right. That she would learn to be a better wife to me." He stepped close again. "I never complained. Believe me, I loved her the way she was. But Earl has developed this way about him where people can't say no. He promises happiness like no one else can give. Even God."

"What became of your wife?" She leaned closer to hear his soft voice.

Rick raised his head and glanced at the cross. "She killed herself."

A gasp shot from Kate's mouth. "I'm sorry." She turned her attention to Seth. Glared at him. Why did he bring them here? Rick was an old man, filled with sorrow for a wife who left him.

"Oh, but don't be sad for me, miss. She's in a better place than the one she left. I trust God for that knowledge." Rick returned to her side and placed his gnarled hand on hers. "I've been plotting how to stop Earl since that day. Now that you two are here, I think we can succeed."

###

Kate listened as Rick spelled out his plan. None of it made sense. An old man's hope, nothing else. Why did Rick think he could deliver anything else? His own hope, that's why. Hope for revenge against an ideal that stole his wife. From the way Seth looked, he felt the same way as her. Probably sorry he brought her here. Kate lowered her eyes.

"With all due respect, Pastor, I don't think there are enough people left unaffected in the Bend to do what you're asking," she said. "Earl has his thumb on most everyone. Including Tim, my editor. If we arranged a town meeting, invited everyone to it, Earl would shut us down. He'd find a way. In the meantime, women will continue to join in hopes for a better future."

"You aren't listening to me, dear." He hoisted himself from the pew and climbed the three steps to the lectern. "This church was once filled with true believers. Week after week, they filed down this aisle to confess their sins, and give their lives to the only one who can make a difference. They are not totally lost. Just confused. Troubled. Afraid. If we offer them hope, they will turn away from the path Earl set them on."

"But hope in what? He offers the men in the Bend a changed life. A life with a spouse who meets their every need. Your plan won't work. I'm sorry we bothered you." Kate stood, glaring at Seth. What was he thinking? Meeting with a man who thought throwing a town meeting and offering an alternative lifestyle for the people would convince a cult leader to stop his plan? Rick must have lost his mind being holed up like this.

Rick's shoulders dropped at Kate's words. Had he been waiting all these years for someone to listen to him?

Seth approached him, shook his hand. "Thank you, Rick. We'll think about your plan."

Kate frowned. An empty promise. His plan wouldn't work.

"God has power to change lives," Rick said, as though in answer to her thoughts.

She looked away. Tell that to Earl. The Bend was not going to change. She had moved into a town that preferred evil over good. Winning was not an option.

Once they were inside the Jeep, Seth spoke. "I'm sorry. I thought he could help. He's one of the few remaining men who haven't fallen under Earl's web of promises. I didn't realize how much he's changed."

As she turned over his words, an idea struck her.

Kate faced him. "So are you. *You* are one of those remaining men." Her pulse throbbed. She grabbed his arm. "You, Seth. You are the one. Why didn't we think of it before? You can make the difference!" She wanted to run back inside and hug Rick. Maybe his idea wouldn't work but talking with him had triggered one that might.

"What are you talking about? Gone crazy on me, Red?"

It didn't even bother Kate that he called her Red. In fact, she kind of liked it now. She smiled and pointed at him. "You can go undercover. Isn't that what reporters do? They go to the story. In the story. You're single. You want a partner for life, and where better to choose one? From Brother Earl's Club. Be sure you order the right ring size."

He pulled onto the road. "You really are crazy. I'm not going undercover for a wife. Earl would smell me coming a mile away. Let's face facts. My article is our ace. I'll send it around to all the papers. Someone will take notice."

"He wouldn't expect a thing. You've never written anything negative about them, and you've lived here almost two years. You aren't an outsider. You aren't dating anyone. And your only run-in with them is at the funeral but you were out of it that day."

Seth shook his head. "I don't know. Won't they wonder why I haven't approached them before?"

"Befriend David. I know that's hard, but the two of you have never spoken at length, right? Then ask him about it. Once you are given the *real* grand tour, you can find out who is doing the training. It will make a better story. Think about it. An expose′. *Reporter undermines cult by joining.* You will be famous." She didn't know about the famous part, but the expose′ might go further with her share of the story. If only Seth would agree.

He rubbed his chin with his free hand. "Famous, huh?"

Kate punched his upper arm playfully. "Get back on track, Seth. You could save lives. Make the Bend what it used to be before Earl took hold."

She could tell Seth was mulling over the idea by the way his faced looked—all serious-like.

"What's the first step?"

"Call David. Tell him you need a mate. You're tired of living out of cereal boxes and pizza." She smiled. "But you have to be careful, okay?"

He stuck out his ring finger. "I always wanted to wear gold."

74

She spent too much time with that reporter. The Trainer had to get rid of him. The risk that he might come looking for Kate was too strong.

The Trainer nibbled on cold fries. Shoved the plate away. He didn't appreciate interference. Not when he had a plan—a specific plan—and time was running out. Until Kate became his, he could not move forward. And moving forward was vital. He'd waited his entire life for this event. Prepared for the moment when it would happen. Dreamed about it. Wrote about it. Life comes full circle.

He and Kate.

He tapped the sticky table with his finger. Getting rid of the reporter would not be easy.

The long-legged waitress stopped by his table for the third time. "Dessert?" She smiled down at him like they all did. He had inherited his mother's looks. Curse or not, it helped.

"Are you offering?" he asked, with a slight lift to his lips.

She giggled, wiped a few remaining crumbs from his table. "I get off at five." She glanced over her shoulder toward her boss, Art, a scrawny, disgusting man. Like she needed his approval or something. Harlots did what they wanted. No one was going to stop them.

An intense heat tightened his stomach. Maybe his plan for Kate could hold a few days. A little more practice wouldn't hurt. Another week remained until the event. He could train Kate in that time on her part of the plan.

He handed the waitress cash for his bill. "I'll wait across the street. Come straight out. I know a private place for dinner."

Another pitiful smile meant to seduce him. She draped one finger across his shoulder and sashayed toward the counter. The Trainer waited, watched as she whispered to her coworker. Like always. It didn't take much to seduce a woman like that. He bet she called her mother and yakked to her about her date tonight too.

The Trainer stood, brushed his pants off. He glanced down at a spot. Gritted his teeth. That stupid waitress. She'd dripped ketchup onto his clothing. He constrained his anger and left the diner before his irritation grew.

After he climbed into his truck, he applied sanitizer to the spot, cursing as he did. Then he drew a long breath. Don't worry, he told himself. By tonight, the blood would cover it.

75

Seth popped a TV dinner into his microwave. Exhausted from the day's events, he looked forward to a good night's sleep. As if that would happen. Not after what Kate suggested. Infiltrate the cult? Go undercover?

She'd read too many books.

Sure, he might be able to convince David of his need for a companion. But would the guy believe him after catching Seth snooping around the cabins? Fat chance.

He pulled out his oven mitt and plopped dinner onto a plate. What he'd give for a home-cooked meal.

Maybe Kate was right. Let David think he was tired of bachelorhood and wanted a woman who could cook, clean, and meet all his needs. He could contact David and meet him at the diner. Convince him how wrong Seth was about Brother Earl and that he'd come around to their way of thinking. What else did they have to try? Kate didn't think sending his article the way it stood would do much good. But if he had an insider's point of view…

Seth gulped down his glass of milk. Patted his stomach. A home-cooked meal. Not a bad idea.

Kate's dinner consisted of a piece of cheese wrapped around leftover turkey from lunch three days ago. She needed to get control of her life. The last twenty-four hours had kicked her butt. She tugged off her shoes and poured herself a glass of water. A shower and a quick call to Jackie, and then she would sleep until ten in the morning. Saturday couldn't come soon enough.

After eating, she pulled out her phone. Her fingers hesitated over the screen. The last time she spoke with Jackie, Trevor had started chemo. How many weeks had passed without an update? It was her fault. She couldn't bear to hear painful news.

She set her phone aside and strode over to her computer. She pulled up her photos and scrolled through them, searching for the last one she took of Trevor. The one that showed her something was wrong.

Her scrolling came to an abrupt halt. The aura was no longer there.

She shut her computer. Was he worse or dead? What did it mean? She reached for her phone, her hand shaking. What kind of friend doesn't call? She stared out of her window as the sun set behind the row of trees. Her *gift* had caused nothing but pain for her for twenty years. Knowing when her family or friends might die. Knowing that time had run out for many. Maybe with Trevor. Her begging Jackie to get him to another doctor's had changed nothing. Or had it?

She reopened her computer. Found the picture of the church taken weeks ago. The aura had grown darker. Almost sinister looking. Like a mushroom overshadowing the building.

Was this photo giving her the opportunity to save lives?

The only way she would know would be to make the call.

She pressed the contact button.

Seconds later, Jackie answered. Her voice high-pitched. "You never called back!"

Kate swallowed. "Tell me about Trevor. Please. How is he?" She tightened her grip. Afraid to listen.

"Ask him yourself."

A familiar young voice came over the phone. "Aunt Kate? I miss you."

Kate dropped her head to her knees. "Hey there, Trevor. How are you doing these days?"

"Are you coming home to my party? Mom says we can invite the whole team."

"Party? What kind of party?" She squeezed her eyes shut. Prayed. *Please . . .*

"I don't have to go back to the doctor's anymore. I'm healthy. A miracle, the doctor said. Mom says it's all because of you, Aunt Kate. You saved my life."

Seth met David at nine a.m. at the diner. Earl's sleaze brother wore a fat grin with his hair dripping in girly product. If Seth had eaten his breakfast as planned, he'd puke his guts out right now. Instead, he stood and shook the weasel's hand.

"Coffee, please," Seth told the overly eager waitress when she made it to their table. David raised two fingers. She barely nodded before dropping a gusher of a smile into David's lap. Why not climb into it? Seth gritted his teeth.

After she returned and set the steaming cups in front of them, David spoke first. Of course. He was used to being in charge. "You're tired of the bachelor life, huh? Need a good woman to cook your meals, clean your house, and keep you warm at night."

"Something like that." Playing nice would not come easy. David came off like a politician making a bid for the White House.

"What makes you think I can help you?" The guy folded his hands together. Seth zoomed in on the ring. A new addition? Or he finally had the guts to wear one.

"Why not? I've lived here long enough to know something. I hear you can find me the right girl. A trained girl. Someone who will follow the rules." He pasted an earnest look on his face. Controlled his gag reflex.

David laughed. Guess he didn't believe him either. "What about Kate? She dump you too?"

"Why bring her into this? She works for the paper. Period." He stopped short of growling. "But if you need to know, she isn't interested in me." He might as well play it all the way. "I thought she was different. She's not."

"Ah, someone's got a crush on the wrong girl." He stirred two packets of sweetener into his coffee. "She's a tough one to crack. I'll give you that. So, we're talking rebound? The women you normally go after aren't taking the bait."

Seth curled his fingers around his mug. If he wasn't there for a noble reason, he'd smack that smug grin right off David's his face. "Something like that. Well, are you going to help or not? I don't have all day."

He waited—hoped he'd convinced him he was serious.

David sipped his coffee. Set it down. Wiped his fingers on a napkin. He pulled his wallet from his back pocket and plucked out a business card. He tossed it to David. "My email's on it. Send me a reminder. We meet tomorrow night at the house. If you're lying, you'll be sorry."

"We?"

"The boys. You can decide then if you're in or out." He stood over the table. "Leave the recorder at home. We frown on reporters." With that being said, he turned and moseyed out of the restaurant like he owned the place. Probably did.

76

When Kate saw David coming out of the diner, she ducked. She should have parked further down the street. After a few minutes passed, time enough for him to get into his truck and drive away, she raised her head. All clear. She got out and hurried inside.

Seth was hunched over a plate of potatoes and eggs. She slid across from him. "Well?"

He looked over his shoulder then slid her a card. "He carries these on him," he said between bites. "Like he's important."

The engraved business card did look important. David's name, phone number, email, and a short blurb filled it. "Don't wait for contentment in the next life, find it in this life."

She wanted to crush it. Instead, she discreetly slid it back across the table. "Are you in?"

"Sort of." He wiped his chin, tossed the napkin to the side. Another glance around the diner. "I've been invited to a meeting tomorrow night. At the big house. They'll probably sit around the coffins comparing rings." He rolled his eyes.

"I know I'm the one who suggested doing this, but I'm not so sure anymore. Maybe we should rethink this." She didn't want to be responsible for endangering Seth. She didn't need that guilt on her plate as well.

"Too late. I'm going. You've made me believe that getting on their good side might be the answer to ending their power. Once I find out what I need to know, I'll write a story that will bring every Fed and cop down on this place like ants to jelly."

"I don't know if we have that much time. Remember the rally is next week. That photo . . ."

She was certain, after talking with Trevor, that if she moved quickly she could save people when she found the aura around their photo. How—she wasn't sure. But at least it gave her a fighting chance. Maybe the curse had been a blessing all along. Unfortunately, because of her fear, she hadn't done anything with it.

"Where did you go?" Seth's voice brought her back to the restaurant. The smell of bacon was stirring her appetite.

"I didn't eat. I'm getting hungry. How about calling the waitress for me?"

He shook his head. "I'm not David. Won't do any good." He motioned to where the young girl was swooning over another male customer. "She didn't like me."

"That's nonsense." Kate called out to the waitress in a singsong voice. The waitress headed her way. Kate gave a hefty order, adding another plate of eggs for Seth. "You'll need your energy."

"What are you going to be doing while I'm learning how to play nice with the cultists?"

"I'm going to contact Shelly's friend, Mandy Baker. I need to know if she's ever been found."

He set his fork down. "Want me to go with you?"

Her breakfast platter arrived before she could answer. The waitress slapped the food on the table before turning away. "I'll go alone. Something doesn't fit. I can't believe that Earl or David would harm anyone. They might be trying to take over the town and people's minds, but hurt someone?" She shook her head. "Call it a gut feeling. David has charisma like Earl. I think that's all they have. Besides a messed-up worldview. Can you imagine David strapping on a bomb?" She had sat up half the night thinking about that possibility. David wanted people to follow him. She couldn't see him killing someone for that purpose. If he had, he would have come after her by now.

It took Kate forever to find the Baker house, as it was so far out, it was almost into the next town. She caught her breath when she rounded the corner. A two-story farmhouse surrounded by acres of fenced green pasture. A couple of horses grazed near a barn as she drove toward the property. Money for sure. She parked in front of the four-car garage.

Kate checked her face in the mirror before getting out, hoping she look presentable. This ranch didn't look a thing like the rest of the houses in the area. Must be big money. She had found out that Mr. Baker was a CEO in New York City and commuted home on weekends. Mandy was their only daughter. Mrs. Baker served on the hospital board until a few years ago, then dropped out of sight.

"Can I help you?"

Mandy rode toward her on a beautiful palomino. Kate recognized the fiery red hair, a shade darker than her own. "Hi, Mandy. Do you remember me? Kate, from the newspaper."

Mandy slid from the saddle. She tied the reins to a fence post and sauntered over to where Kate waited by her car. Mandy's hair hung loose, and her shiny boots complimented her tight jeans. She looked like she'd dropped in from a photo shoot for a horse magazine. Mandy shook her hand.

"What brings you out here?"

Kate searched for a place to talk besides the middle of the driveway. Mandy saw her look and motioned for her to follow toward the massive front porch. They sunk into comfortable chairs separated by a wicker stand.

"I'm here about your friend, Shelly. Have you heard anything from her?"

Mandy's pretty face grew dark. "I was hoping you had news. She's never called, and her parents refuse to believe that something may have happened. They think Shelly ran away. I don't believe that. I think someone took her."

Someone took her? "Why do you say that? Was there anything in her past that might make her vulnerable? Maybe problems at home or with people in general?"

"She was always down on herself. Believed she wasn't pretty enough or smart enough." She caught Kate's gaze. "She was, though. I wanted to look like her." Her tone grew louder. "I'm the one who's stuck in this mausoleum with parents who haven't a clue that maybe I want more than to inherit their dumb money. Like college."

Kate straightened. Not expecting the conversation to go in that direction.

"Tell me about Shelly. Was she easily swayed by men?"

"Sorry, yes. She had been dumped earlier this spring by a guy she fell for hard. She would do anything a guy told her to do, even when I warned her to be careful." She picked at her manicured nails. It seemed Mandy was unhappy with her lifestyle in the same way Shelly had been.

"You know Brother Earl."

"I've met him." She glanced over her shoulder toward the house. "My mother knows him better. She goes to all his rallies. Tries to get me to attend, but I won't. Who wants to hear that old guy go on and on about cell phones and movies?" She rolled her eyes. "Actually, my father took my mother to the first one. Then she went to some dumb camp for a month or so and came back a different person." She leaned closer to Kate. "I think something more serious is going on with the Bend."

Kate hesitated. Should she confide in this young woman what she knew? Would it save her life? "I agree. Something is different about Brother Earl. I think he's started a cult or a group that likes to control others. Please be careful in your interactions with them."

"I knew it. Ever since my mother went, she's been different. Talking about

Earl as though he's God. Do you think that's where Shelly went?"

"I honestly don't know. I haven't been able to figure that out, and it seems like no one is talking." She stood, anxious to leave. She wouldn't find her answers here as she hoped. Mandy joined her, and they walked toward the steps. "If I hear anything at all, I'll contact you, okay?"

As she lowered her foot to the first step, one of the double front doors opened. An older version of Mandy joined them. But unlike Mandy, this woman was dressed in a dark skirt that fell near the ground, and she gripped a black Bible with both hands.

77

The Trainer gunned his truck's engine. His fingers gripped the steering wheel as he careened over the back roads toward his house. Heat filled his vision. He had never once changed his plans, but today he did. All because of Kate.

If only he had taken her when he planned instead of befriending that waitress. When he saw his next candidate sashay—the only word to describe her disgusting promenade—out of the restaurant, he knew she was a bad candidate.

No one could fulfill what he needed from Kate. The urge to move forward with his one and only plan destroyed his previous desire. It was time. Time to proceed with his master plan. The plan that would meet all his desires—not these temporary ones that his candidates gave him over the years.

He slammed his fist against the dash. Practice. That's what his father told him to do. Well, he was done practicing. How many had he sharpened his tactics on? He couldn't count nor remember especially when his vision burned with Kate's image.

He was ready for her. His focus would only be for her.

The Trainer's breathing slowed. Control. Yes, that's what he needed. Control over the entire situation. Monday morning. No later. No sooner.

He turned into his driveway. Shut off his truck. Stalked to the building behind his house. He unlocked the padlock. Entered the dark interior.

A smiled discovered his lips.

Let no one ever say he hadn't prepared.

78

Mandy's mother stepped between them. Kate smelled the strong odor of whiskey before she could clear her brain.

"What are you, a reporter, doing on my property?" She spit her words into Kate's face.

Mandy placed her hand on her mother's arm. "Mom, Kate's a friend. We were talking about Shelly."

Mrs. Baker glared at her daughter before turning her angry face toward Kate again. "Get off my porch. You don't belong here."

Kate raised her hands, palms outward. "I'm sorry. I didn't mean to intrude. I was trying to help find your daughter's friend." She glanced at Mandy, hoping for further back up. She wouldn't get it. The young woman's face had turned red. Embarrassment or anger. Kate couldn't be certain.

"Do I have to report you to Brother Earl? He doesn't like nosy women." She raised her Bible. Waved it between them. "Read what the Lord has to say about the virtuous woman. It's all in here." She slapped the front cover like it was a baby's bottom.

Kate took a step backward, navigating her feet on the flight of steps. Mrs. Baker followed, pressing her, holding her Bible as she quoted verse after verse.

"I'm leaving. I'm sorry." Kate threw one last desperate look at Mandy and then spun around, hobbling down the steps as quickly as her lame leg allowed.

Had everyone in the Bend fallen for crazy Earl's garbage? She didn't want to wait around to see if Mr. Baker had, too.

Kate locked her car. Shot down the driveway.

Away from this craziness. Away from this insanity. Toward the Bend. Into more of the same.

###

Seth recalled his last trip to Earl's funeral home. Amy's funeral. A dismal day. Like today. He rolled up to the double gates, waited as they slowly opened. He'd dressed simply but neatly for this occasion. Dark pants and a white shirt. He wouldn't wear a tie. Brother Earl or not.

But he must convince his skeptics he had decided to join them. To find a willing woman. Cross over to their darkness and ways.

He spit the remainder of his lollipop into the cup holder. What he'd give for a cigarette. He flexed his cramped hands. Scanned the parking lot. At least a dozen vehicles filled it.

The good old boys.

The cream of the crop.

Ready or not. If this is how he was to get the story of a lifetime, then so be it.

His sister's doe-like eyes rose into his thoughts. Yeah, he'd do it for her too.

After locking his Jeep, he strode up the steps to the entrance marked Private. He raised his knuckles to knock. David opened the door before he struck wood. "Greetings, Seth. We were waiting for you. Earl is about to begin." The smile David gave him didn't reach his eyes. Seth forced a matching one on his face. He shook David's hand with a strong grip.

The men sat in the living room, surrounded by photos and a baby grand piano in the far corner. If he hadn't known the real reason he was there, he might think he was attending a men's Bible study. Seth nodded to the hardware store owner, to Doc, to the guy who hooked up his internet, to the owner of the bakery, and to a few other men he'd met in passing. Good thing he'd dressed up. Not one pair of jeans in the crowd. These men met business.

So did he.

Seth finished his greetings, took a comfortable chair in the far corner next to a plant dripping with leaves. He placed his back to the corner. On purpose.

Earl came through the doorway that led into the hall. He was wiping his face with a napkin. Late dinner? Seth watched the way the man navigated the room. Eye contact. Pats on the shoulder. A few atta-boys. When he stood in front of Seth, his cheer faded. Seth jumped from his seat and offered his hand.

"Heard you were coming tonight. Be ready to give your testimony."

After ignoring Seth's outstretched hand, Earl retreated to the front of the room where he stood behind a music stand turned into a lectern. Handy. Seth dropped back into his seat. What did he mean by a testimony? He shot a questioning glance to David who politely ignored him. In fact, everyone ignored him. Except Earl who stared at him a full minute before slapping his Bible onto the stand.

"It's good to be together like this. The Lord is blessing us as I speak. Can you feel his presence? He knows we are doing great work. Upright work. His work! The work that will save our sweet Bend." He paused, took a deep breath.

One by one, the other men began to clap. At first in rhythm, then it grew louder. A few whistles, catcalls, and then all out shouting as they jumped to their feet. Earl, still locked behind his makeshift podium, raised his hands in the air and shut his eyes, "Yes, Lord, yes Lord, we hear you. We are doing your work!" And then, as though on cue, the men dropped to their seats and stared at the door behind Earl.

Seth had remained seated during the ruckus, unsure as a newbie what was expected of him. David reached over and touched his knee. He pointed in the direction everyone had set their interest. With increasing alarm, David watched as a petite woman clothed in dark clothing that showed nothing but her white face, crossed the threshold and stood in front of Earl. She bowed her head,

Who was she? Seth strained to identify the woman but most of her features were covered with a head cloth.

Earl turned back toward the group of still men. The only sound Seth heard was heavy breathing near him. Doc. His thoughts made him want to scream.

"Gentlemen. Gentlemen. Our newest candidate is ready. She's gone through extensive training. Prepared not only in her mind and soul, but in her body as well." Earl looked at Doc. Nodded. He tipped his head in agreement.

Seth swallowed. He clenched his fists in his lap. Was this woman to be auctioned off like a cow at a fair?

"As we always do, we must first pray over this young maiden. She's changed her life for the welfare of the Bend. Tells me she is ready to step into the world a changed woman. A woman who wants to serve the Lord though serving man and procreation." He clasped his beefy paw on the woman's shoulder, spun her around. Like a prize.

It was all Seth could do to remain seated. He schooled his thoughts, straightened his lips. A story. That's why he was there. Not for some noble reason like Kate wanted. No, a story so he could get out of this forsaken town.

79

Kate tried calling Seth's cell twice before going to bed. Tomorrow, she could quiz him all she wanted while at work. Besides, if something important had happened, he would call her. Despite her best efforts, she trusted Seth. More than she first did. Maybe it was the way he acted like he cared about her well-being without showing it. Or the way he spoke about the missing women.

She pulled off her jeans and shirt. Tugged her sweatshirt over her head. Seth had changed this summer. She remembered the first time she met him at that rally. A real oaf. Never would she have pegged him for a man who would put others' needs first. Nope. He had been on a mission to sell a big story. His story of the year, or century. Whatever.

After brushing her teeth, she sat in front of her computer. Another glance at her photos wouldn't hurt. Maybe there was a clue she had missed. Something. The Bakers had been no help. They had been sucked in. Yes, sucked into Earl's lies like dogs to trees. Except for Mandy.

Her pictures came into focus. Kate kept her work photos and personal photos on this computer too. She found Mandy's. Waited. Nothing. A sigh left her throat. She hoped nothing would happen to that girl since it was evident she was in direct opposition to her mother's beliefs. Kate had read about cults that did away with family members who discarded the teachings. Mandy was smart. It wouldn't surprise Kate to learn that she left town one day. With a mother like hers, Kate couldn't blame her.

She scrolled through several other pictures until her cursor stopped on the one she'd taken of the church. The aura still circled it. But it had grown darker. The rally was planned for next week. Maybe she was wrong. Maybe this aura had nothing to do with that rally. She shoved her fist against her forehead. Think. Why else would it be there?

Kate zoomed in closer. Several people were milling around out front. David's face focused first. To his left, she saw Doc and Mary. David had waved to her that day. Did he know what was going to happen? Was he going to harm all those people?

Her thoughts raced. Maybe David wanted Earl's role. Maybe he was tired of being second. Isn't that what Cain did to Abel? From the little she knew about David, it was obvious he liked to win. Maybe he didn't like being under Earl's thumb. Maybe that family plot might add a few more bodies. She peered closer. The aura didn't quite reach David.

80

"Sorry you weren't ready, Seth. She would have made a fine wife for you." Doc stood next to him by the Jeep. The other followers had already left the parking lot, leaving Seth in Doc's company.

"I need a little more time. I'm sure she would have made a great wife. And yes, I'm looking for one. After Amy . . ."

"The new theater owner, right? I heard you were sweet on her." Doc removed his glasses and wiped them on his shirt. "Surprised me to hear you wanted to throw your lot in with us. Especially after the way you spoke to me." He returned his glasses to his face. Stared at Seth a little longer than needed.

"Mary's a sweetheart. Why wouldn't I want someone like her?" He ached to get into his car and get out of there. After seeing that woman paraded in front of him, he had better plans. Plans to get out of town. Story or no story.

"I guess I thought your someone special was more like our Kate."

Our Kate. His fingers tingled to crush that look from Doc's face. Instead, he shrugged. "She's a little too opinionated for my taste."

"Got to agree with you there. Not sure any man would want to take that fox on."

"Listen. I was wrong about Kate. She's a know-it-all, but I have to work with her. That's all. There never was anything romantic between us." He frowned hoping to sound convincing. This whole evening had been a long shot. They were probably playing him like he was them. He was stupid to have tried. Tomorrow they'll probably run him out of town.

Seth slapped Doc's arm. "I got to get going, Doc. Back to work tomorrow."

"Yes, the news. Sorry Tim couldn't make it tonight. I bet he'll be pleased to see you've joined the boys and me. Tim played a key role in getting our little group organized."

"A key role? How long has he been involved?"

Doc laughed. "Sounds like the reporter I know. Hard to break old habits, eh, Seth? You might want to start writing the real news. I'm sure Tim will point you in the right direction." After a pat to Seth's arm, Doc turned, and poked his way over to his truck.

Seth followed him out of the compound. He unwrapped another Tootsie Pop, changed his mind, and tossed it back into the bag. Candy wouldn't— *couldn't*—take away the rancid taste in his mouth.

###

A cup of tea didn't ease Kate's worries. She scuffed across the living room in her slippers to her kitchen fridge. Maybe a plate of cheese to take her mind off those pictures? And David. What if he was planning something?

She swung the fridge door shut. Crazy. Crazy thinking, her grandmother would say when Kate started with her fears. Valid or not, her fears kept her safe from the media. Maybe her fears could prevent someone from dying. She glanced at the window in her front door.

A flash of light?

Since her road received little traffic, a car passing alerted her no matter the time of day. She crossed into her living room, pulled back the curtain as a knock sounded on her door. Kate jumped, dropping the fabric.

"Who is it?" She scanned the room for her knife. Grabbed it from the end table where she put it before changing.

"It's Seth. Are you awake?"

Seth? The meeting. Something must have happened. She snapped the lock. Opened the door.

"Do you always dress so well?" He glanced down at her running shorts and torn sweat shirt.

Kate stepped aside to let him enter. She eyed his outfit. "Do *you* always dress so well? Let me guess. You don't own a tuxedo."

"I dressed to impress. Not sure it worked." He kept walking straight toward her kitchen. When he got there, he picked up one of her cheese slices and tossed it into his mouth. "But they offered me a woman."

Kate stopped her movement toward him. "They what?"

"Got any crackers?" He opened the cupboard over the stove.

"By the sink. What do you mean they offered you a woman?"

Seth pulled out a packet of saltines. Stacked slices of cheese on several. "Just what I said. Want one?" he asked through a mouthful of crumbs.

She sat at the table. Seth joined her. "Tell me what happened."

"Peanut butter?"

She nodded. "Tell me first. Or I'll never be able to understand you."

Seth chewed, swallowed. He wiped a few straggling pieces from his chin. "They did everything I thought they would. Earl preached then brought a woman out. For me. Already been trained and packaged to go. The poor girl didn't say a word. It was disgusting. I was waiting for Earl to open her mouth and show me her teeth."

"Did you recognize her?"

"No one I knew. But that's not saying much. She could be anyone's daughter. "

How did you say no?" She reached for the cheese.

"Told them I was still learning about their expectations. Didn't want to mess anything up. They bought it. At least they acted like they did. Probably playing me but I'm on the inside for now."

"When is the next meeting? We're running out of time."

"David will contact me. Guess they like to keep the meetings secret until right before."

"Why bother? Everyone in the Bend knows what he's doing."

He shoved the crackers aside. "Yeah, even dear old Tim."

"Tim?"

"Seems he's been involved since the beginning." Seth's expression darkened. "I believe that's another whole story to investigate. If I stick around long enough."

"What do you mean? We have to stop whatever is going to kill those people."

He ignored her question and unscrewed the top to the peanut butter jar. She wanted to yank the knife out of his hand. Wisely, did not.

"I don't think I can do this again. I hated tonight."

He hated tonight? What about doing what's right? "It was one night. Please hang in there until we figure out if they are going to hurt hundreds of people."

Seth shoved his food aside. "How do you figure to do that? I didn't learn a thing tonight, and time is running out."

Of course he was right. But she couldn't stop trying. Even if he did.

81

Kate woke with a pounding headache. Thinking about her conversation last night with Seth sickened her. What craziness did Earl do to the Bend? Training women to be better wives. Setting up the men as gods. She slipped her feet to the floor. Facing Tim at work today would not be an easy task. Not after discovering his bigger part in the cult.

She doubted she could work for him much longer either.

At least Seth had agreed to not leave yet. At least until he broke the story. Then she was getting out of town as fast as she could right with him. Maybe she would head south. As far as Florida. She'd never been there before, but with winter coming, it might be the place to go.

She ambled into her bathroom. Studied her tired expression for a moment. No, it would not be easy to smile and pretend much longer. She turned from the sink and started the shower. A half hour later, dressed, and nibbling on a bagel, Kate was startled by a loud knock on her front door. She checked her watch. Too early for mail.

Kate crossed into the living room and peered out her front window. The delivery truck. Her heart slowed. She opened the door and immediately recognized the driver who had delivered her file cabinet weeks ago. "Morning. You're out early. Lost?"

She eyed a large box on a hand cart.

"Delivery." He held up his device for her signature.

Kate opened her door. "I think you have the wrong address. I didn't order anything." A huge box. She read the label. Her name was printed on it. "Is there a return address?"

He punched numbers into his device. "Michigan."

She let out her breath. Jackie sending something for her place. She opened the door. "Thanks. It looks heavy."

Her front door blew shut. The wind, kicking up. Another storm.

"It's about to get a lot heavier," he said, stepping closer.

"What?" Instinct gripped her. She shifted backward. "You better leave. I have to get to work."

He didn't leave. Instead, he reached into his back pocket. Brought out a syringe. "So do I."

A scream formed in her throat. It was soon cut off as his hand clamped down on her mouth. She kicked her foot into his shin and reached for her pocket knife.

No! She rolled backward as he overpowered her. She clawed at the air, shock surging through her veins. Then black dots until she hurtled into final darkness.

When ten o'clock rolled around and neither Tim nor Kate had showed up for work, Seth strolled out to where Rhonda was checking her phone. "Did Kate call in? She was supposed to go with me to the first-day-of-school ceremony. It's late and I've got to run."

Rhonda had the decency to put down her phone. "She didn't call, but I remember her talking about not feeling so well on Friday. Maybe a girl thing."

He didn't want to hear about a girl thing. She could catch up with him when she came in. He grabbed his gear and left Rhonda to her nails. She had already set up her equipment by the time he brushed out the front door.

With school back in session, the Bend's streets looked more like a ghost town except for the flyers pasted on every storefront window. Earl had certainly covered the territory. Probably the entire town would show up for the rally. Who wouldn't? Free snacks and face painting for the kids? A regular three-ring circus.

Seth turned toward the elementary school. He drove up the hill and parked next to a line of buses. A light breeze caught his hair as he hiked toward the brick building. Fall. He could not spend another winter here. Once he exposed Earl and his followers, he'd write his story, send it to the big papers, and leave.

Hopefully, he'd land a better job from the article. A first-rate job. Maybe with *The Times*. He clamped his thoughts off as the principal met him at the door. A homely woman with a hook nose, dressed in the familiar garb of the Bend—a dark skirt that covered her knees, raised her palm to him. "We aren't letting reporters in today for the assembly. Private matters only for the kids."

"Private? This is a public school. I've covered events here before." Miss Quiver, or Quigley? He couldn't remember. He remembered only that when he did run into her, she always wore a frown. Like she did now.

"Sorry. Not today. We have important information to cover that doesn't need to be spread all over the county." With that spoken, she slammed the door. A burly-looking guard with a missing side-tooth took her place. He crossed his arms.

Message received.

Seth turned and stalked back across the parking lot. Now they were brainwashing the kids. He cranked the Jeep's engine and drove toward town and the office. Maybe Tim would be there, and they could talk.

Tim was in his office sorting files when Seth knocked.

His boss looked as though he hadn't slept in weeks. Too busy making plans for Earl? Seth controlled his expression as he sat across from the man.

"Don't I give you enough assignments, Seth? Shouldn't you be at the school today?"

So he didn't know.

"The principal wouldn't let me in. Seems they are having a private, first assembly this year."

Tim met his look, then shifted his eyes to the side. He shoved his glasses to his forehead. "Times change. We'll catch their mid-assembly."

"I didn't see you last night." Might as well wade in.

Tim tipped his face toward his stack of papers on his desk. "Got busy. How did everything go?"

"How come you didn't tell me you were part of Earl's group? I might have joined sooner."

"I doubt that."

Seth shifted closer. If he couldn't get Tim to believe he'd gone over to the dark side, no one would. "I need a woman. It gets lonely living like I do." He shrugged. "What better woman than one who can meet all my needs. Home cooked meals. Clean clothes. A man gets tired of doing for himself. Why not take what's available?"

Tim snorted. "That's hard to believe. I thought you liked the single life."

Seth shrugged. "I mean it, Tim. I'm tired of being on the outside. Earl promises the kind of life every man wants."

Tim's eyes narrowed. "What about our girl, Kate? She might be available. Too tough to crack?"

Our girl? Seth flinched at the words coming from Tim's mouth. His fist clenched below the desk. What right did he have calling Kate *our* girl? First Doc, now him.

"She drives me nuts. Never on time. Always has her head in the clouds. You should never have hired her. She's detrimental to the paper."

"Harsh words for someone who wants a wife."

"Yeah? Maybe, but she isn't my type."

"That's right. The movie lady. She was your type."

Seth swallowed hard. He looked away. At least that was the truth.

Tim rose from his chair and crossed the room to stand near the ancient radiator. "Looks like a big storm on the horizon." He rocked on his heels. Seth loathed his nerdy black shoes. Something his grandfather wore.

"Kate didn't come in today. Maybe she got tired of this place."

Tim turned around. Dug his hands into his pockets. "Should have asked her last night."

What was he talking about?

"When you were at her house."

Seth jumped. "What are you doing? Spying on people now?" He growled with annoyance. "Last I heard, that's against the law. Oh wait. You're above that, aren't you?" He couldn't stop. Maybe it was his annoyance at the school, but Earl and Tim had gone too far. "Tell me you aren't following me."

The twerp strolled to stand in front of him. A sick grin grew on Tim's lips. "It's my job to know the news."

His job. To spy? To watch him like a criminal?

"News flash. Something you missed. Congrats. You're minus one reporter. I quit. Put that on your front page." Seth controlled his boiling urge to spit on those ugly shoes, and instead, marched to the outer office, gathered his belongings, and stormed out the front door.

82

It was too easy. Almost. When he saw her expression turn to fear, he almost changed his mind. The Trainer didn't want Kate to be afraid of him. He wanted her to obey him. Follow him to their glorious end together. After she fell into his arms, he stuffed her limp body inside the box.

Perfect. Anyone driving past would think he was taking a package for delivery.

Exactly his plan.

He wedged open the front door of her house with his foot.

A heavy wind pushed against him as he wheeled the box back to the street, up into his waiting truck. He ran back to shut the door, stopping for a moment to look around.

Sparse furnishings. Nothing to show the world who she was.

He closed the door.

Like him. Waiting to finish what the world started.

His chest tingled with anticipation. When she awoke, he would be ready.

Then he would ready her.

Seth couldn't quite believe he'd quit his job. He spun out of the parking lot like a man bent on a mission. What had he done? Blown everything he told Kate he would do. He'd never be invited into the group now. No, old Tim would see to that. Seth slapped his steering wheel with his palm. Why couldn't he control himself? Was he that fed up with the Bend?

He drove through the downtown. Few people littered the streets. A mother hauled a screaming kid into the grocery store. Another woman dressed in prairie skirts rushed by the burned-out theater with her head down.

He turned down Pine Street. Cruised past the bigger houses. Watched workers touch up gingerbread trim and helpers rake fallen leaves. A part of him would miss the Bend. Small town living had appealed to him when he first arrived. Now? Too small a town. Buried with its crazy followers of a man who was nothing more than crazy himself.

He continued out of town until he came upon the church. The one in the photo. The one where the rally was to be held in two days. He pulled across the road. Rolled down his window. Two cars were parked beside the building. Pastor? Secretary? He debated going in and telling them what he knew, but he understood that this church had fallen under Earl's spell too. Rumor led him to believe that the pastor had sent his wife to the camp for the finishing touches.

He thought of what Kate told him.

Maybe her aura nonsense was just that. Nonsense. Who saw stuff like that on pictures? How could he believe that everyone in that church might die in two days? Maybe he was going as crazy as Earl and his zombies.

He shifted into reverse. He'd talk with Kate. Get her to tell him the truth. That her gift was all a lie. Something she made up for attention. He flicked his turn signal and tore over the bridge. He'd lost his job because of her. The least she could do was be honest with him.

Kate weighed less than his other candidates, yet his breath came in spurts as he carried her inside his work room. He laid her gently on the quilt inside her own personal coffin. Not that she would ever get to use it. There wouldn't be that much of her left.

A groan escaped her lips. Soft lips. Kissable lips. Lips he had dreamed about as a boy of twelve. Now they belonged to him. He bent over her still body, stroked her cheek with one finger. "My dear Kate. Finally, we are together. Soon we'll be together for eternity."

When he finished tying her wrists to the sides of the box, an enormous hunger overtook him. He hadn't felt this alive in years. Not since his father died. Is this what his final plan would feel like? Euphoric? The Trainer brushed his hands down his pants. He must take care of himself before the day arrived. Nothing must get in the way. He paced the room, scratched his head. Grabbed a pad and pen that waited on a wooden chair in the corner.

It must go as planned. No one must stop him.

Next, he checked his knives. Felt the blade sting his palm. Looked over his shoulder toward Kate.

Soon.

When she woke. He wouldn't rush it.

Only then would he begin the training.

83

Kate's lips throbbed. She tasted them with her tongue. Parched. And why did her wrists hurt? She pried her eyes open. Remembering. A hand. Then blackness.

Still blackness. She raised her fists, but they pulled tight. Where was she? Her pulse surged into her throat as she yanked again. Cords dug into her wrists. Why couldn't she see anything? Her heart sped up. Her legs. Kate raised one as far as she could—her toe bumping into something solid. She raised her other foot, smashing into that same wall. Why couldn't she move? She squeezed her knees together and kicked both feet upward. Bang! What was she in?

With nothing left to try, she opened her mouth and screamed. "Help me! Please! Help me!" Her voice sounded muffled. Locked in the prison with her. Tears flooded her eyes as she willed herself to breathe. She must not pass out. Whoever did this to her would return. The delivery man? Why would he do this to her? Again, she screamed. Screamed until she gagged on her spit.

A bright light flooded her eyes. She blinked—focusing about her.

The delivery man. Peering down. Smiling.

Kate opened her mouth again to scream. But nothing came out.

###

Seth pounded on Kate's door. Harder this time. He checked his watch. Strode off the front porch to the side driveway. Her car was parked next to the house.

He peered inside. Nothing out of place. Her silly briefcase and an empty soda can.

He scanned the house again. Something wasn't right. Maybe she'd fallen in the shower and hit her head. It wasn't like her not to answer her door if she was home. The back door was hidden behind a few large bushes. Seth made his way to it and tried the screen door. It opened with ease. The storm door didn't. He eyed the kitchen table. Kate's purse. Open. He remembered her words about Debbie. No woman goes off without her purse.

He jiggled the knob then made his decision.

He took off his coat, wrapped it around his arm, and smashed the window. Glass poured into the house and scattered at his feet as well. He would fix it later. Right now, he wanted to be certain she was okay. Seth pulled open the door and stepped over the shattered pieces into the kitchen. The lights were turned off. Her dirty breakfast dishes sat in the sink. He ran his finger over a coffee cup. Cold.

From there, he made a pass through the bedroom and bathroom before ending up in the front living room.

He wasn't a detective, but something felt off. He dropped onto the ugly couch, probed the room again. Chunks of fresh mud coming from the front door led to the center of the room. He'd never seen Kate wear boots. He crossed the room and knelt to inspect the tracks in the mud. Wheels? His gaze caught on a piece of cardboard. Almost invisible but at this level, he made out a torn box corner.

Had she been packing? Was she leaving town like him?

She was as frustrated as him but was also passionate about the upcoming rally. Hundreds might die, she'd said. He rocked back on his heels. No, she would not leave with that hanging over her head. She had more conscience than he did.

A buzzing sound caught his attention. Seth lunged for the purse, opened it, and found her phone lit up. A caller from Michigan. He punched accept.

"Kate?"

"This is Seth. I work with her. Are you a friend?"

"Where's Kate and why are you answering her phone?"

A feisty friend.

"Listen, when's the last time you spoke with Kate?"

"Is something wrong? Put her on now."

That answered that. He hung up. Her close friend didn't have a clue about Kate's whereabouts either.

His pupils filled his eye sockets. Kate stared at her abductor. Waited. "I see you're awake. Good. We can begin the training." He disappeared from her line of vision but returned moments later with a large knife. Kate clamped her teeth together. Was this the man who had taken the other missing women in the Bend? Was it her turn?

"Let me go. Now." She tugged her arms, glanced down and noticed the binding around her wrists.

She was helpless. Like a rat in a cat's mouth. A wave of panic washed through her as she envisioned her own death. Not like this. No, Lord, not like this.

"I've waited a long time for this moment, dear Kate."

A long time? "Please, let me up. Let me talk with you." She'd reason with him. Find a way to convince him to let her go free.

He waved the knife over her pounding heart. Kate clamped down on her bladder. She would not die a victim. The Bend was full of them. Not her. Please not her.

He moved the knife to her wrists as she tried not to squirm. Snap. He cut her wrist free, and then did the same to the other. Kate struggled to sit up. When she did, she discovered she'd been trapped in a long box made of wood.

Her captor stepped back. Still that sick smile covered his face. He crossed his arms, the knife blade pressed against his bicep. "Feeling better?"

Kate scanned the dark room. A small overhead bulb cast a shadow of light. A barn? A shed? Nothing else in the room except a chair, her box, and a bucket. A chain attached to the wall with an ankle shackle on the loose end lay next to the bucket. The horror of what he intended for her crashed into her mind. "Let me go, please. I won't tell anyone."

"Funny you should say that. I did that once. She lied. I don't do that anymore. Besides, I need you. I've been waiting for you a long time."

"What are you talking about? Why do you need me? I don't know you. You're my delivery man, that's all."

He held out his hand, ready for her to get out of her prison. Kate flinched when he grasped her fingers and pulled her upward. At first her legs melted, but she steadied them, climbing out onto the packed dirt floor.

She faced him.

Something tickled her memory.

"You're remembering, aren't you, my Kate?" A satisfied smug formed.

Remembering? She scoured his features. Where did she know him from besides the Bend? Had he been following her before? A reporter? "You want my story, don't you? I'll give it to you if you let me go."

He laughed. Threw his head back and laughed out loud. Maybe someone would hear him. Rescue her. She stepped to the side. His laughter died. "Don't try it. I always win."

Still her memory cells pricked her brain. One by one. That nose. Those eyes. Why did she think he looked familiar? "How do I know you?"

"Good girl. Now we're getting somewhere." He pointed to the lone chair. "Over there. Now."

She hobbled the ten feet to the chair then collapsed into it. Her mind raced for answers. They knew each other? Impossible. She would have remembered a man who looked like him. Handsome in a rugged way.

"How do I know you?" she asked again.

"Oh, you disappoint me, Kate. I've never forgotten you. How you picked your pepperoni off the crust, laid it to one side and then washed it down with your chocolate milk. And then there was Susan, your best friend, who tittered whenever a boy walked past. But my favorite memory is you on the playground jumping rope. You had little talent in that department."

Her mouth opened. It couldn't be.

He stepped closer, dangling the knife in front of her. "Keep thinking. You're almost there."

"Todd Logan." The name slipped from her memories. She stared into his wide-set eyes. His too handsome face. "The boy who should have died too."

84

Seth couldn't go back to the newspaper. Not after the way he'd behaved with Tim. No, he was on his own in the Bend. He did another quick tour of Kate's house, checking that she hadn't packed her suitcase and taken off. When finished, he left the way he entered, getting in the Jeep and turning left.

He would visit David. The only other person Kate had formed a relationship with in the Bend.

When he pulled up to the intercom, he almost changed his mind. He told himself he was overreacting. Should wait a day and call her tomorrow. But the sight of her purse and phone unattended told him otherwise. Too many women had gone missing since he'd arrived in the Bend. Kate was not going to make that one more.

He pressed the button. "May I help you?"

Earl's wife. "I need to talk with David. Is he home?" A lengthy silence ensued, followed by David's voice. "I'll meet you out front, Seth."

The gates opened. Seth drove through and parked by the visitor entrance. A light rain had begun when he left Kate's house, and now it had beat itself into a regular storm. Seth ducked and ran for cover beneath the porch. David met him at the door.

"Come on it. Looks like quite a storm. We'll be lucky to have power by dinner." Seth didn't answer but followed him into a room filled with books, and furniture out of the Victorian era. He didn't want to sit but paced in front of David who had seated himself by the fireplace.

"What's up? Change your mind about the woman?" David gave a relaxed stretch. He was kidding, right?

Seth was sure he didn't look like a man hoping for just any woman.

"No. I didn't. I figured you had gotten a call from Tim by now." Might as well throw it out there.

"A half hour ago. But a man can change his mind."

"I won't. I'm here on a different matter. It's about Kate."

David sat forward. His interest in her still obvious. Seth stopped. Did lover boy feel something for her? He wanted to ask but kept his mouth shut. It wouldn't do anyone any good. He pressed forward. "She's missing." He watched David for clues that he knew more than he let on.

David stood, furrowing his brows. "What are you talking about? Did she move?"

"No. I was just at her place. Her car is still there. So is her purse and phone." David's eyes widened.

"How long?"

"I saw her last night. She didn't show up for work, so I checked on her." He stepped closer to David. "If you did something to her, I swear I'll kill you."

David's mouth twisted into an angry scar. "You know better. I'm not a murderer, nor do I abduct women. You might not like some of our tactics, but we don't kill people to get what we want. It's much simpler than that."

Seth found himself in a stare down contest.

He looked away. He no longer believed the cult was capable of murder. Not after seeing Debbie and after attending the meeting. They wanted people to submit to them and had found a way through lofty promises. That's all it took.

"Will you help me find her?"

David let out a sigh. Guess he didn't want a fight any more than Seth did. "She broke it off with me."

Seth rolled his eyes. "Your point?"

What makes you think I can help? That's my point. I don't know any more about her than you probably do. Maybe she left her purse for a reason. A second purse?"

Seth hadn't thought about that possibility. He'd been so certain something was wrong. Did she have a friend he didn't know here in the Bend? Someone picked her up?

"A possibility." He eyed David again. Watched for some sign of guilt. When he found nothing, he frowned. "Sorry for busting in like this."

David dropped his hand on Seth's shoulder. "Call me tomorrow if she doesn't turn up."

Sure. He'd get on his high horse and trot right out here again. Seth nodded, left the house as fast as he could without running. He got back into his Jeep and punched Kate's number in the phone. "Pick up. Please pick up."

Nothing.

He threw his cell down. What woman leaves the house without her phone?

###

She remembered him, all right. Fresh chills rolled through Todd's body. She remembered him. All those years of thinking about her. Planning for this day. This moment. She remembered him!

"I never forgot you." His tone sounded almost accusatory. He didn't want it to. She remembered, and that was all that counted. "Now we can move forward."

The chain lay at his feet. As he bent for the clasp, a thunder of pain shot through his head. He rocked back on his heels as Kate leaped from her chair and rushed to the door. Todd recovered from her kick and threw himself at her. Tackled her to the floor with a heavy thud. "You aren't getting away that easy. Not after all this time," he whispered into her ear as she panted beneath him.

"Let me go. Please, Todd. Let me go, and I won't say a word."

He hauled her to her feet. "Begging doesn't become you, Kate. I've seen you in action." He shoved her back into the chair and snapped the heavy chain around her leg. Sweat dripped from Kate's face, marring her beautiful profile. Pity. He didn't like messy women.

She grabbed his arm. "What do you want from me? Can't we talk?"

He shook her off. "We'll have plenty of time to talk. I've waited twenty years." He laid his hand on her flaming red hair. Stroked it.

But first he had other work to do. Final preparations. With a last lingering look at his final capture, he flipped off the light switch and left her in the darkness.

He crossed the yard to the house he'd rented when he came to the Bend days after Kate arrived. Like hers, the rooms were bare, filled with garbage furniture his mother would have demanded his father haul to the dump. He liked it like this, though. Easy to leave. Easy to forget.

He moved through the living room toward the second bedroom. The room he used to prepare.

He turned on the light he purchased at a junk store. With three one-hundred-watt bulbs, the light glared down on the folding table also purchased when he got here. He kicked aside a stool, preferring to stand over his work. His best work. Wires, tools, and enough explosives to blow up three buildings.

He hadn't spent his entire life interviewing candidates.

Meeting JC when he was fifteen changed his life. The kid with hair down to his shoulders and a scar across his left cheek found Todd behind the high school the day Todd skipped history class because the teacher pointed out his stupidity about WWII.

JC promised to teach him something better.

They crossed the empty football field, climbed the bank, and ping-ponged through a grove of elm trees until JC opened cellar doors to a house that needed more than a paint job. Cobwebs attacked Todd's mouth as they descended. He soon forgot the nastiness when JC showed Todd his *work.* Seems JC had big plans like his old friend Burke, whose pieces lay beneath an unmarked stone in Ellis Cemetery.

JCs eyes glowed as he showed Todd how the parts could change the direction of his life. Their lives.

Only Todd had a direction already. Her name was Kate.

He spent the remaining afternoons, when history class commenced, deep in JC's basement learning.

Soon he would put that schooling to good use.

He shut the door on his room. His stomach reminded him he hadn't eaten all day. He opened the fridge and took out a pepperoni pizza. Thirty minutes later, he shoved the last piece of crust into his mouth.

Kate would be starving by now.

Instead of taking care of that small matter, he showered and climbed into bed.

85

Going home was not an option. Seth finished the rest of the can of tuna he found at the back of Kate's cupboard before rummaging through a closet for a spare blanket. Instead, he found a quilt that looked like she'd dragged it across the country. He stretched out on the couch, immediately regretting his decision to not borrow her bed, but he was too tired to get up.

Her phone had not rung again. He charged it up as soon as he returned and scanned the contact list for a clue. Only three numbers were listed. The paper. Him and her friend. What kind of life had she lived? Running from the media. Unable to make long lasting relationships for fear of moving or telling someone about her curse.

Sympathy was not Seth's strongest point. But something about Kate—the way she'd pushed to find the missing women and stop Earl from taking over the Bend—impressed him. He hated to admit it but he believed her about the church and what might happen.

The day after tomorrow.

Maybe he could get Earl to cancel.

Sure. As if that would happen. The man thrived from social adoration. He'd never give up the chance to further his agenda. His adoring followers will probably beat the church doors down to get a front row seat.

He shifted the pillow beneath his head, trying for comfort.

Kate's phone rang. Seth lunged for it. "Hello?"

"It's me, David. Seth?"

Seth let out his breath. "Do you have news?"

"No, I was hoping you did. Listen, I spoke with my brother. He's willing to help you find Kate. He took a liking to her."

"I'm not sure that's a good thing."

"Listen to what I'm saying. He said at first light, he'd put the word out among town that she's missing. The sheriff will probably come by her place. Can you let him in?"

Seth looked around the dark room. "Not a problem. I don't think he'll find much. She lives like a monk. The only thing I found was packed dirt and a shred of cardboard. Like she'd gotten a recent delivery."

"A delivery?"

Seth smacked his pillow with his fist. "Why didn't I think of that? Who delivers the mail on this side of town?"

"Old Joe. He's been with the postal department over forty years. Kate could touch him with her finger and he'd fall over. Listen, you might be on to something though. Let me run it by others."

Seth hung up but couldn't fall back to sleep. A delivery man? Why would that even be a possibility?

But it was.

86

Kate's ankle burned where the shackle cut into it. Her throat felt as though someone had torched it. She slumped down onto the chair where she'd spent the night, being careful with her bad leg. After slamming her feet into Todd's head, her leg might never recover.

A sliver of light crept under the door and around the blocked window. Would she see daylight again?

Her lips trembled with uncertainty. She strained one more time to loosen the bolt on the wall with no success. Although he had left her hands free, he'd made certain everything around her was more secure than a bank. And it was cold. Ice could form in this room. Downright miserable. Already her chest wheezed.

And her stomach. Beyond hungry. Would he leave her to die of starvation or thirst? Surely that wasn't his plan. But what was it? She tried to remember Todd as a boy, back when she knew him. A distinct memory of him helping her when she fell outside bobbed to the surface. There had been kindness in him. After the blast, she changed schools. What had become of him? The shock that she knew her captor still had not worn off.

Yet if there was one ounce of kindness left in the man, she would find it. She'd convince him to let her go. Let her return to what little life she had.

Footfalls outside the door slashed into her thoughts.

A larger cone of light shone in as the door opened. A shadow of the man who threatened her life stood in the doorway. She bit back the whimper that rose to the back of her throat. No. She would not give him what he wanted.

Instead, she straightened her back—pressed it hard against the chair.

Waited as the light grew stronger.

Seth woke, shook his hands and feet. The horsehair couch had been harder than the floor. He checked the time. Early. Sunlight filtered in through the curtains.

Where was she?

The longer she didn't return, the more likely she wouldn't. Exactly like the other women in the Bend. Seth shook his thoughts. He would not go there. Not yet. Besides, the sheriff would show up here later, and maybe he'd have a better explanation.

He considered again the idea that a delivery man might have played a part in her disappearance. Seth turned on Kate's computer and punched in delivery services for the Bend. Nothing. His fingers paused above the keys. Unless. The hardware store accepted and shipped packages. How come he didn't know that?

He plunged out of the chair and grabbed his wallet and keys. He'd make a quick visit to town before the sheriff got out of bed. Seth climbed into his Jeep, turned left as he pulled out of Kate's driveway, and headed across the bridge. Hank's Hardware store was located at the east edge of town along the river. When Seth moved to the Bend, he thought the rundown building was a feed mill, but upon further inspection, learned Hank sold everything from shovels to light bulbs. For Easter, he invested in dozens of colored chicks for brats to buy and let die ten days later. Did the same at Christmas with puppies. A woman in the neighboring town ran a puppy mill and sold her runts at half price. Rumor had it. Seth had never been able to confirm that with Hank.

He pulled into an empty parking space out front. Two other pickups were parked near a loading dock. Seth sidestepped three buckets in the walkway and detoured around a couple of ladders. He found Hank behind the wooden counter drinking a Coke.

Hank brushed his balding head with his palm, then held out his hand toward Seth. "If it isn't our popular newsman. What brings you my way, Seth?"

Seth shook the offered hand despite his urge to ignore it. Any information Hank could offer about Kate's whereabouts was worth a few germs. "I saw online you run a delivery service out of here. News to me. Want to tell me about it?"

Hank puffed out his shoulders and pulled on his belt until Seth was certain he'd given himself a wedgie.

"Been doing it now for about six months. Got a deal with UPS in the city. People can drop off packages, and my delivery man makes the runs. Doing quite a bit of out-of-town business now too." His smile produced gaping spaces at the back of his mouth.

"Mind telling me who does your local deliveries?" Seth leaned against the counter. Plunked a toothpick in his mouth. What he wouldn't give for a cigarette right now. He could almost eat the thick smell of nicotine that blasted from Hank's skin.

"Got me a good guy. Always on time. Punctual. Keeps his nose clean." Hank glanced toward a door behind the tool section. "He didn't show today, or I would introduce you. Said he had a prior commitment he needed to deal with. Okay by me as he never misses. Why the interest?"

A prior commitment? A rush of fear for Kate overtook him. Could David have been right? "Can I get his name and where he lives? It's important."

"Now, you know I can't do that. Private information. Confidential, I think they call it. Come back in tomorrow, and I'll introduce you." Hank reached for a jar filled with peppermint candies and popped one in his mouth. He held the jar out to Seth.

"I promise I have a good reason." He was not going to tell this buffoon what his concerns were yet. If he was wrong . . .

Hank held up his ink smeared hands. "Sorry. Like I said, come back tomorrow and I'll introduce you."

Tomorrow. Another twenty-four hours. His frustration built. "Thanks anyway, Hank." Seth turned and charged out of the store toward his vehicle. Maybe the sheriff would get the information for him. Confidentiality. Seth spit into the road. Like that idiot knew what the word meant.

He roared out of the parking lot. He had another idea.

87

The Trainer opened the door to find Kate, his beloved, waiting for him where he left her the night before. Sure, she looked a little peaked. A little worn. But he'd fix that. He'd fix everything eventually. In his right hand, he grasped a bottle of water. Couldn't let her suffer too much during the training process. He needed her to be able to walk upright tomorrow.

"Good morning. How did you sleep?"

Kate remained rigid in her chair. Good girl. Trying her best to appeal to his sense of right and wrong. How quickly she'd discover that only what he wanted would appease him. He held up the bottle. Jiggled the water.

Her tongue came out and licked her bottom lip. Someone was thirsty. They all came around sooner or later when they got like this. He set the bottle on the floor two feet from her. "Hungry, too? If you're good today, I might be able to drum up a slice of pizza or a sub from the deli in town. I hear they make a mean Italian."

"You're being cruel, Todd. That's not how I remember you. What happened to the boy who helped when I fell on the playground?"

That memory of them surged through his chest like fire. "I'm not being cruel. I'm doing what is best for you. For both of us."

"Kidnapping me? Tying me up like an animal?" Her eyes shone with unshed tears. Good. He would let her vent awhile longer. Get her anger out of her system. Sometimes they needed to do that. But especially Kate since she was the special one.

He slipped the knife from the holster he'd attached to his belt and moved closer.

Kate gasped.

Just like he wanted. Maybe her training would be finished sooner than he expected. He wiped the blade across his thigh. "You aren't an animal, Kate. On the contrary, you're special to me. We have history. We have purpose together."

"What are you talking about? We were friends once. Is that our history? Friends don't do this to each other, Todd. Do they? You must remember how you walked me home from school. How you sat with me in the cafeteria, and I shared my rolls with you. Don't you remember how you liked me?" Her voice escalated. Struck a nerve inside of him.

Of course he remembered. Why would he spend all these years on anyone else if he didn't remember? But she'd forgotten the most important aspect of their past.

"Keep digging. Maybe you'll remember the most crucial part of our history."

She was dealing with a crazy man. Kate kept her shoulders firm, determined to show Todd that she was strong. Not a woman who would give in to his threats. But she was so thirsty. Hungry. How dare he bring water and set it at her feet where she couldn't reach it.

She twisted her gaze to the knife he held in his hand. Surely, he wouldn't hurt her. She must keep talking—get him to remember the old Todd—not this monster before her.

"Do you remember the day my mother and I stopped by your house when you didn't show up to school for a week? I was worried about you. Me. Only me. My mother spoke with your mother as I stood next to her." She would tell him what she knew about his sordid life.

Her captor flinched.

Kate pressed on. She needed to find that crack that would make him release her.

"Your mother. I saw your mother that day. I never told you because there wasn't a chance. She could hardly talk. She was drunk, Todd. I discovered your secret—why you wore clothing that needed washing. Why you never brought a lunch to school or had enough money to purchase one. She didn't take care of you, and you hid it from me."

His face caved in. He sucked in air and wheeled away from her toward the door where he had entered.

"I cared about you! Me! And now I hope you'll care about me the same way!" she shouted at him, her throat raspy from her earlier screams.

Todd twisted around—his face a mask. "I do care about you. That's the whole reason I must do what I will do tomorrow. You'll see then. You'll see how much I do care." He swerved toward her, plucked up the bottle of water, and tore from the room.

Kate trembled, felt her fears rising to the surface again. What did he mean about tomorrow? What sickening plan did he have for her that he must keep her tied like a wild animal? She strained again on the bolt in the wall and collapsed into her chair.

###

Seth parked in the newspaper parking lot. Another storm ripped across the skies, hurling leaves around his feet. Did the sun ever shine in the Bend? He hunched down and ran the final steps to the door. Rhonda glanced up when he entered. "I thought you quit," she said. Three bottles of nail polish were lined up on the most recent edition of the paper.

"I did. Now I want to see Tim again."

She nodded toward the back area. "He was screaming in his phone the last I heard. See for yourself."

He brushed past the front desk. Tim was staring out the window when Seth tromped into his office. He didn't turn to acknowledge Seth but spoke. "That didn't take long."

"I don't want my job back."

Tim's gaze swung around to meet his. "Kate?"

"You heard?" He dropped into the chair across from the desk. Like old times. Only nothing was the same. His boss belonged to a cult that owned the town. Tried to own him. "She's been missing since yesterday. Do you know anything?"

Tim chuckled. "So now you have me pegged as a kidnapper? Funny. And here I used to think you would one day be a star reporter. You're on the wrong scent, Seth. I don't know where she went or what she's doing. For all we know, she's disappeared on purpose to draw attention to herself or to Earl's cause. She didn't strike me at first as that kind of girl, but now that I think about it . . ." He removed his glasses and placed them in the empty space between them. "Let it go. Let her go. She'll show up one day, and we'll wonder why we worried for one minute."

Tim's tone crawled inside his gut. How did he work for this piece of dirt for over a year? He stood. "If it doesn't hurt too much, call me if you hear anything. You're wrong about Kate."

"Like I was about you?" His lips curled over his teeth.

It was all Seth could do to restrain himself from punching those suckers down his throat. Instead, he stormed from the room to the outside. Rain pelted his bare head as he raced to his Jeep. He'd return to Kate's to wait for the sheriff.

The ten-year-old Pontiac that passed as the Bend's only official vehicle was parked out front of her house when he arrived. It looked like the sheriff had just gotten there. He hadn't left his car yet. But then Oscar did as little as he could. Passed go and collected his two hundred bucks each week. The

Bend couldn't afford more than that, so Oscar tended bar at Billy's Pub two nights a week along with the money his wife collected as a bank teller.

Seth tapped on the car window. The rain had changed to a light drizzle, but water still dripped from his nose. "Coming in?" He tilted his chin toward the house

Oscar huffed, grabbed his clipboard. He lumbered after Seth through the back door where Seth had broken the window. Oscar paused, looked down, and then eyed him. "Going to have to report this."

Seth didn't have time for dramatics. "I'll pay for it."

He led the sheriff through the kitchen into the living room. "I found this." He showed him the piece of cardboard he'd discovered on the floor. "What do you think?" Oscar got into character and scouted the room like Sherlock Holmes. "I also found mud that looked like it came from treads."

When the sheriff completed his round of the cottage, he stopped in the middle of the living room floor and scratched his scraggly beard. "She's gone all right. No woman leaves her purse or phone."

Seth rolled his eyes. "What can we do? I've looked everywhere, and she doesn't know anyone in town. You know, other women have gone missing . . ."

"Now don't go getting all up in arms about Earl. Those women choose their lifestyle. It's for the best. We don't force them to go."

Seth was wasting his time. He ought to be out knocking on doors—something. "Think I should call the state boys?"

"Now you're overreacting. Let's give it another couple of days. I'll make an announcement at the rally tomorrow. Someone will have seen her. A pretty girl like her doesn't just disappear."

Seth couldn't help but think of Becky and how she looked after being pulled from the river. After Oscar left, he returned to Kate's computer. Fired it up. He clicked on pictures and scrolled through them. He gave her points for organization. Every photo had a location and date attached to it. The library's awards ceremony, the hardware store's annual event, the fireman's parade. He clicked through a few more and came upon the ones she took that day of the theater fire.

His heart slowed. Seth bent his head. Whispered a prayer. It felt unnatural on his lips, but so did the image seared on his brain that Kate might suffer a similar fate.

88

The Trainer changed into his work uniform. He could not let himself become distracted with Kate's words. She was trying to disarm him—make him change his plans—plans he'd developed for twenty years. Tomorrow, tomorrow they would finalize!

He checked the time. He would need to run to the hardware store to borrow the truck. Hopefully, Hank would be occupied with customers and never notice.

The room next to his bedroom held more than his undelivered office supplies. He wound his way to the back table where several boxes were piled. The order for the church's monthly supply of bulletins and paper were stacked in the middle. He'd swiped them from the truck when they came in for delivery. What was one more day? But the important box—the one containing his bomb—waited next to them.

The sun finally came out as he steered his truck across the flats toward town. When he neared Hank's Hardware, he noticed his boss's car was gone. That meant only Sylvia would be working the counter. The ditz had no clue to his real work schedule. All she did was blow him kisses enough to make him gag. If he had more time to spare, he would put an end to that.

He parked in the back next to his delivery truck. Within minutes, he had transferred the load of boxes to the back of the truck. He clambered into the driver's seat and drove the five miles to the church where the rally was planned for tomorrow. As he hoped, only one vehicle sat in the empty parking lot. Evelyn. The church's ancient cleaning woman. The pastor and secretary never worked Tuesdays. He'd done his homework well. A swell of excitement surged through his chest. His fingers tingled as he rounded the truck to the back and loaded the boxes onto his cart.

So easy. This plan was unfolding exactly as he envisioned it, nights lying alone in bed thinking about Kate and how the two of them would be together for eternity. Death—the final chapter of their story.

Evelyn looked up as he opened the side door. She put her mop aside. "Don't slip. I just mopped and don't want to pick you up." She showed her nicotine-stained teeth.

"Would never want to do that to you, darling." The Trainer gave her a gentle pat on her arm which produced the expected giggle. Fat old broad. He hoped she showed up for the rally.

"You men. Never could get my work done with a handsome character like you around. Go right on with those packages to the storage room where you always put them." She shook her head with her annoying smile once more.

The Trainer saluted and gave her what she wanted—another seductive stroke on her arm. Then he wheeled his special delivery into the room that was filled with two long, folding tables. With as much care as he could muster, he stacked the boxes on the table but placed his special one beneath the table against the sanctuary wall.

Evelyn's whistling drew closer.

The Trainer looked over his shoulder. He could finish Evelyn off now. One less person later. Her inane conversation was pushing him to the limit. He stuck his head out into the hallway. "Darling, do you have a minute? I'm having trouble in here."

His voice echoed down the empty hallway.

"Evelyn?"

He tipped his head. Listened.

Nothing.

The Trainer unfolded his fingers. Shrugged. One more day. What did it matter?

89

Her stomach roared from hunger. Kate lifted her head from the cold floor of her prison. When would Todd return? Would he bring his knife with him? She fingered her jeans' pocket. Yes, it was still there. Her pocketknife. She'd tried using it to cut through the chain but thought better of it after two strikes. Why dull the blade? She might need to use it on Todd.

She rose to her knees, wincing at the pain that shot through her leg. He hadn't patted her down either. He acted almost afraid to touch her. That realization gave her hope. Perhaps because of their long-ago friendship, he would discover he couldn't hurt her.

Very little light crept beneath the doorway any longer. When would he return?

She licked her cracked lips again. She would ask for a drink. A sip. Anything. She would tell him that she would not be able to do what he asked unless he cared for her basic needs.

Kate thought of Seth next. Was he worried about her? She didn't show up to work yesterday or today. Would he look for her like they did Debbie and Shelly, or would he say good riddance? She had grown to care about him, though she hated to admit it. Seth could be a huge pain at times—always looking for the next big story. Acting tough when he was worried much like her. She thought about their trek through the woods to the cabins. She'd been scared but didn't want to show it. Seth made sure she succeeded.

She wiped her eyes. If only she was climbing that mountain again. Not this. Trapped and tortured. Her jaw trembled as she considered her fate. Would he return soon? To kill her?

As she struggled to rise to her wobbly legs, the door opened. The last rays of orange sunlight filtered in behind Todd. Her breath caught in her throat. She backed up to her chair. Todd crossed the threshold and shut the door. He flipped a switch and a more powerful overhead light bulb illuminated his handsome features. Yes, he was handsome. Not the homely boy she remembered.

"Please may I have water? It's been so long."

He pulled his hand from behind his back. A bottle of water. A bag she recognized from the diner as well. "If I give you this, will you behave?"

She would jump through hoops for water. Exactly what he wanted. "Yes. Please. I'm so thirsty."

Satisfied with her promise, he tossed the water to her feet. Kate lunged for it like a dog for a bone. She opened the cap with fingers that had lost their life. Finally. She poured it into her mouth, swallowed, coughed, and gagged.

"Slowly or you'll throw it all up."

She followed his orders. Drank slower. Felt the refreshing liquid coat her parched throat. When the bottle was empty, she held it out for more. Like he wanted.

Instead of answering her, he moved to the far wall and crouched. With slow deliberate movements, he pulled out a juicy burger and raised it to his mouth. Kate sunk into her chair. The beefy aroma reached her nostrils, torturing her. She would faint soon. Maybe that would be best. She could black out this horror.

Todd chewed slowly. Took another huge bite. When he was nearly finished, he tossed the remaining piece to her. Kate once again lunged from her chair and scooped up the dirty piece of burger. She forced it between cracked lips, chewed, and mercifully swallowed. The tiny offering did nothing to satisfy her. She eyed the floor for crumbs. Seeing no more, she remained seated on the floor while Todd watched her.

How long would this torture last? She must think of a way to escape. But her body was so weak now. So hungry. She didn't have the strength to move back to the chair.

Todd laughed. "Sorry I don't have more to share. But tomorrow you won't care. Neither will I."

"What do you mean? What's tomorrow?" At least she had one more day to find a way out. If only she could gain her strength. But that's what he was counting on. That she would grow weaker and weaker and beg him to kill her. She fisted her hands. Never.

Todd pushed up from his squat and stood. He reached into his back pocket and pulled out a worn leather wallet. "I've carried this picture for twenty years. Do you remember when it was taken?"

He tossed the photo to her. Kate watched it flutter to a dead stop. A black and whiteout-of-focus picture. Before picking it up, she glanced upward to her captive. "What are you doing? Please let me go. In God's name, stop this before it goes any farther."

A hard look filled his dark eyes. "Pick it up, Kate."

She picked up the creased photo. Blinked. Tried to clear her vision. "I remember this day. Mrs. Graham took it. At play practice." She studied the way Todd looked as a twelve-year old boy, his shoulder touching hers as he smiled. This was the last photo her teacher took. The last photo taken of Kate when she was loved by her parents and a brother. She fought back burning tears. Licked salty ones that escaped.

"You do remember. I see that now." Todd's voice came to her in a whisper. "You remember how close we were. More than good friends, my Kate. Much more."

She shook her head. He didn't remember the sadness connected with this photo at all. He remembered a deeper level of friendship that never existed. She poured over the picture once more. Torturing herself. Then she gasped. Dropped the picture to the floor. No! It couldn't be.

The auras. She'd seen the auras.

Around both of them.

90

Seth threw his cell phone to the counter in his kitchen. Daisy gave a low rumble when he shifted her off his lap. The second night since Kate had left them. Where was she? Why didn't she call?

He strode to his fridge to take out one last piece of pizza. Thin circles of pepperoni clung to it as he folded it into his mouth.

He'd called David again, and the sheriff and Doc, but no one had any idea about Kate's whereabouts. It was as though she had disappeared into thin air. If no one came forward with news at the rally tomorrow, he would call the State Police. Forget what anyone thought. Something was wrong.

He reached to turn off the lights when a light tap at his door stopped him. Seth grabbed a knife from the drawer. His breathing surged. No one but Kate knew where he lived. Kate and whoever clobbered him over his head. He inched closer to the door, his knife raised.

Another tap.

He heard a cough and then shoes shuffling on his porch. Whoever it was didn't care that they were heard. He flipped on the outside light.

Let me in, Seth. I'm going to ruin my hair in this mist."

Rhonda. "What are you doing out this late? Get in here." Of course. Tim and Rhonda knew where he lived. He'd given them the information for the files. Rhonda wore a light raincoat and carried a pointed umbrella that looked like it could do damage should she freak out. She stomped her feet on his catchall rug before pushing past him into his kitchen.

"Nice place. How much do you pay in rent?" She opened his refrigerator, then perched her behind on one of his two chairs. Really? he wanted to ask. His rent?

She patted the chair next to her. "Sit. I didn't come all the way out here for you to be rude. I would have called but my phone died. Imagine. I bought it six months ago. Besides, who took such good care of you with Tim? Me."

She was right. Rhonda detoured Tim away from him on more than one occasion. He owed her politeness. He straddled the chair across from her. "Is it about Kate?"

Her face clouded. "I can't believe she's missing. I don't want her to end up like that other girl did. Dumped in the river without a breath left in her." She picked at her long nail. "It might be nothing, but I was all tucked into bed when I thought of something that might help. I would have gone to our illustrious sheriff, but he's tending bar tonight and well, you know how that will go."

"Rhonda—what do you know?"

Again, she studied those ridiculous nails. Purple today. Did the woman ever think that natural might not be so bad? He growled like Daisy.

"Okay, okay. I was lying there in bed, watching the Wheel. It's my favorite show, you know, when this little niggling thought kept tap-tapping away at my mind."

Honestly, he wanted to reach over and strangle her.

"Then I thought, this might be something. Seth is the one to tell."

"Rhonda, you're killing me. Get it out. What do I need to know?"

She waved her fingers at him. "Okay, okay. You see every day at about two, we get our deliveries. Sometimes it's only a few items, other days it might be a bigger order I placed. Remember when you wanted those black pens that didn't stick when you clicked them?"

Seth left his chair. Stood over her. "You got them. I remember."

"Well, getting to my point . . ." she said. "Every time the delivery man dropped off my supplies he asked me about Kate. I finally asked if he knew her and why didn't he talk to her himself. He kind of blushed and said he was shy. Can't believe that one. What a hunk of a man he is. If he had only looked my way . . ."

Seth stopped pacing. "You say he asked about Kate? More than once?"

Rhonda nodded. "All the time. It was like he was obsessed with her or something. Wanted to know where she ate lunch, where she shopped, but I didn't tell him where she lived. No sir, I didn't." She looked up at Seth. The woman had tears in her eyes. "Did I speak out of turn?"

Seth dropped his hand on her shoulder. "I know how you feel about Kate. Thank you. This helps." Another pat. He needed to get her out the door, so he could get into his computer. He would find where Hank's guy lived with or without Hank's help.

91

Kate did not want to believe her eyes. Two bright auras. Around Todd and her. She met his gaze across the room. He planned to kill both of them.

What are you going to do?" She must know. It would be the only way she had a chance to live.

Todd stepped closer, swooped to snatch up the picture. "I don't need this anymore. I have the real thing." He tore the photo in half and tossed it to the ground again. "Sleep tight, my sweetheart. Tomorrow is going to be a big day for you and me."

Wait, don't go! Tell me what you've planned. I . . . I want to be excited too. It's been so long since I've seen you. Can't you talk with me? Please?" She hated groveling.

He liked it. He leaned against the door and crossed his arms. "I'm actually excited about it. It's been twenty years in the making."

"Twenty years? What are you talking about?"

"Surely you don't remember? You who have been running from what happened all this time. Avoiding the press, lying to friends and coworkers afraid of your own shadow." He tsked with his tongue. "Not a pretty way to live your life."

"The bombing. You're talking about that, aren't you? But you weren't there that day. You stayed home. I remember." After the killings, her grandmother had told her about the one boy who remained in her class. At the time, she hadn't cared. All she cared about was her family who would never tell her they loved her again. "You were spared, Todd."

He moved nearer, his eyes glazing over. "Is that what you call it?"

"But you lived. You didn't lose everyone like I did."

"No. I didn't lose anyone. Only my entire class and teacher and the only support system I had in the world. You of all people must remember how it felt to have someone shove a microphone in your face and ask how you felt being one of two survivors. How it felt to go to bed at night burdened with guilt because you survived and no one else did! You of all people must understand!" He screamed his last sentence. Tears shone in his eyes.

Kate scrunched backward as though he had physically struck her. Survivor's guilt. Todd wished he had died with everyone else. Like her.

He left her huddled by the wall the entire night. She was hungry and thirsty, and every part of her body ached. The dread of what Todd planned to do lassoed her throat. After the bombing, her grandmother made her attend a support group of other accident survivors. Cars, fires . . . your-run-of-the-mill accidents. Nothing like the one she lived through. No one understood the depth of her grief nor how badly she wished she had died too. No one but one person.

Her name was Julie. She was fifteen. A few years older than Kate. Julie's mother had died in a bus accident along with twenty-seven other victims. Julie was thrown clear when the bus smashed into a guardrail and tumbled down an icy hillside into a river. She had come to long enough to watch the bus sink taking her mother with her. She attended the support group with Kate three times. At the fourth meeting, the facilitator asked that they say a short prayer for Julie. She'd tried to kill herself.

Kate never returned to that meeting. She didn't want to know what happened to Julie. If she succeeded or not. Kate told her grandmother that she was dealing with everything better now and wanted to return to school.

Her grandmother believed her. Eventually, Kate believed herself.

Todd didn't. He may have been planning her capture for twenty years. But what was his final mission to be? She tried to remember what day tomorrow was. Wednesday. The rally.

She pulled herself to her feet and shuffled to her chair. What would the rally have to do with Todd? It would be packed. Brother Earl always spoke to a good crowd.

Her thoughts froze. A big crowd. Like their school.

A frenzy of fear grasped her. No. He wouldn't do that. She stood and pulled again at the chain that bound her leg to the wall. *Please,* she whispered. Nothing. By now, the day's shafts of sunlight had almost disappeared. Kate forced herself to calm down. She must think. Somehow she must stop him from killing her and other innocent people. But how?

Minutes later, the door opened again letting the remaining light fall onto the empty box in the middle of the room. "I thought I might better prepare you for tomorrow." He dangled the key to her chains in front of him.

"Please, don't hurt me. Please. Let me go. In the name of our friendship, let me go." She would get on her knees if she had to in order to convince him to stop any crazy plan he might have. He ignored her pleas and unlocked the shackle from her leg. It fell to the floor in a heap. The instant relief she felt was cut short as he dragged her broken body toward the box. He lifted her in.

"A little time in here will make you much more willing to work with me tomorrow. Nite nite, Kate." He slammed the lid shut—casting her again into darkness. She heard another lock before she heard footfalls leading to the door.

She'd never liked being confined to narrow spaces. She dug for her knife and popped it open. Inch by inch, she tried unsuccessfully to fit the blade into the crevice of the lid. When nothing worked, she tried to control her breathing. Inhale. Exhale. Slowly. Purposely. She counted from one hundred to zero forward and backward. She imagined sunny days by a lake. Picnics near waterfalls. Anything. Anything at all to keep her worst fear from coming true. Dying in a coffin.

92

The brief show of sun didn't last. Instead, the sky over Seth's cabin filled with clouds as he raced to his Jeep. He hadn't slept at all last night after finding nothing about Hank's delivery man. He'd considered calling the sheriff first thing this morning but changed his mind. He was probably sleeping off a drunk. David had contacted Seth early though, telling him again how sorry he was that Kate was missing and that he would announce her disappearance today at the rally.

He didn't sound too positive. Seth figured everyone thought Kate took off. Left her life behind and took off because she couldn't deal with the Bend's way of life.

Stupid. That's what he thought of that theory. Kate was no more afraid of the cult in the Bend than she was of dying. She was taken and that was that. Where, he didn't have a clue, but he was determined to find out. First, he would see Hank again. He would find out more about that delivery man if it meant a fist between him and Hank.

His stomach growled as he drove out his driveway. He hadn't stopped to eat breakfast. Plenty of time to stuff his face later. Right now he needed answers.

As he drove through town, he studied the few people who littered the streets. Stooped, dressed in clothing that hung on bodies bent over by the coming storm. Where were all the people who had not followed Earl? Had they moved on? Left what they had and disappeared?

After he found Kate, he would be history here too. He probably had stayed too long as it was. Why he hadn't discovered Tim's involvement before now angered him. Seth prided himself on being sharp. That he could read people. But he'd seriously messed up with Tim.

Had he Kate? His foot touched the brake. What if Kate had gone to the cottages on her own? What if David and Earl were hiding the fact that she now lived behind their funeral home? Seth swerved to the side of the road.

Stranger things had happened. Like Debbie? She'd left her car open, her purse behind. When they finally found her, she said she was happy. Wanted to live there.

"Foolish," Seth whispered to himself. But was he the fool or Kate?

He backed up. Turned his Jeep toward the west.

It wouldn't hurt to turn over one more stone.

93

Kate couldn't breathe. The darkness in her coffin pressed down upon her chest like a bag of rocks. Her mind played tricks on her too. She thought she had died and this was hell. No light. No sound. Nothingness. She could still hear her breathing in her ears. In and out. Labored. Torturing her. Louder and louder. She pounded on the lid. She clawed the wood with fingers raw from attempts. Her feet ached from kicking.

Nothing.

No one.

Was not even God going to help?

If she could will herself to die, she would. If only her breathing would not come so loud. Over and over and over in her ears. Filling the space between her and freedom.

Please.

Please.

Her ears filled with tears that no longer stung as they rolled from her eyes. She would die in this box. No one would ever find her until the skin had rotted off her skeleton. They would find her knife, rusty with age, beside brittle bones.

Her knife. Of course.

She felt for it where it lay next to her. Useless with the hard wood. Her fingers flipped the blade open.

Did she have the energy to slice as deep as she needed? She raised her wrist to her chest. Steadied the knife next to it.

Yes. Dying by her own hand would be better than this torture.

What little sanity remained in her fought her decision at first. Then reason overtook her. She pricked her skin. To see how it felt.

A warmth filled her. Yes, this is how she must do it. She wouldn't let a madman take credit for her death. She would decide.

Now. It must be now before he returned.

Kate lifted the knife and pressed it to her wrist.

###

The Trainer checked the clock over his refrigerator. It was time for the final part of his plan to begin. He gathered the two bags he'd filled earlier, then he grabbed the keys to the shed. His mounting excitement coursed through every vein in his body. The weather was perfect, too. Overcast, dark. Exactly the kind of weather that drew people to a rally. No reason to stay home. No, they would come out in droves. Fill the church to the rafters.

He laughed out loud.

Foolish, stupid people.

Like lambs to the slaughter, like his father said about the cult in his town.

Only this time he would be doing the slaughtering.

He crossed the yard, kicking dead leaves with his boots. It wouldn't be long before winter descended. His least favorite time of the year. He never was able to forget how cold he had been walking to school without a proper coat. Neither his mother nor father worried about how he dressed. But his classmates did. They teased him at every opportunity.

Except Kate.

Darling Kate.

To die with her in his arms would be an honor.

He hoped she was ready to comply with his wishes. He didn't want to force her but would do what it took to finish this day as planned.

He unlocked the shed. Set the bags to the side and crossed the room to the coffin. He swiftly unlocked it and raised the lid.

"No!" he shouted at the bloody raised arm. Kate stared up at him with open eyes, blinking. He pressed both hands against her wrist. "You aren't going to die this way! Not like this!" He let go of her and raced for a piece of clothing from the bag. He pressed it against the gash, holding it until he was certain it stopped the bleeding.

"I'll die by my own hand. Not by yours."

"Then you should have tried harder, my love." Todd yanked her upward. Kate gasped as he lifted her from her coffin and carried her to the chair. He found the knife still clutched in her other fist.

"You have cost me time." He yanked the knife away from her and threw it outside the shed. After chaining her to the wall, he returned with bucket of water and a rag.

"Clean yourself up," he said. He kicked the bag of clothing with his toe. When you're done, put these on. It's almost showtime."

He unlocked the chain around her ankle one last time. Squatting in front of her, he smiled. "You will do as I ask from here out. If you don't, your friend Seth will pay the price. Do you hear me? I know where he lives. And let's say that I know his house, his car, his routine intimately. Do you understand me? A bomb can easily be activated."

She was smart enough to nod her head. Good girl.

94

Seth pounded on the private entry door to Earl's house. When he didn't get an immediate reply, he burst into the dim hallway uninvited. He'd been lucky the front gate had been open when he arrived. A funeral for old lady Dennis—the sign announced on the front porch. Only three cars. He met her once. Never smiled. That's what she gets. A private funeral.

Organ music sounded through the walls. He ignored it and worked his way through the dining room toward the kitchen. If Kate was here, he would find her. He sidestepped a pile of books and headed toward the back door. Seth exited the house, crossed the porch, and stormed toward the path that led to the cabins. All clear. So far. He looked over his shoulder expecting David to tackle him any second. No one.

Satisfied he hadn't been noticed, he punched in the same code Kate used when she got into the compound. He was in. No stranger to the layout, he circled the area until he found Debbie's cabin near the cluster of trees against the mountain. Still he passed no one. A part of him wondered where all the women and children had gone.

He knocked hard on her door. Debbie opened it, staring at him with a curious expression. The same long skirt and white blouse. "What are you doing here, Seth? I meant what I said." She stepped outside and peered around. "Go, now."

Instead of leaving, he stepped closer. No brainwashed woman was stopping him today. "I came for Kate. Where is she?"

Debbie slid her hand into her pocket. "She isn't here. You must leave. Now."

"Listen, she's been missing for two days. She left everything. Like you did. Please. If she's here, you have to tell me," he said with a growl. Seth drew closer, hoping maybe a little physical presence might scare her into telling him.

"I said go home. She isn't here!" Debbie drew her hand from her pocket. She clutched a silver whistle. Seth watched as she put it between her lips and blew. A shrill sound reverberated from the trees and cabins. She blew harder.

Seth heard doors open. Women and children dressed in their ridiculous costumes stepped out of each cabin like zombies ready for combat. One by one, they pulled whistles on cords from their pockets. They joined Debbie in their shrill whistling.

Seth restrained himself from covering his ears.

"Get out of here now, Seth or you're going to regret it," Debbie shouted at him.

The parade of women glared at him. Robots. That's what he was dealing with. He wouldn't find Kate here. She would die before she turned into one of these circus freaks. He cast a final harsh look at Debbie and pushed past two bigger women near him. Seth stomped to the front of the compound where he found David—armed with a shotgun—leveled at Seth.

"This is private property. I warned you once before."

Seth stumbled to a halt. He raised his arms. "I came about Kate."

"I told you before. She isn't here." David lowered his weapon. A smile formed on his face. "You're going to have to believe me for once. I told you I would announce her disappearance today. But I can't have you running crazy on my property. There are women and children back there who deserve peace. I plan to make sure they get it."

He'd had it with David's sick talk about his women. He had seen how many were pregnant. Breeders. That's all they were for the men in the Bend.

"I'm leaving. I won't be back."

David nodded, giving a wave with his free hand. "Good plan, friend. I'll see you later."

Seth shot David one last look before rounding the house to his car. The service had ended and he was the only visitor left. He hoped he would never be a visitor again.

She hadn't been able to kill herself. A mere scratch. When she'd placed the blade against her wrist, reason had returned. Or her will to live. A stronger resolve to see this plan to the end had overtaken her even though her body felt weak. Maybe she would have a chance to escape today. She bent toward the water, bringing a handful to her dry mouth. She sipped and sipped before running the refreshing water over her face and hands. Then she opened the two bags, and discovered in one a wrapped peanut butter and jelly sandwich. A last meal? She didn't care. She shoved piece after piece into her mouth, savoring the nutty taste. When she felt her stomach would not up heave its contents, she opened the second bag.

Clothing. A long dark skirt and a white blouse. She threw it down in distaste. Was he dressing her to look like the women in the cult? Was he part of it? No. Todd was acting on his own. But for some reason he wanted her to blend in with the crowd. She picked up the shirt, fingered the Peter Pan collar. He wanted others to think she had joined the cult. But why?

He would return soon. She knew he would. Gingerly, she peeled off her filthy jeans and shirt and donned the unfamiliar garments. She tugged the tie at her waist tightly so the skirt would not slip down over her hips. He'd done well with sizing the blouse. When dressed, she rummaged through the bags a final time. A comb and a Bible. Apparently, she was to carry the Bible like the other women filing into the church. She slid the comb into her pocket.

Then the waiting began. Without a sense of time, she resorted to pacing the shed while sitting when she grew tired. The sandwich had done little to restore her full energy. It didn't matter though. She was living on adrenaline. If Todd meant to take her to the rally, she would have a chance. That's all she needed. One chance.

95

Seth shoved a cherry Tootsie Pop into his mouth. He should have known Kate would not go to that compound. At least not willingly. He found it hard to know what to think now. But he had one more bone to chew. The hardware store. He checked the time on his dash. One o'clock. Where had his day gone? The rally started at three. Two hours. Did he have enough time to find the delivery guy? He parked his truck next to the store entrance.

A couple other trucks were there, too. Seth recognized the black Ford that belonged to the barber who gave him his last haircut. Dan was a nice guy. Moved here a couple of months ago. They'd hit it off from the first cut. Dan was looking for a woman to settle down with. Said he'd heard the Bend had an abundance, and so he'd moved there to start his business. Seth wanted to warn him but hadn't. Maybe he should.

"Hey there. What project you going to work on today?" Dan slapped him across the back as Seth approached the counter. As usual, he wore his plaid shirt and his hair was cut in a military style. Yeah, he fit into the Bend better than Seth did.

"Not much. I need to find Hank." He scanned the store.

"He's out back. Getting me a bucket of nails. Say, are you going to the rally today? Heard there might be something special going on." He winked.

"What do you mean special?" Seth glanced toward the back again. Where was Hank?

Dan leaned closer. Seth couldn't understand why, since they were the only two near the counter. "Going to be a ceremony of sorts. For the men." Another wink.

Seth imagined what kind of ceremony would take place. His stomach turned. "You want to be part of that group? I'd be careful, if I were you."

"What are you talking about? I spoke with Earl's brother there a while back, and it sounds like a soft deal to me. Ready-made wife. All I got to do is sign the check."

Seth inhaled. "They charge you?"

Dan backpedaled. "Not really a charge. A donation to the cause. Earl knows what he's doing. Actually he's pretty sharp. Plans to turn the Bend into a community that people will be begging to get in. I'm glad I moved here when I did." He stopped talking when Hank returned lugging several sacks with him.

"Sorry it took me so long. My delivery guy messed with the supplies in the back. At least I think it was him. When he gets in tomorrow, he might find himself looking at the exit door." He shook his head, exhaled. Slapped the bags on the counter.

"I need his address, Hank. Now." Seth leaned over the counter.

"Told you before. Against the rules to give out personal information."

"Blast the rules! My friend is missing, and I need to find her." He grabbed Hank by the shirt and yanked him over the counter toward him. Hank was no slouch and ripped Seth's hands off him. Dan grabbed Seth by the shoulders and pushed him back against a rake display.

"I'm calling the sheriff. This boy doesn't have any manners." Hank reached for the phone.

Seth shoved Dan off him. "Listen. Kate is missing. Your delivery guy knows something. If you don't give me that address now, I'll be the one calling the cops. They might be interested in that gambling thing you've got going here too."

At the suggestion of illegal activity, Hank put the phone down. His face reddened. "You aren't going to hurt him, are you?"

Seth stepped closer, eyeing Dan as he did. "Not if I don't have to."

Ten minutes later, he was speeding across the flats along the river. Hank said he wasn't exactly sure the address was legit, but it's what he had on record. The scrap of paper and Seth's GPS on his phone lay open on the seat next to him.

He wasn't sure what he would do when he found the guy. Maybe pound his face? Threaten him? Rough him up a little? Seth cringed. Sure didn't sound like the guy who had moved here to find the big story. Rough someone up? He hadn't been in a brawl since high school. He lost that one.

It didn't matter. He'd do what it took. He was the only one, it appeared, who cared enough about Kate's disappearance to do anything. At least he was trying. He braked as a deer ran across the road. His English-speaking GPS woman told him to turn left onto a dirt road. He followed her orders, sliding his wheels in the gravel.

The trees grew larger as he followed the road deeper into the woods. Anyone who lived this far back had to be crazy. He swerved as two rabbits leaped in front of him. He'd be lucky to leave with an intact bumper. The further he drove, the voice on his phone counted the miles. Finally, he heard the words he had waited for. "Your destination is on the right."

He braked to a dead stop.

In front of a cemetery.

Kate waited. Plotted what she would do when Todd returned. Kick him again? Go for his throat? Thrust her thumbs into his eyes?

She gave a weak laugh. What little energy she had left would not allow her to swing at him. He'd done his training well. Starved her. Isolated her. Threatened her. There was no doubt in her mind that Todd had done this exact same thing to other women. Maybe not.

She thought about Shelly. Did he practice on her only to ensure everything would go well with Kate? She wiped her eyes.

She would not give in. Not until the end.

The door to her prison opened with a squeak. Todd filled the opening. He had changed his clothing too. He wore dark dress pants and a long-sleeved, white shirt. Was that to blend in? Or because today was so special for him.

"I see you're ready. Good." He crossed the threshold. Held out his hand. "Let's go. We don't have much time left."

His words chilled her soul. "We don't have to do this, Todd. You can let me walk away right now."

His lips curled into the grin she had come to loathe. "Do what? We're going to church together. It's what couples in the Bend do together. You're my new girlfriend."

The cemetery was barely recognizable. It reminded Seth of the one that housed Earl's relatives. Overrun with weeds, and the stones were crumbling from age. Seth got out of his vehicle. Why did the delivery guy give this as his address? He searched behind him and peered into the plots. A distinct path cut through the center of the cemetery. Curiosity drove him to follow it. He'd come this far. It would take minutes to check it out.

The path wove in and out through larger burial plots and some that dated back to the early 1800s. He ducked beneath an overhanging branch, lost his bearings for a second, then pushed forward. He didn't know what he was looking for but felt in his gut that he would soon find it.

He was right.

Ahead of him lay fresh mounds of dirt.

His girlfriend. She never liked him in that way. But he did her. She'd had an inkling when they were in school, but at twelve? Kate allowed herself to be led outside. She blinked hard from the light peeking through the clouds. If the day had been sunnier, she doubted she would have been able to see. She shaded her eyes with one hand while he dragged her with her other. When they reached his truck, she flinched. She recognized his vehicle. Dark red. She'd seen it pass her house many evenings while she sat on her front porch. She also saw it downtown near the paper.

He'd been carefully stalking her. Why hadn't she been more alert? He said he'd been following her whereabouts for years. How did she not see? Was she so absorbed in staying away from the media that she missed Todd's attempts to watch her?

"Get in." He shoved her onto the seat. Kate struggled to climb into the truck as her skirt refused to cooperate. Her bad leg made moving more difficult but she managed to get in. He pulled a pair of handcuffs from the glove compartment. Snapped them on her wrists. "A little precautionary measure."

She could not have run far if she tried. No, he'd seen to that. Starving her. Her legs felt weak as newborn kittens. She wasn't sure how she was supposed to walk unnoticed into the rally like he told her she must. But she would not die willingly. She'd find a way to escape.

Why did he choose the rally? For the crowd? Like their school?

He joined her in the cab. When the truck roared to life, she heard him sigh. "It's time, my darling Kate. It's time for us to finish what was started."

96

Seth dropped to his knees. He scoured each mound for signs of recent digging. As he drew closer, he discovered fresh weeds growing from each. No, they weren't made for Kate. But perhaps if he dug deep enough he would find the remains of other missing women from the Bend.

He brushed off his pants. Another dead end. Literally. His only recourse was the rally and hope that someone had seen her or noticed something out of the ordinary. What better place to ask than a gathering of the town?

He trooped back through the overgrowth to his truck. He should make it to the church in thirty minutes or less if he pushed it. He wanted to be there early to scan the crowd. Maybe his delivery guy drank the Kool-Aid and would show up.

By the time he crossed town and drove into the church parking lot, it was half full. Another van of women and children pulled in behind him. Earl's crew he guessed. He watched the ladies descend the bus steps, lifting their skirts or holding a youngster's hand. After nine or ten descended, he recognized Debbie. She wore a look of uncertainty—not that look of determination she shot at him when he showed up at her cabin. No, she was definitely ill-at-ease. First time in public as a new convert? He looked closer. A dark bruise on the side of her cheek. He hadn't noticed that before. David's punishment? A fresh surge of anger washed through him. They controlled their women like mangy dogs.

He hung his head. Until he found Kate, he had no desire to blast the cult all over the papers. He was starting to wonder if anyone would believe him.

Kate did.

He grabbed his phone and left the Jeep. More cars arrived as he skirted past people he knew. He wanted to speak to Earl before the show started.

###

Instead of driving directly to the church, Todd took a detour onto a back road. Kate glanced at the scenery, her pulse pounding in her neck. What if he changed his mind? What if he meant to kill her out here instead of going to the rally? She slid her hands to the door handle. She would jump out. A chance. Any chance was better than dying from his hands.

"Thought we would take the time for a little heart-to-heart conversation. There is so much I want to say to you, but I fear there won't be time."

"We have the rest of our lives to talk." She twisted in her seat toward him.

He looked sad, almost forlorn. "We have now. Only now. I've waited my entire life to be with you like this, but the seconds are ticking away as I speak. I promised myself I would be swift and not frighten you."

"What are you talking about?" She forced her gaze on his. "You're frightening me now."

He touched her knee. Kate willed herself to not pull away.

"We are survivors. What happened that night twenty years ago at our school changed our lives. You lost your family. I lost my friends and school. My safe harbor. You. Did you know you were my best friend? Surely you didn't. You were surrounded by best friends. I watched you walk home from school with them, go to the library, spend time at their homes. You know some things about my mother. Let me tell you the rest." He frowned. Licked his bottom lip and stared out the window for a flash of a second. "She had to leave me and my father shortly after you visited. So I understand about loss. I also understand about fate." His grip on her knee tightened.

"You and I, we're alike. Both of us should have lived different lives. I can't change all that. But I can change our future. Make it what it should have been."

He lifted his hand from her knee.

Kate exhaled, remaining as rigid as a rabbit spying a fox.

Todd started the truck again. "It's time. I'll tell you the rest later."

The rest? What was he planning?

She would scream for help when they reached the church. Someone would take him out and save her.

"Oh, and in case you get any funny ideas when we get there? Don't forget about your friend. If anything goes wrong with my plan—he dies."

97

Seth found Earl holed up in a back office with David. The last person he wanted to come face-to-face with was David, but he had no choice.

Earl put down his papers and took off his glasses when Seth walked in. "I wanted to talk with you a minute before you go on."

David nodded and stepped out of the room. Standing this close to the scumbag made Seth boil with disgust. Instead, he pushed his anger down. He needed Earl. Or at least what Earl could do.

"Will you make the announcement about Kate right at the beginning? If anyone knows anything, the quicker I hear, the better chance I have to find her."

"Of course. But have you considered another scenario? Maybe she doesn't want to be found. Maybe she walked away from her life like many people quite often do."

He'd considered that scenario dozens of times. Maybe she faked her disappearance because she told him the truth about her auras. Maybe she was afraid he would rat on her. Maybe another reporter found her and she ducked out of town.

"It doesn't matter. If that's the case, I'll eventually find out. But right now, I need your help. The Sheriff never got back to me, and I've dead ended every other lead. If no one in town knows anything, I will take your advice and consider that option."

The only response Earl gave him was a long sigh. Like Seth was asking the impossible of him. Maybe he would stand up in front of everyone himself. Push Big Wig out of the way and take over. A smiled formed. Kate would love to see that.

With nothing else to say, Seth left Earl and wound his way to the front of the sanctuary. The crowd trickled in. Children ran around the front altar, and mothers in their prairie get-ups huddled in groups, talking about laundry. Or something mundane. Seth took a seat in the far back. He wanted to watch who came in. Plus, he intended to leave after Earl announced Kate's disappearance.

Seth dies. She believed Todd would follow through on his threat. Especially when he pulled up next to a cemetery not unlike the one Seth and she traipsed through the past summer.

"Do you see that path?"

She nodded. Of course she did. It skirted the edge of the overgrown field.

"If you follow that path, which we don't have time to do now, it takes you to three unmarked graves. A shovel waits behind a nearby pine tree, so I can easily dig a fourth grave as well as I did the first three."

She gagged. He planned to kill her. Them.

Satisfied that she understood, he turned around and drove toward town. Kate's nails dug into her arm. She had been afraid before, now she was paralyzed. Surely, he wouldn't hurt her in front of a packed church. Or would he? Did he care? He said their lives had been changed. They were both survivors.

She inhaled. He planned to kill both of them to finish what the bomber started. The question she couldn't answer was how.

###

The church parking lot was full when Todd pulled in. He parked his truck near the back corner next to a van. Like before, he shut off the engine and faced her. "You will not scream, nor shout, nor act in any way I wouldn't like. You will walk next to me, and if anyone you know says anything to you, you will answer briefly that you are with an old friend from the Bend." He stroked her jaw. Kate twisted away. "We are good friends, aren't we? Now, now. You better start behaving for me immediately." His voice turned deeper with a menacing growl. "Today is our destiny, darling Kate. It's the day that has been saved for us for the last twenty years. The two remaining survivors of the Canton Bomber. Can you imagine the headlines?" His eyes glowed from eagerness.

She glanced around her. Would anyone help? Sweat poured down her back. A heavy cloak of fear choked her as she contemplated what the next few minutes would bring. Would he kill everyone here too? Like her school?

"You still don't get it!" He grabbed her shoulders, causing pain to shoot through her back. "This is the moment! Our time together! We should have died with everyone else. Now we will! No more reporters hounding you. No more running. You will be set free! I will be set free!"

She was trapped with a maniac. "You can't believe that. We lived for a reason. We have to find that purpose. Not this, Todd." Her voice shook as she pleaded with him. Tried to reason with whatever logic remained in his warped brain.

"Time's up. Let's go. It's showtime, love." He unlocked her handcuffs and gave her one final warning look.

She would follow his instructions if it meant saving lives. But would she be able to save her own? He helped her from the truck like he might a real date. His actions sickened her. Then he hooked her arm on his and pointed them toward the church where several people still straggled in.

Her feet would not move, and more than once, he had to pull up on her. As they neared the structure, she focused on the cross hanging above the doorway. *Please, please, God.* She begged Him to hear her prayer to let someone stop this crazy man from what he was about to do. She sought the faces around her, hoping to send a message.

Todd opened the double door. She tripped on the sill, but he caught her. He put his mouth next to her ear. "Don't blow this or everyone in here is gone." He led her in with a crowd of people, whispering to her to keep her head down.

She scanned the auditorium, filled with children, women, and men from the community, as discreetly as possible. Maybe if she screamed. No, he was so crazy he'd kill her in a second and those around them. There had to be another way.

As he pushed her toward the middle row, she searched the pews behind her. She froze.

Seth. Sitting in the last row. But he didn't see her due to a crowd of people behind her.

Todd motioned her to sit. Kate swallowed hard. She could smell her fear it was so thick. The voices around her laughed and called out to each other as they waited for Earl to start the show.

And what a show it would be.

Todd kept a firm grip on her arm and with the other, a grip on a briefcase he'd brought with him. If only she could signal someone. Her brain struggled to form a plan, but nothing came.

Kate? What are you doing here?" She looked up. Seth.

He stood at the end of the pew, glaring at her. Todd's grip on her arm tightened. "Answer him, my darling."

She cleared her throat. Forced the tears in her eyes to stay put. "Hey, Seth. I'm sorry I haven't been around. I've been with an old friend." She tipped her head toward Todd. "Todd. A friend from my old school." She gave a weak smile.

Todd stood, letting go of his hold on her to stretch out his hand. "Good to meet you. Seth, is it?"

His acting sickened her. Seth glanced at her, confusion written all over his face, and ignored Todd's outstretched hand. Didn't he recognize Todd?

"I've been looking everywhere for you. You look sick. Are you ok, Kate?"

Her heart broke. How could she save him from her abductor? "You know me. Of course I'm fine." She blinked fast. Would he recognize her fear? "Seeing Todd and meeting up with him happened so fast. I dropped everything."

Seth's face reddened. She knew that look. He was disgusted with her. No, she couldn't let her life end with him angry at her. "Thanks for the notice. Have a good life."

"Wait, Seth." Todd's hand returned to her arm. "Tell Tim I won't be back."

"I don't think that decision is yours anymore."

"You're right. Okay. Thanks." She gave a slight wave of her hand. The sign for H.

Would he remember?

Seth worked his way to the back of the church. He wanted to curse at Kate for making him worry like he did, for acting like a fool searching for her. And now she pranced in like a princess on the arm of some guy from her past. He stared at the back of their heads. He would have to find Earl and stop the announcement. No need looking like a bigger fool.

He pushed past a mother and three kids to get to the aisle that led up front. He couldn't help another look at the guy by Kate's side. Something about him pricked his memory. He stopped.

The delivery guy from work.

The guy he'd teased Kate about having a crush on her.

His heart zoomed to his throat. He stepped closer to the wall, watching. Kate didn't look like she was enjoying a reunion with an old friend. She looked like she did that day at the bowling alley. Cornered.

Kate turned his way again. Gave another quick wave. Was it a sign?

And then he remembered the story she told him about her grandmother. How Kate used the sign letter H for help when she found herself in a situation she couldn't handle.

She had given him that same signal.

He glanced to the podium where David was sorting papers. He glanced back at Kate and her friend. If he was wrong . . . no, he wasn't. He slid along the wall. Worked his way toward one particular area. His hand connected with cold hard metal—the solution that might save Kate.

He pulled the fire alarm.

98

The earsplitting shrill of the fire alarm penetrated Kate's fear-ridden brain. Around her, men and women, crying children bolted toward the marked exits screaming *fire!* Todd clamped onto her waist as she struggled to rise. "There's a fire! We need to get out." She met his penetrating stare. His pupils had widened but his face remained calm.

"It doesn't matter for us. The show just got better."

"You're crazy! I'm not doing what you asked. You can't blow everyone up now. Let me go! Your plan is ruined!" She shoved at his arm, but he was stronger than her. He forced her to stand and dragged her toward the front of the church where a ten foot cross stood.

"It's our time—with or without anyone else!" he screamed at her. "This is our destiny!" He shoved her to the floor.

She watched in horror as Todd opened a briefcase and brought out a remote. "No! Please don't do this! Please!"

Seth was pushed, with hundreds of others, out the church doors into the parking lot. He shoved past men in a desperate attempt to return to Kate like a fish swimming upstream. He'd seen the crazed look in her captor's eyes and knew he had little time to save her. He would not fail. He stepped over another woman who had fallen in her haste to get out of the building. Seth continued to push forward until David grabbed him by the shoulders.

"You're going the wrong direction. There's a fire in there. Are you crazy?"

"Get out of my way." His chest heaved with exertion. "Kate's in there!" He ripped David's hands from his grasp and hurled himself back through the doors.

"Kate!" he shouted. "Kate!"

He saw her. Up front at the altar. Rising from the floor.

"Run, Kate!" She met his stare and bolted toward him.

Todd held something in his hand high above his head, a murderous grin on his face.

Instantly, Seth knew what Todd planned to do.

Blow them up.

"Noooo!" he screamed.

The blast threw him backward.

Hands pulled at him. Tugged him into the grass. The roaring in his ears split through his brain. His arms ached. His back felt as though it was on fire. "Are you okay?" Was that David? Yelling at him?

Seth opened his eyes. He was surrounded by people. "Where is she?" He pushed from the ground. Struggled to rise.

Heavy smoke filled his vision. The church. In shambles and flames. Distant sirens faded in and out of his consciousness. Where was Kate? Did she make it out? He stumbled forward while hands tried to hold him back. Kate. She was inside with that monster. He lunged forward again and pushed past the anxious bystanders. One side of the church still stood along with a large part of the roof.

If there was a chance. He bent his head down and blasted into the blackened remains. His soot- filled eyes struggled to take in the chaotic scene before him. "Kate? Kate!" The sanctuary—torn apart. Pews shredded like paper. No one could have made it out alive. He tore his glance to what remained of the front. The gold cross had crashed to the floor crushing a body.

He searched the aisles. Heard a low moan. Kate. Behind a nearby pew.

Seth pushed as quickly as he could through the rubble.

He dropped to his knees beside her still body. He scooped her into his arms and as he did, he heard a small gasp.

David and a few other men met him as he reached the exit. "She's alive!" Seth forced fresh air into his lungs. "She's alive."

99

The bag of Tootsie Pops slapped Seth's desk as they landed. He looked up with a smile tugging his lips. "Chocolate?"

"Twelve in the entire bag. It was the best I could do." Kate gave him a crooked grin. The bruises on her face had been artfully hidden with makeup. She couldn't look more beautiful. Seth tore his eyes from her. Typed a few more words into his computer. Since moving to Dallas, it was all he could do to stay on top of the news.

She rolled up a neighboring chair, her camera slung over her shoulder. "Do we have something?"

He typed a few more sentences. Spun toward her. "I think so. Give me five and I'll meet you in the Jeep."

She rolled her eyes. "Not going to let me drive yet, are you? Aren't you excited to ride in my new car? Smells so fresh." She inhaled and giggled. After the accident, (they preferred calling it that), she rid herself of everything that reminded her of the Bend. Even her old car.

But then she could afford it. Finding the killer of those other girls paid a handsome reward. Seth preferred to hang onto his share. He never knew when this new job might blow apart like others.

"Hey." She shoved his arm. "Daydreaming again?"

"Just debating if my ace photographer is up for this assignment. This cult sounds as evil as Earl's."

She shrugged. "All cults are evil. Besides, I'm tired of covering everyday news. That's why they hired us. Let's do it." She spun out of her chair and danced down the newsroom's hallway while blowing kisses back to him.

She hid her fear well. He gave her that much. When he found out she survived with only a few cuts and bruises, he'd wept harder than when his mother passed. Something about Kate stirred him. After placing her in the ambulance, he had returned to the blown-out building. The firemen had long since doused the flames and were carrying a body out on a stretcher. Todd.

"Wait." He flashed his palm. Flipped back the sheet. He wanted one more look at the man who tried to destroy his world. Seth held back a curse.

Flipped the sheet into place. He didn't need to see the monster's face any more. There would be plenty to replace his.

###

Kate pushed the elevator button as she waited for Seth. She strolled to the large window and watched fresh flakes float to the street below. Since moving to Dallas for the job Seth and she managed to wrangle together, she found little time to think about the events that led to her leaving the Bend.

When she could have visitors at the hospital following the explosion, she had found Seth at her bed. "You scared me," he said.

"I'm sorry. I promise I won't disappear again." Smiling hurt, but she had tendered him her biggest grin.

"They found the bodies of four other women. I guess he practiced before you, cutting women up. Torturing them. They found a journal he kept. His father dismembered his mother after killing her. Todd wrote that cutting and torturing gave him a feeling of power. Guess his mother would not have won the mother-of-the year award from the sounds of his ramblings."

Kate shivered. "I almost feel sorry for him. He did me a favor though."

Seth's eyebrows rose. "Seriously?"

"Seriously. Before he took me to the church, he showed me a photo of us as children. I saw auras around us even though I didn't take the picture. But I didn't die. My curse doesn't always mean death. It means I might be able to help someone because of it."

"What if it's gone? What if the blast knocked it out of you like when you first got it?"

"I guess time will tell. You aren't going to write about that part, are you?" Seth would get the long-awaited credit for the bombing story but she hoped he wouldn't share the part about her auras.

He shook his head. "That's between you and me. Never know when I'll need you to use it again."

"What about Earl and his craziness?"

Seth moved closer. "That's all covered. Looks like his promoting of women is over. He might be in some deep legal trouble for nonpayment of taxes on his business. The Feds shut his place down after a little chat with me. Found out he'd stolen his father's money and there's a possibility they died with a little help from him. But it also helps that we made the front page of the *NY Times*." He reached behind him. Pulled out a newspaper.

The headline said it all. **Small Town in PA Subject of Cult-like Operations**.

He had bent down and kissed her forehead before leaving the hospital.

She thought of that one kiss as she waited for him to ride down to the street. She touched her forehead.

"Hey, Red!"

She looked up.

Seth held out his hand in the familiar sign for H. A warmth exploded in her chest. If he hadn't listened to her that night . . .

"I gave you candy, what more do you want?" She held the elevator door open with one foot.

Seth breezed past her. "Just testing. Never know when it might come in handy again."

The door rolled to a shut. The elevator lurched. She smiled at her new partner as the elevator carried them down to their next assignment.

Thank you for purchasing this book. If you would take a moment to rate your experience with *The Bend*, I would appreciate it. Every review on Amazon points another reader toward my books.

If you would like to learn more about my writing and life, please check my website at territiffany.com.

11.99

CPSIA information can be obtained
at www.ICGtesting.com
Printed in the USA
BVHW031018300619
552280BV00002B/335/P

9 781542 746854